Other books by Malco

Bridges, Islands and Villag
(Lang Syne Press,

Scottish Battles
(Chambers, 1990)

Scottish Myths and Legends
(Chambers, 1992)

Scottish Animal and Bird Folklore
(St Andrew Press, 1996)

Sixpence for the Wind: A Knot of Nautical Folklore
(Whittles, 1999)

Across the Pond: Chapters from the Atlantic
(Whittles, 2001)

Soldier of the Queen
(Fledgling Press, 2003)

Winner of the 2005 Dundee Book Prize
Whales for the Wizard
(Polygon Press 2005)

Horseman of the Veldt
(Fledgling Press, 2005)

Aspects of the Boer War
(Fledgling Press, 2005)

Mother Law: a parchment for Dundee
(Fledgling Press, 2006)

Selkirk of the Fethan

by

Malcolm Archibald

Cover illustration by Keir Murdoch © Copyright 2003

ISBN 0 95 441213 3

Note: With the exception of historically recognisable people, all the main characters in this book are purely imaginary. Any resemblance to real people, living or dead is coincidental. Some places are real, others in the imagination of the author. Any errors are those of the author.

Published by Fledgling Press 2005

Printed by Digisource GB Limited in Livingston, Scotland

Selkirk of the Fethan

by

Malcolm Archibald

For Cathy

Contents

Chapter One : Cape Colony – February 1902 1

Chapter Two : Cape Town – Late February 1902 11

Chapter Three: Cape Town – February 1902 29

Chapter Four Northern Transvaal – March 1902 54

Chapter Five : Akersdorp - March 1902 67

Chapter Six : Akersdorp – March – April 1902 77

Chapter Seven : Akersdorp And The Veldt, May 1902 94

Chapter Eight :Northern Transvaal - May 1902 112

Chapter Nine: Northern Transvaal - May 1902 123

Chapter Ten :Northern Transvaal,May – June 1902 139

Chapter Eleven :Northern Transvaal - June 1902 146

Chapter Twelve :Northern Transvaal – June 1902 153

Chapter Thirteen :Northern Transvaal – June 1902 167

Chapter Fourteen :Edinburgh - October 1903 177

Chapter Fifteen : Edinburgh - October 1903 190

Chapter Sixteen :Fethan Valley, October 1903 195

Chapter Seventeen :Ettrick – November 1903 204

Chapter Eighteen :Ettrick – November 1903 210

Chapter Nineteen :Ettrick – November 1903 221

Chapter Twenty : At Sea – January 1904 231

Glossary 232

Historical Note 232

Chapter One : Cape Colony – February 1902

The rain had started in late afternoon and by midnight it was falling in a continuous downpour that thundered on to the corrugated iron roof and wept into the pools that had formed on the ground below.

'Bloody Africa!' Haig pulled his bush hat further over his face and glowered into the dark. 'Who said that it was always hot and sunny?'

'A man who had never been here. Watch your front.' Sergeant Campbell looked upward. 'If I was Piet, this is the type of weather I would choose to cross the line.'

Haig grunted. 'Maybe Piet's got more sense. He's probably tucked up in a nice dry farmhouse toasting his arse in front of a fire.'

Lieutenant Selkirk was standing behind Campbell, his field glasses methodically scanning the veldt. Between the dark and the rain there was not much chance of him seeing anything but, as Campbell said, this was exactly the sort of weather that the Boers would use to cross the wire. If they did, Selkirk did not want to be known as the man that failed to stop them. He swivelled left, focussed on the wire entanglements that protected the low sandbag wall around the blockhouse and followed the gleam of wet wire to the next post half a mile to the north.

He had heard that some blockhouses had searchlights that would penetrate even the darkest of nights, while others even had telephones that allowed them to communicate with their neighbours. Selkirk found such technology incredible. This war was certainly different from any other in history.

The rain increased in intensity, drumming on the roof until it sounded like half a dozen Maxims firing simultaneously.

'Do you know what Hansie says about weather like this?' Campbell cocked his head to one side to increase the efficiency of his hearing. 'She says that it was raining hard enough to kill the big devils and cut the legs off the little ones!'

1

'Sort of thing a Boer would say. This is bloody monsoon weather!' Haig inadvertently gave away some of his past. Automatically he checked the bolt action of his Lee-Enfield carbine.

Selkirk ignored his grumbling. He knew that Haig hated everybody, most of all himself, but he would watch all night, whatever the weather, out of sheer bloody-mindedness. Haig was a soldier, pure and simple.

There was no movement out there, either to right or left. Nodding to Campbell, Selkirk opened the door, with its corrugated iron shield and slid on to the back of Ben, who had been waiting patiently in the rain. 'Just one more to inspect, Ben,' Selkirk fondled the horse's ears, 'then we can rest for the night.' He tapped with his heels and splashed along behind the wire, keeping well to the rear of the blockhouses in case some sentry mistook him for a suicidal Boer who had strayed across the line.

He was in charge of four of these blockhouses, each manned by an NCO and six Reivers. The men were unhappy at being back in the Cape Colony after months of roving across the veldt, but there was nothing that he could do. Everybody knew that the Boers were beaten, that there were only a few thousand 'Bitter-enders' left, but everybody also knew that the war would last for ever. Some of the Reivers claimed that these last Free Burghers were busily breeding a new generation of men to continue the struggle. Having hard experience of the Boer mentality, Selkirk nearly believed it.

He was very aware of the Boer commandos under Smuts and Van Deventer that threatened Cape Colony. Striking at the heart of the British defences, these hard riding burghers called upon the Cape Dutch, men of their own blood and language, to rebel against the British. The British responded with columns, armoured trains and lines of blockhouses.

Selkirk halted at the next of the blockhouses under his command and frowned when there was no immediate challenge.

'Are you asleep in there?'

'Just watching you waste your time sir!' Donnelly's familiar Arizona drawl sounded from inside. 'Do you want some coffee?' There was usually coffee on the fire wherever Donnelly halted, and Selkirk accepted the chipped mug with gratitude. Blackdown and

Applewood grinned to him from the circular recesses of the blockhouse, then remembering where they were, straightened to attention.

'Stand easy.' Selkirk again scanned the blackness with his field glasses. 'Do you think that they'll come tonight?'

Donnelly shook his head. At one time he had been Selkirk's superior officer in the Kimberley Light Horse, but had lost his rank when that unit was disbanded. Since then he had joined Selkirk's own irregular unit, Selkirk's Reivers, and had been promoted from trooper to sergeant. Selkirk had great faith in Donnelly's military expertise. 'They won't come tonight. Brother Boer's strength is his speed and mobility; but even his horses can't move quickly with all the drifts flooded and the ground a quagmire. Maybe tomorrow.'

'Aye.' Selkirk focussed on a lump on the veldt, an area of greater blackness amidst the black. 'And maybe they'll expect us to think like that. Buccleuch took Carlisle Castle on just such a night.'

Donnelly nodded. After two years, he knew all Selkirk's stories. 'Maybe so, but Buccleuch was a Borderer and they're all mad.' He poured more coffee into Selkirk's mug.

'That's good, coming from a man who's risking his life in a war that has absolutely nothing to do with him.' Selkirk could see the lump better now; it was some animal, possibly a duiker, or even a kudu, but more likely a jackal. He was becoming knowledgeable about African wildlife.

Donnelly slurped his coffee noisily. 'Somebody has to look after you Limeys. God knows what would happen to your Empire if we weren't here to help.'

Selkirk moved the field glasses. He could see nothing but darkness beyond the animal. Even as he watched the rains stopped. In the sudden hush he could hear the night sounds, the baying of a hyena, the squeak of the frogs and the thin hiss of wind through the wire. He did not envy the Boers, camped out on the veldt on a night like this, knowing they were outnumbered, knowing that there were British columns hunting them. He thought of Helena Van Vuren, tough, determined, resourceful; what would she do if she had to invade the Cape Colony? Probably capture Cape Town and hold it to ransom.

'So how long are we here for, sir?' Donnelly broke into his train of thought.

'Until we're ordered elsewhere.' Selkirk grinned, 'look at it as a wee holiday.' He had been asked that question at least three times a day every day since they had arrived at the blockhouses. That had been six weeks now, weeks of tedium and boredom, weeks when the boredom of garrison duty in the middle of nowhere ground away the fighting edge of his Reivers.

It was in March 1900, nearly two years ago, that Field Marshall Lord Roberts had first proposed using blockhouses. He had just captured Bloemfontein, capital of the Boer republic of the Orange Free State, and was concerned about his army's main supply route, the railway that stretched all the way to Cape Town. Rather than institute patrols, Roberts had ordered a line of blockhouses. Initially these were large, stone built affairs, two storeys high and armed with a machine gun. When these blockhouses guarded a river crossing, the railway was safe. Only the largest Boer commando had the firepower to overcome a defended blockhouse, and few commandos would risk a prolonged firefight that would certainly attract a relief column.

With the success of the blockhouses proved, Lord Milner, the British High Commissioner at the Cape wanted to build more. He wanted blockhouses strung like washing on a line, all across the veldt. With de Wet and de la Rey proving too elusive for the cumbersome columns, the British hoped for permanent features that would restrict the Boers. The idea was to use the columns to drive the commandos against a fixed line of blockhouses, where they would be trapped and brought to battle. However, a parsimonious government baulked at the cost of thousands of stone buildings. They wanted a cheap and speedy alternative.

Major S. R. Rice of the Royal Engineers came up with the idea of corrugated iron. While the stone blockhouses could take up to three months to build, a skilled team could erect one made of corrugated iron in six hours, at a cost of under £20. The double skinned iron, with sand and rubble between, was proof against rifle and machine gun fire, although Selkirk doubted that it would withstand the impact of even a one-pound pom-pom shell.

4

The garrison peered at the same patch of land out of slits lined with steel. They baked in the sun, froze at night and had to fight boredom more than the Boers. Selkirk had heard stories of men who had been posted in blockhouses for months on end. Some had taken to gardening, so that their iron strongholds had become as decorative as any provincial railway station and khaki clad men had carefully watered and tended their colourful flowers while their rifles had slowly rusted with neglect. Other men had taken to drink or gambling while their discipline gradually crumbled. One or two unfortunates had gone 'sand happy' with the heat and the flies and the monotony. Selkirk had vowed that no such sickness would afflict his men.

Accordingly he had ordered his Reivers to mount offensive patrols, practise their marksmanship and make their defences as formidable as possible. They grumbled at the extra work and cursed their officer in the endless letters that they wrote to the families that many had not seen for years, but at least they retained something of their fighting potential. Even at this stage of the war, the men used codes in these letters home, for the Boer commandos still had the capacity to capture the mail. In his letters home, Selkirk had evolved a system of replacing African names with those of familiar Border towns, so that his sister Jenny would know where he was.

'Do you think that they'll come this way sir?' Hetherington was too good a soldier to move from his post. He peered into the dark, automatically keeping his carbine sights in line with his direction of sight.

'No telling, Hetherington.' Selkirk could see nothing save the night. 'Just listen for the rattles.' The Reivers had tied an assortment of empty tins and bottles to the defensive wire to act as alarms while Campbell, the ex-Clydeside engineer, had set trip wires attached to loaded rifles. Up to date the traps had accounted for two springbok and one hyena that had blundered into the wire and been summarily dispatched by the Reivers. The fresh meat had proved a welcome addition to the normal army rations.

'When did you last sleep sir?' Donnelly asked. 'Properly sleep, I mean. You check these pepper-boxes every night and you're up all day.' He leaned closer, so that only Selkirk could hear. 'We're quite capable of looking after ourselves, Selks, and you're no good to anybody if you're exhausted.'

Selkirk knew that Donnelly was right, but the thought of spending comfortable nights in his tent while his men stood sentry against the Boers was not appealing. 'Maybe tomorrow,' he said, but still allowed Donnelly to usher him back on to Ben. The rain had started again, making a miserable job worse. He knew that he would lie awake half the night, listening for the crack of Lee-Enfield carbines or the rattle of Boer boots against the trip wires, but that was the price of command.

His tent was central to the small encampment of the Reivers, a pyramid of white canvas whose walls wept with condensation but whose interior offered some sanctuary. There was a folding camp chair and a portable desk with official papers and a small lantern. There was a camp bed on wooden legs and a couple of books that he tried hard to assimilate, for Selkirk was deeply aware of his lack of education. With no idea of what to read, he accepted anything that was offered, and pored over the lurid penny novels that were common among the other ranks. He was constantly astonished at the antics of the characters, and wondered that he had never noticed so much romance and so many shady goings-on in the world.

His maps were here, showing the frontier between the old British colony and the annexed lands that had lately belonged to the Boers. The letters that he received were also here, for one advantage of blockhouse life was a regular supply of mail. He lifted the top letter again, with the writing that was now so familiar, and read the news of the Fethan with a nostalgia that never faded.

Jenny was fit and happy, but constantly worried about her brother out at the war. His father was still working in the fields of the Mains, and his mother continued to attend church and organise everybody's life. His other sisters, shadows of their mother, were living their own lives; Margaret was already married, Agatha was engaged, both to decent farm labouring boys from the area. Jenny wrote that their mother wished Selkirk well, although she remained bitterly disappointed that he had gone for a soldier rather than becoming a respectable working man.

Selkirk held the letter close to him as he fell asleep, reliving the sounds and scents of the Fethan, where the Ettrick hills slithered to the burn, and cattle lowed their milking call in the cool dim of the morning. That was how a man should live, following the seasons of nature, not waking to the blare of a bugle and checking the bolt of his rifle in case it was blocked with dust

Selkirk was still in that position, sprawled across his camp bed with his uniform on and the letter clutched against his chest, when the bugle for reveille sounded. He scrambled up automatically, buttoning his tunic as he stared into the glaring African dawn. In other units an officer would have a servant, but not in the Reivers. Irregular horse could not afford such luxuries.

'You should have wakened me,' he accused Donnelly, who nodded agreement.

'Yes, sir. Shall I order stand to?'

The notes of the bugle haunted the line of blockhouses; men dashed from tents to their posts and a score of birds rose skyward. Selkirk inspected his men, ignoring the minor faults in their appearance but being far more particular with their weapons. His unit was for fighting, not decoration.

It was already a habit to drink coffee with his sergeants as they stared over the veldt and discussed the possibility of action that day. In the daylight he could see the tracks that various animals had made during the night, and wonder anew that nature and man could co-exist in the middle of a war. Already the sun was warm and would get much warmer so that men would pant for breath within the baking tins of the blockhouses. Usually they would ride into the veldt but this morning an alert sentry interrupted their routine.

'Riders approaching, sir.' Macpherson was perched casually on top of the blockhouse roof, confident that he would see any Boer long before they could sight a rifle on him.

'From what direction? How many?' Campbell glowered up at Macpherson. 'Have you not learned how to make a decent report yet?'

'Hard to say, sir.' Macpherson was known as 'Kirky' to the men because of his predilection for studying the Bible, but he had evolved into one of the best scouts of the Reivers. His only rivals were Donnelly and the Australians, Cobb and Grey. 'Three men I think, coming from the south west.'

'Probably British then.' Campbell's words eased the tension. Although the Boers were bold, it was unlikely that so small a group would approach the blockhouses.

'Cover them anyway Macpherson.' Selkirk gave the order casually, for he knew that Kirky would not be satisfied until the riders had adequately proved their identity. The Reivers had extensive experience of Boers masquerading as British soldiers, and had even acted as Boers themselves.

There was no point in speculating who or what the riders might be, so Selkirk climbed up beside Macpherson, coffee in hand, and scanned the veldt with his field glasses. He saw nothing but the flat plain, with the same small kopje that had been there for a hundred thousand years before ever Boer and Briton disputed its ownership, and which would be there a hundred thousand years after both Boer and Briton had been forgotten. There were no trees in sight, just the brown landscape that stretched into the infinity of Africa with the sky clear and blue and vast above.

Selkirk cursed the rising steam that hazed the rough grass as the sun sucked away the moisture of the night's rain. Poor visibility always made observation difficult. 'Applewood!' He gestured to the fastest of his horsemen, an Englishman from the New Forest. 'Dash off to the Reivers' blockhouses and tell them to be wary. Piet might come in under cover of that haze.'

As Applewood galloped away, the three riders cantered in. 'That's Major Scott sir,' Macpherson reported, raising his carbine, 'and two men that I don't recognise.'

'Thanks, Macpherson.' Draining the dregs of his coffee, Selkirk vaulted down from his perch on the roof of the blockhouse and straightened his uniform. Although Major Scott had always been friendly, he was still a superior officer and even after he had held his commission for nearly two years, Selkirk believed he should look his best.

'Selkirk.' Scott looked relieved to be off horseback. He was a short, round, red-faced man with a casual air that belied his efficiency and a smile that did not disguise the sharp intelligence of his eyes. 'How do you like blockhouse life then?'

'The boys are getting a bit restless sir.'

'Already?' Scott looked incredulous. 'I'd have thought that your lot had experienced enough excitement to last them until the peace.' He shook his head mockingly; 'some units have been in blockhouses for a year or more.'

'Yes, sir. Maybe we're just not suited to garrison life.'

Scott nodded and gestured to the two silent men who stood at his back. 'These are Lieutenants Cloete and Windrush. They will soon be attached to the Reivers.' He looked around the bare veldt, where a warm wind was moaning through the strands of barbed wire. More than one Reiver had edged closer, still facing their front but obviously listening to every word that was being said. 'Is there somewhere we can talk?'

There was thirteen feet of space between the corrugated iron walls of the blockhouse, and Lieutenant Cloete had to stoop to ease his six foot three under the ceiling. The interior smelled of stale sweat and rifle oil and already there were a dozen green-bodied flies buzzing around. Somebody had left a pair of socks stinking against a loophole.

Scott, a fastidious man who preferred fine wine and gentle living to life on campaign, screwed up his face. He waited until the heavy door was closed before easing himself on to the single, roughly made chair in the middle of the room.

'I'll be brief Selkirk. Colonel Hume wants to see you in Cape Town. Your Reivers too. You can say farewell to this luxurious living for a while my boy; it's back to hard tack and cold water for you.'

The two lieutenants stared at him through expressionless eyes. Neither said a word as Scott produced a silver flask from his inside pocket, unscrewed the lid and slowly sipped at the contents.

'What's it all about, sir?' Although Selkirk was as averse to danger as anybody else was, the prospect of escaping the tedium of blockhouse life was very appealing.

'No idea, Selkirk. You know the Colonel, tells you everything except what you need to know. Probably something rough and ugly though. You didn't expect to grow old, did you?' Grinning, he took another sip. 'In the meantime, I'll allow these two officers to gape at your men, then take them away again.' The grin remained. 'Things are hotting up Selkirk, old boy, things are hotting up.'

Chapter Two : Cape Town – Late February 1902

The mob of struggling men exploded from the dockside tavern and crashed on to the sun-hardened ground. The smallest of them all ducked beneath the swing of a seaman's fist and butted his forehead into his assailant's face. As the seaman yelled and pulled back, lifting his hands to his shattered nose, the small man kicked upwards with his steel-shod boots, once, twice and a third time so the seaman squealed in anguish and curled into a foetal ball on the ground.

'Bugger you, Jack Tar!' The small man roared, spat on his writhing victim and straightened his khaki tunic.

A second seaman, witnessing the demise of his shipmate, detached the knife that hung at his belt, flicked it open and launched himself at the small man. Yelling gutterally, he slashed the blade toward the small man's forehead. The small man grinned, ducked beneath the sweep of the blade and rattled his fists off the seaman's ribs. He was a veteran of many bone-crushing encounters and knew the old Scandinavian trick of cutting the forehead of an opponent so that the blood would stream blindingly into his eyes.

'And bugger you too, Dansker!'

More seamen poured out of the tavern, some so befuddled with alcohol that they could only lean against the door post and gape, others who spewed as soon as they reached open air and one or two who joined in the general melee.

'Time we were out of this Haigie.' The second khaki clad man spoke with a more refined accent than would normally be expected on the Cape Town dock front. He placed a restraining hand on the thin shoulder of the small man and pulled urgently, but the small man tugged violently away.

'Bugger off Newie! Did you hear what these bastards called me?' He swung his boots again, crunching them indiscriminately into ribs and legs and bellies. 'They said that I was only a dwarf Tommie! Me!' Rolling along the ground, he kicked out with his heel so that a sailor screamed and clutched both hands to his shattered knee. 'I'm Haigie of the Reivers!'

Somebody in the crowd threw a bottle, which smashed against the wall behind them. Haig did not flinch as a shard of glass opened his cheek and blood seeped out. Another seaman emerged from the tavern. Taller than most of the others, he glanced across to where Haig and Newman stood, hitched up his trousers and smiled.

'Here! Soldier boys. I want a word with you.'

Haig looked over to the seaman. While the others in this brawl had only been drunken maulers, he recognised that this newcomer was a fighting man. Haig was not articulate enough to say how he knew. Perhaps it was in the set of the shoulders, the shape of the out-thrust jaw or just the expression in the sailor's eyes, but there was something of the predator about him as he approached, softly stepping over the sprawled bodies on the ground. An iron ring on the forefinger of his right hand betrayed him as a Brigger, one of the men who had helped construct the railway bridge that spanned the Firth of Forth in Scotland.

'Haigie! Let's get out of here.' Newman flinched as the sailors took heart from the appearance of the tall man and began to clamber to their feet. One swarthy, ear-ringed man lifted the neck of the broken bottle and advanced on them. African sunlight caught the cruelly jagged edges of the glass. 'Come on man, footslack.'

'Footslack be buggered! I want him! I want to cripple that arrogant tarry-arsed bastard!' Sweeping aside the challenge of the ear-ringed man with a backhanded punch that sent him sprawling to the ground, Haig beckoned to the tall sailor. 'Come on son, come to Haigie!'

'Haigie is it?' The man looked even taller as he approached, walking softly and with his arms loose at his sides. 'It's good to know the names of the men I break. Scotch, are you?' His fists thrust massively from forearms that were as broad as Haig's thighs, while his smile revealed a mouthful of even white teeth. They were ill matched combatants, the tall, broad seaman with his handsome, tanned face and the diminutive, scarred soldier in battered khaki. Yet it seemed natural that the seaman should extend his hand as though in respectful friendship.

For a second, Haig looked surprised, then he advanced with his own hand out and a strange, almost shy expression on his face. As he approached the seaman Haig smiled, then used the prostrate body

12

of one of the earlier victims to launch himself into the air. Newman watched in disbelief as Haig leaped a good six feet above the ground and kicked out savagely. His steel toecap smashed squarely into the mouth of the seaman. He landed on both feet, pivoted and landed a volley of punches into the belly and groin of his staggering adversary. The seaman stiffened in his agony, and Haig turned and ran, grabbing hold of Newman as he passed.

'Come on Newie, we can't hang about here all day playing with the tarry arses!'

'What?' Still shocked by his rapid destruction of the giant seaman, Newman stumbled as he followed.

'Can't you see them coming? Even I can't fight that lot.' Haig gestured with his chin and Newman glanced to his left. The word must have spread that two soldiers were systematically demolishing Britannia's pride, for it appeared that all the seamen in Capetown were roaring down upon them in a bid to exact summary vengeance.

They ran through the dockland area, passing painted women who peered from shabby doors and men of half the hues of the world who cheered or cursed them, depending on their view of British soldiers and state of sobriety. Twice policemen shouted for them to halt but one backward glance revealed enough for Haig and Newman to keep running. Filling the narrow streets with a dense mob of angry men, the seamen did not look likely to heed the Rule of Law.

'Up here!' Newman had taken charge, pulling the smaller man up hill, further away from the docks in the hopeful belief that the seamen might not wish to leave their native element too far astern. The rising roar of oath-laden abuse behind them confirmed his mistake. They ran up Strand Street, hesitated at the elegant Lutheran Church as Newman momentarily pondered asking for sanctuary but speeded up as a marlinespike rattled in front of them to protrude, vibrating, from the ground. Haig stumbled over a loose stone, staggered and swore foully.

'I don't think they bastards like me very much.'

'At the minute, Haigie, I don't like you very much either. Run!'

Far ahead of them, Signal Hill and the Lion's Rump rose spectacularly to the bright blue sky. The hills were majestic, vaguely reminding Haig of Arthur's Seat in his native Edinburgh, but higher and sharper in the crisp African air. The granite cliffs seemed to soar toward the white tablecloth of cloud that dripped so gently from the summit. A bottle splintered against the iron railings that surrounded the church.

'Kill the shite coloured bastards!' The seamen were raucous as they sensed that their quarry was weakening. British seamen were renowned for the trouble that they caused in the seaports of the entire world. From the West Coast of America to the Rocks of Sydney, from Bombay to the Broomielaw, drunken British seamen had brawled and cursed and spread their distinctive brand of mayhem.

Fighting a couple of soldiers in Cape Town was nothing special; it was far easier than shovelling coal in a tropical stokehold where the temperature topped 120 degrees and men went mad with the heat. It was far easier than balancing on the yardarm of a slab-sided Clyde built barque, when the Screaming Fifties lifted great Cape Horn greybeards as far as the eyes could see, and the sky hurled bitter sleet into your face. It was far easier than enduring the endless tedium, short rations and tuberculosis of the forecastle for month after torturing month while a bully mate hazed you during every working moment. Indeed, brawling in Capetown was quite an enjoyable pastime for Britain's merchant seamen.

The mob was gaining ground as the effects of their three-day binge in the brothels and disreputable taverns began to take effect on the soldiers. Haig coughed, shook some of the blood away from his face and felt the painful rasping of his breath in his lungs. He felt sick.

'I cannae go on, Newie. We'll just have to stand and fight.' He looked around for a handy wall against which he could plant his back.

Newman nodded, nearly past speech. The sailors were slowing down as the front-runners waited for the main body to catch them up. After witnessing Haig's clinical demolition of their colleagues outside the tavern, nobody was keen to be next. Haig backed against a white washed wall of a flat roofed house in a narrow street that climbed steeply uphill. Oriental looking men in smart suits and red fezzes stared at this intrusion into their neighbourhood. Women in long dresses hurried wide-eyed children inside the deep doorways.

14

'Come on then you bastards!' Haig slipped the bayonet down from his sleeve. He was not normally a knife man, but the odds were stacked against them. The sailors shuffled forward in a motley semi-circle, encouraging one another to make the initial rush. Haig flourished the bayonet, flexing his wrist so the eighteen-inch blade made little circling motions that attracted the attention of each man in the gradually closing ring. 'Come to Haigie.'

There was a low growl from the throats of the seamen and a couple of missiles arced through the air. Neither landed on target although Newman flinched as a brown bottle that had once contained Bass Pale Ale rolled noisily over the rough ground. The seamen edged closer still, many sliding knives from their sheaths or weighing marlinespikes in hands that were calloused from years of hauling on ropes and lines.

'God help us,' Newman muttered, 'here they come.' He straightened his back and lifted his fists in the boxing stance that he had been taught in one of the best schools in England.

The sound of galloping hooves echoed from the low houses as two riders kicked in their spurs and shouted above the roar. 'Reivers! Selkirk's Reivers!' They rode knee to knee up the street, ploughing through those sailors who did not immediately scatter. One unfortunate man, too stubborn or too befuddled to move, was ridden underfoot and squealed as the steel shoes sliced into his leg.

'Haig! Come up behind me!' The rider on the inside reached out a hand and grabbed the small man by the collar. 'Newman! Go to Donnelly!'

Haig was no weight as he threw himself astride the horse, swearing and lashing out at the sailors with his boots. 'We were fine. We were just getting the better of them!'

'Keep your mouth shut Haig. You're in enough trouble.' The rider kicked in his spurs again so that his horse reared up, flailing his front hooves at a group of seamen who had rapidly gathered to oppose their progress. He waited until Newman was safely behind the second rider before hauling round his horse and heading back down the hill. Baulked of their prey, the sailors voiced their frustration in a terrible shout, followed by a shower of anything on which they could lay their hands. Spattered by stones and mud, and with bottles bouncing from the flanks of their horses, the two mounted men lost no time in their withdrawal.

'Keep moving, Donnelly,' Selkirk, the leading rider ordered.

Donnelly grinned. 'Reckon that's what I was planning to do.'

'Thank you, sir.' Newman sounded genuinely grateful. He gestured backward with a jerk of his head. 'Whatever Haigie says, I think that we were in trouble there.' He kicked sideways, catching Haig a glancing blow on the leg. 'Haigie will say thanks too.'

Haig glared at Newman, then at the lieutenant. 'Aye. Maybe, Selks.'

'That's maybe, Lieutenant Selkirk, sir!' Lieutenant Andrew Selkirk matched the glare until Haig looked away.

Still riding two to a horse, they rode into the centre of Capetown, ignoring the curious glances of passers-by. Even although it had been a British military garrison for the best part of a century, the wartime influx of khaki had changed the city. From a nautical and trading centre, Cape Town had become the base for many of the rearmost elements of the British Army. While the fighting forces were a thousand miles to the north, supporting troops, intelligence men, supply convoys, reinforcements and the sick filled the sun-lit, boisterous streets.

Selkirk's Reivers did not fit into any of these categories. As a free ranging force of irregular horse, they were the personal tools of Colonel Hume, who ran a part of the intelligence operations of the British army. Since Major Scott had ordered the Reivers to Cape Town, Selkirk had waited for the summons to Hume's headquarters, but the Colonel had been busy with other work. In the meantime some of Selkirk's men had succumbed to the pleasures of the city that had once been dubbed 'Tavern of the Seas.'

'Right, off saddle, you useless, drunken bastards.' Selkirk waited until they had dismounted. 'Can I not leave you for five minutes without you causing havoc? Is fighting the Boers not bad enough, without you starting a new war with the sailors?' His anger was genuine, partly because Haig and Newman were two of the finest soldiers in the Reivers when they were sober, and utterly unreliable if they touched anything alcoholic. Haig he could understand, for the man was a product of one of the worst slums in the Old Town of

Edinburgh, but Newman had less excuse. He was an educated man, a gentleman ranker who rather than descending the ladder rung by rung, had leaped off into infamy. The fact that he was the unwanted and unrecognised brother of Charles Drongan did not help matters.

The Honourable Charles Drongan was the middle son of Lord Drongan, who owned tens of thousands of acres of the Scottish Borderland and was one of the chosen beings of Creation. Lord Drongan was also the landlord of Selkirk's father when he grew up in the Fethan Valley. The Honourable Charles had been Selkirk's main rival in the annual horse race in Ettrick, and had been very frustrated when Selkirk had defeated his favourite during a ploughing competition. Accusing him of horse theft, Charles Drongan had intended to have Selkirk imprisoned, but instead Selkirk had taken the Queen's Shilling and joined the Royal Borderers.

A Christian mother and a Rechabite father had decently reared Selkirk, but years of living and fighting with the rankers of the British army had educated him into a choice variety of obscenity. He used it all now, delving deep into his repertoire to call his wayward men every insulting name he could. They took it quietly, standing at attention at the roadside as the curious crowds watched. Just as Selkirk reached his full potential, bawling his disgust at their actions and likening them to the foulest creatures that his angered imagination could conjure, he became aware of an elegant coach passing by.

Drawn by a matched pair of horses, whose glossy black coats seemed to reflect the sunshine, the carriage was open to the bright sunshine of the Cape. The driver wore a livery of dark blue, with gold epaulettes and buttons that gleamed. The paintwork of the carriage matched the driver's coat, while the two people who sat in the back looked very much in love.

The man wore the brilliant scarlet dress frock of an army officer and smoked a long cheroot, while his companion wore a dress of shimmering blue silk. A double string of pearls enhanced her throat, while pearl droplets swayed softly from her ears, emphasising the tall, beautifully worked set of her dark hair. Although she was not facing Selkirk, he was immediately aware of her presence and stopped his tirade in mid sentence.

He had known Georgina Drongan, now Georgina Montgomery, since his early childhood. Despite being the brother of the Honourable Charles, she had supported him when he took part in the horse races and had encouraged him in the Merse ploughing matches. More recently, Georgina, as head of a group of gentlewoman nurses, had instigated a brief affair with Selkirk, only to drop him for James Montgomery, the wealthy landowner with whom she now shared the carriage.

The contrast between their positions could hardly have been greater. Selkirk was a jumped up ploughman, a private soldier risen one step from the ranks, dependant on luck and idiot courage to sustain the privilege of rank. Georgina was a gentlewoman of money and leisure, the pampered cream of society. Selkirk was dressed in faded and stained khaki, his face weathered to mahogany, his hands calloused from years of carrying and using rifles, while Georgina wore the most fashionable satin and silk that Cape Town could offer. Selkirk was soaked with sweat, his own and that of the horse, while Georgina looked pristine and fresh, as though she had only that instant stepped from a deep perfumed bath. Selkirk was shouting coarse oaths in a voice designed to shake the composure of scarred veterans of the North West Frontier and Magersfontein, while Georgina had the liquid tones of an angel and would certainly not understand the terms that Selkirk bellowed so freely.

'They're married, you know sir.' Newman spoke quietly. In common with all the Reivers, he was well aware of Selkirk's attraction to Georgina. 'Best leave well alone.'

More direct, Haig spat on to the ground as the carriage rolled sedately past. 'Bloody Mount Nelson dragoons! You're too good for them Selks, though she's no' a bad looker.'

Selkirk opened his mouth to blast away the insolence of his men, but the anger had dissipated. Instead he pondered on the aptness of Newman's words. When the armies of the Free Republics had precipitated war by invading British territory, the Uitlanders, the rich mine owners and financial speculators of Johannesburg about whose rights this war was ostensibly fought, had moved en-masse to Cape

Town. While thousands of the khaki-clad army had died of Mauseritis and typhoid, the Uitlanders, known to the British as Randlords, had settled into the most comfortable hotels of the city. The wealthiest had taken over the Mount Nelson, spending so much time in partying and riotous living that bitter British soldiers had termed them the Mount Nelson Dragoons. Now Haig hinted that Georgina and her new husband had adopted the same lifestyle.

As the carriage rolled smoothly toward the more upmarket areas of Cape Town, Selkirk surveyed his men. They stood at attention again, chins lifted and eyes staring expressionlessly past his shoulder. 'Come on then you useless bastards, let's get back to work.' He sighed softly, 'I've no idea what Colonel Hume wants, but I doubt that he'll be giving us all a free ticket home on a lavender boat.' The Union Castle Liners that sailed between Britain and Cape Town were renowned for their distinctive lavender coloured hulls. 'In the meantime, Sergeant Donnelly will take care of you.'

He felt, rather than saw, the slight shift in their expressions as both men looked toward Donnelly. They had known him as an efficient trooper and liked him as a comrade, but Donnelly was one of the hardest sergeants that Selkirk had ever met. The two errant troopers would not enjoy this next period of their lives.

Selkirk allowed Donnelly to take command of the rapidly sobering soldiers as he rode slowly through Cape Town. He remembered his last meeting with Georgina, when she had laughed at his hope for a lasting relationship. He remembered his deep hurt when he realised that Georgina regarded him as beneath her, but he also remembered her attempts at kindness. Although Georgina had welcomed a quick tumble in bed, she found the idea of a permanent liaison between the son of a tenant farmer and the daughter of a lord vastly amusing. She did not consider Selkirk as a real officer, unlike James Montgomery, who owned great swathes of Berwickshire and spoke with the affected drawl of Eton.

So here he was, an officer who should be a ploughman, a leader who should be a follower, a soldier fighting against men whom he respected and admired more than he did his own superiors. For more than two years, he had ridden across Africa, fighting for his country with every ounce of his muscle, every thought in his head. He had achieved some successes, and had suffered some failures, but overall he had done his best. What was it all about? Was this war being fought to retain the privileges of the Rand Lords? Or was it really fought to defend British interests and to spread civilisation that much further?

Selkirk looked upward, past the modern cable cars to the massive mountains that hemmed in this coastal city and wondered at the mixture of beauty and barbarism that was Africa. Why was he here? Who was he?

The answer to the latter was simple. He was Drew Selkirk of the Fethan, whatever other people thought. Automatically Selkirk straightened his shoulders and stretched his legs so his feet slid into the long stirrups that he wore Boer style.

'Aye, aye, the lieutenant's back.' Newman jerked a thumb toward Selkirk.

Haig grunted. 'Better with his bint than here.'

At one time Selkirk would have growled at them to keep quiet, but now he had enough experience to pretend he had not heard. The three wise monkeys had many lessons to teach a green lieutenant.

There was another commotion as they made their way back to the small encampment where the Reivers were temporarily based. A slow procession made its way across Greenmarket Square toward the Castle of Good Hope, watched with little sympathy by the good people of the city.

With naked bayonets weighing down their rifles, four immaculately uniformed Guardsmen escorted four creatures that shuffled in bareheaded shame in their campaign-stained rags. Handcuffs on their wrists made it obvious that the four were prisoners, and the Guards ushered them with some force as they tried to retain a military bearing. Despite himself, Selkirk stopped to watch, for he was well aware of the story behind these men. Indeed, their trial was second only to that of Breaker Morant, and for much the same reason.

'Who are they sir?' Newman was one of the most intelligent of the Reivers, but was more inclined to lose himself in one of Oscar Wilde's plays, a Dickens novel or the bottom of a glass than pay any attention to the common gossip of the barracks. He listened attentively as Haig filled in the details.

'That's Nat Blunt and his boys. They're like us, they're irregular horsemen, see, patrolling out on the veldt to make sure that the big poncy occifer buggers are safe in their open carriages.' Selkirk recognised the swipe at Montgomery and the indirect vote of support for himself in the matter of Georgina. 'They catch some Boers see, wearing British uniforms and all.'

'I see.' Newman nodded encouragingly. He knew that it was often difficult to get the monosyllabic Haig to speak, and once the small man realised that people were listening, he would either descend to a mutter of obscenity or bask in the limelight. It all depended on his mood.

Haig glanced at Newman to ensure that he understood so far. 'You know that old Kitchener gave orders that all Boers caught wearing British uniforms were to be shot.'

Newman looked to Selkirk before he nodded. There was no secret that Kitchener was alleged to have given that order, but the Sirdar was notorious for his bad communication skills and as he seldom, if ever, put anything on paper, there was no proof.

'Well,' Haig continued, 'that's what they lads did. They took some Boojers prisoner, took them out to the veldt and shot them like dogs.'

Selkirk stirred uncomfortably in his saddle. He knew exactly how difficult it was to draw the line between humanity and duty, between obeying orders and crossing the line between a professional soldier and a murderer. He had been given similar instructions before leading the Reivers to Bechuanaland to forestall an incursion by German troops. The fact that he had not obeyed still made him feel guilty, although he realised that he would have felt much worse if he had shot his prisoners out of hand.

'So if they were obeying orders, why arrest them now?' Newman shook his head, puzzled at the workings of the military mind.

'How the hell should I know?' Haig's limited patience ended abruptly. 'Ask the occifers! Ask Breaker Morant; ask the bloody King! Ask anybody but me.'

About to add, 'ask Gideon Scheepers', Selkirk decided to keep quiet. This war was complicated enough without adding more controversial evidence. Scheepers had been the commander of a Boer commando who had burned farms, flogged African natives and murdered turncoat Boers. Never denying his maltreatment of the Africans, Scheepers had reported that under British rule 'everything is for the kaffirs; their own soldiers go short and the barbarian, the kaffir, gets all the benefits.' Nor did Scheepers deny shooting the Afrikaners. He had caught two spying on his men, made them draw lots and shot the loser. Scheepers had been executed on 17 January 1902, to the disgust of the Guardsmen who had to carry out the sentence.

War was never pretty, but this one was taking an ugly turn and most British soldiers just wanted it to end. They had no hatred for the Boers, no desire to burn farmhouses and took no pleasure in shooting brave men.

Silently, the Reivers watched the unhappy column file past. The four men only glanced once in their direction, but the expression of defiant hopelessness would remain with Selkirk for a long time. One of the men walked slightly apart from the others, with his shoulders stubbornly square and the corner of his mouth lifted in a sneer. He spat as he met Selkirk's eye.

'Learn your lesson, Lieutenant.' He spoke with the broad, flat accent of the English Midlands, 'remember what Poore said and shoot the Boers before you take them prisoner, not after.'

Selkirk held the man's eye. Provost Marshall Robert Poore was Kitchener's Chief of Police, a man feared by all the military malcontents in Africa. He had interpreted Kitchener's order, and had helped decide the fate of these four soldiers. Like Scheepers, they were to be shot as an example to the army and the world.

'That could have been us,' Donnelly said quietly.

Selkirk nodded. Much of the army believed that although Nat Blunt deserved all he got, Breaker Morant had been used as a scapegoat for the faults of his superiors. While the higher ranks gave the orders, it was those lower down the scale who had to carry them out. Men such as Morant or himself, were the natural victims of any military malpractice. Men with no connections, no influence; men whose death would improve the image of justice that Britain liked to project, but without harming anybody that mattered.

There were many in the army hierarchy who would delight in removing an upstart lieutenant. Georgina's husband was one, and her brother another. It seemed that he was safer fighting the Boer than when spending time with his own people. He touched spurs to Ben. 'Let's trek.'

The Reivers were formed up in all their glory on the flat ground of Green Point Common, with the great Atlantic rollers splintering white and frothy at their back and the slopes of Table Mountain rising above the city. Selkirk stood in front, uncomfortable in his newly pressed uniform and with his boots gleaming in the early morning sunlight. While most officers of the British army had a soldier servant to help them present an immaculate appearance, Selkirk had to rely on his own efforts, with the occasional help of a woman from the town.

He could feel his men fidgeting as they wondered why they had been ordered to parade at dawn, in their best uniforms. Selkirk was no wiser; Colonel Hume had given the order only the previous evening, leaving little time for preparation. 'Parade on horseback,' the message had specified, 'with all men present.'

The Reivers had been raised specifically for the South African War. They had no dashing dress uniform of scarlet and gold, so were formed up in field khaki, pressed and clean, but certainly not as ceremonial as any established regiment. Selkirk remembered the splendid show that the Royal Borderers had made when they paraded in Dublin immediately prior to departing for Africa, and sighed at the contrast. Battered and faded khaki, however clean, was no substitute for the brilliant scarlet.

As a boy, Selkirk had been astonished at the colours sported by the recruiting sergeant when he made his pilgrimage to the Ettrick Fair. That vocal, loquacious man had epitomised the glories of the Queen's empire that encompassed a quarter of the globe. Selkirk knew that many country boys had been dazzled by the splendour of scarlet in a manner that would never have worked with khaki. A small part of him felt cheated as his Reivers paraded in their field dress, as if these drably clad men were second-class soldiers. He smiled at the concept. Perhaps their picture would never enhance the front of a box of chocolates, but when it came to soldiering on the veldt, his Reivers could match anybody.

He checked them, scrutinising each man. There was Haig, small, scarred and ugly, Hetherington the bluff Northumbrian, Andy Charlton who had been wounded at Magersfontein, Blackdown the massively muscled poacher from the West Country, Ogilvy and Pert from Angus, Cobb and Grey the Australians and all the rest. Hard men, reliable men, good men, his men. These were Selkirk's Reivers.

Selkirk's horse broke wind noisily. 'Sorry lads,' he apologised.

'That's all right sir,' Pert said, 'we thought it was the horse!'

The ripple of laughter proved that manning blockhouses had not damaged the morale of the Reivers.

'Here they come, sir.' Sergeant Campbell spoke from the corner of his mouth. A veteran of Modder River and Magersfontein, he had joined the Reivers after recuperating from wounds and had proven himself an excellent soldier. He was also amorously and honourably pursuing a Boer woman. Campbell had saved the young son of Hansie Fourie from being shot by one of the Reivers and the two had been more than friends ever since. 'Looks like Colonel Hume's in front, sir.'

'Thank you sergeant,' Selkirk said. 'I'm quite capable of identifying the colonel without help.'

The tallest of the dozen riders scrutinised each man keenly, his weary eyes sunk beneath a maze of deep lines. 'All present Selkirk?'

'Yes sir. Twenty five men.'

Leaving his entourage to look out to sea, Hume inspected the Reivers, studying the face rather than the uniform of each man. One or two of the horses were restless, pawing the ground as their riders sought to make them stand motionless for this uncomfortable period. Selkirk could feel the tension behind him as Hume rode slowly along the line, making no comments. It seemed an age before the colonel returned to him.

'A fine body of men, Selkirk.' It was the age-old formula that Selkirk had heard a dozen senior officers utter on a score of parades.

Yet, perhaps because it was the first time the words had been addressed to him, about his men, he felt ridiculously pleased.

'Yes, sir. Thank you sir.' There was already a bite in the sun, so the first sweat of the day started from Selkirk's pores and began its trickle down his back. Within ten minutes his armpits would be damp, within half an hour his shirt would be sodden, and sitting on horseback would be decidedly uncomfortable.

'But a bit bare, don't you think?'

'Sir?' Slightly surprised, Selkirk did not understand the criticism.

'A bit bare. They lack something.' Hume motioned quickly with his right hand and the portly Major Scott moved toward him. The major's broad red face was peeling but there was a smile in his eyes. He removed a broad, blue box from his saddlebag and proffered it to Hume.

The colonel held the box for a good minute, seemingly intent on gazing out to sea. When he spoke, more than one Reiver started. 'Who is Trooper Donnelly? Ride forward please.'

'It's Sergeant Donnelly now sir.'

'As is right and proper,' Hume approved. He nodded as Donnelly approached, with eyes wary in an expressionless face. 'Lieutenant Selkirk recommended that you receive the DCM for your actions above the call of duty while on active service on the veldt.' Opening the box, Hume removed a circular silver medal, whose crimson ribbon he pinned carefully to Donnelly's breast. 'I was more than pleased to confirm the recommendation. Congratulations, Sergeant. From what I've heard, few men deserve it more.'

'Thank you sir.' For once, Donnelly's casual drawl was strained. He saluted clumsily and, avoiding Selkirk's gaze, returned to his position. There was a sound like indrawn breath from the Reivers.

'And Trooper MacPherson?'

MacPherson rode forward slowly. Known as Kirky for his extreme religious beliefs, he looked dazed as Hume also presented him with the DCM. For a moment Selkirk thought that he would refuse to accept it, but instead Kirky smiled and saluted.

'Thank you, sir.'

'These medals,' Hume stated in his quiet, brittle voice that nevertheless managed to penetrate the sound of surf and the raucous calls of the gulls, 'are not presented lightly. They are symbols of extreme bravery, courage beyond that normally displayed even by British soldiers.' He paused to let the words take hold, all the while scanning the assembled men with his expressionless blue eyes. 'The men who wear them represent all of you. You are Selkirk's Reivers, the striking force of the intelligence service, and if I say it myself, the finest fighting force, man for man, in Africa.'

The Reivers were too well disciplined to break into spontaneous cheering, but some nodded their acknowledgement and Applewood, the horse expert from Hampshire, smiled.

'I have one last presentation to make,' Hume continued, and removed another medal from Major Scott's box. 'Lieutenant Andrew Selkirk.'

Selkirk walked Ben forward and allowed Hume to pin the DSO on his tunic. The colonel seemed to take an age fiddling with the pin and ribbon, but at last the thing was done and he could salute and pull Ben back a pace.

Like MacPherson, Selkirk felt stunned. Although he knew the British soldier's studied contempt for all medals except the Victoria Cross, he was aware that something special had happened today. Whatever the future brought, if he lost his commission, if he once again became a private soldier, if he returned to his old life as a Border ploughman, nobody could take away his medal. Henceforth, he was Andrew Selkirk, DSO.

'Congratulations, Captain Selkirk.' Hume held out his hand.

'Thank you sir.' It took Selkirk a few minutes to realise what Hume had said. 'It's Lieutenant Selkirk sir.'

'I don't make mistakes, Selkirk.' Reaching inside the immaculate tunic that looked as if it had been measured in Saville Row, Hume produced a square buff envelope. 'Open this Selkirk and read it out loud. I want everybody to hear.'

Wondering, Selkirk eased away the wax seal and fumbled open the flap. He stared at the Royal Crest at the head of the single sheet of paper and read slowly.

'By order of His Majesty King Edward,' Selkirk deliberately missed out the VII after the king's name. He guessed that it was a number, but his education had never included Roman numerals. 'I am pleased to announce that Andrew Selkirk, lieutenant, commander of Selkirk's Reivers, is of this date appointed and promoted to Captain in the same formation. This field promotion comes about because of his consistent and loyal service to the Crown during the present war in South Africa. On the successful conclusion of hostilities, the said Andrew Selkirk shall retain the rank of Captain within his parent regiment of the Royal Borderers.' Selkirk looked up.

'Who's it from Selkirk?' Scott prodded gently, 'who signed it?'

Selkirk gazed at the mass of words at the bottom of the page. 'Horatio Herbert Baron Kitchener, of Khartoum, G.C.B., K.C.M.G., General Commander-in-Chief of His Majesty's forces in South Africa; High Commissioner in South Africa. That's Kitchener.'

'Must be true then, Selkirk,' Major Scott said cheerfully, 'for the Sirdar never lies.' He grinned and raised his voice, 'three cheers for Captain Selkirk!' He led the way by emitting a cheer that caused two large seagulls to fly screaming into the air. The Reivers followed his example, some grinning with what looked like genuine pleasure, others merely taking the opportunity to make a noise. Haig spat on the ground.

Hume leaned closer. 'As you will be aware, Selkirk, your actions on the Bechuanaland border can never be made public, but they were of great service to the Crown. However, your repulse of the Boer attack on Lord Kitchener was recorded by the newspapers and so must be rewarded. If it were possible to reward all your men, I would do so, but these three medals, plus your promotion, must be taken as being awarded to the entire unit.'

Scott ambled forward. 'I wouldn't wear these medals in the field if I were you lads. Piet likes a good target.'

Now the Reivers were cheering again, and Donnelly was pumping his hand in congratulation. Sergeant Campbell was nearly smiling, as honest Hetherington grinned foolishly and Newman lifted his water bottle in salute. Judging from the glitter in Newman's eye, there was more than just water in his bottle and Selkirk resolved to have all his men checked for spirits as soon as he could.

He felt dazed, as if he had been under an intense artillery bombardment. He was Captain Andrew Selkirk DSO; what would Jenny say about that?

'I want to see you at noon in my office Selkirk. In the Castle.' The atmosphere changed as Hume became suddenly businesslike. 'Medals and promotions are fine in themselves, but we still have a war to win.'

Chapter Three: Cape Town – February 1902

It was strange, and a little humbling, to walk with his new badges of rank and the medal ribbon bright on his tunic, stranger to acknowledge the salutes of lieutenants in the regular army. Selkirk wondered if they would still have treated him with respect if they knew who he really was, but dismissed the thought, as he marched through the classical Dutch entrance into the great pentagon-shaped Cape Town Castle that had stood guard over the southernmost city of Africa for nearly two hundred and fifty years.

He knew little about the Castle, save that it was the oldest building in South Africa, but its size was impressive. Automatically, Selkirk surveyed the bastions at each of the five corners, measured the ten yard high walls and wondered how he would attack such a place. Inevitably it had been Newman who told him of the ghost of Lady Ann Barnard, who was reputed to have bathed stark naked, but Selkirk had little time for such nonsense. As rulers of the Cape, the hierarchy of British military and civilian command now occupied the castle. In Selkirk's eyes it was not dissimilar to the eighteenth century barracks at Berwick, perhaps a trifle cramped for modern soldiers, with limited access to the city, but it was certainly handy for the railway station from where so many troops travelled north to the fighting.

The Guardsman at Hume's door saluted automatically, the creases of his trousers pressed to an edge that appeared sharp enough to cut.

'I want you back in the veldt, Selkirk.' Colonel Hume looked even wearier when he was indoors, with deep lines on his sallow face and grey hair noticeable at his temples.

'Yes, sir,' Selkirk agreed.

He glanced around Hume's office. There was barely room for the battered stinkwood desk and two chairs, yet Hume had his usual pile of buff-coloured files in front of him as well as a collection of books. A large-scale map of South Africa stretched across two walls while a brace of clocks ticked formidably. One showed the local time, the other the time in London, a reminder of how far they were from the centre of Empire. A holstered Webley revolver hung from the back of Hume's chair. A small window looked over the grassed courtyard, where a file of Cape Town Highlanders drilled impeccably. Remembering them from the relief of Kimberley, Selkirk felt a fond familiarity. Hume lifted the folder that lay on top of the pile on his desk. The words 'Top Secret' were stamped diagonally across the surface. The mauve ink was slightly smudged. 'What I am about to tell you must not go any further. Do you understand?'

'Of course, sir.'

'There's no "of course sir" about it.' Hume sounded like a man with a bad hangover, which surprised Selkirk after the morning's ceremony. 'I've been hearing reports about how you command your Reivers. I know you treat them like equals, allow them to give an opinion in command decisions. That will not happen in this case.'

'Yes, sir,' Selkirk agreed.

'Good. That's why I have promoted you to captain and sent you two more lieutenants. I intend to insert a layer of command between you and your men. I also want to increase your numbers from twenty-five to fifty.'

'Yes, sir. Thank you sir.' Despite Hume's brusque words, Selkirk recognised the compliment. He was no longer a junior lieutenant in command of a handful of men, but a captain with quite a powerful strike force. With fifty men, trained up to Reiver levels and Reiver tactics, he could make quite an impact on this war.

'Windrush and Cloete are sound men. Experienced men. Use them well.'

'Yes, sir. May I make a suggestion sir?' Selkirk felt his chin lift in a manner that Sergeant Lithgow had once described as 'dumb insolence.'

'You may.' Hume's eyes were bleak as a November sky in the Merse.

'May Sergeant Donnelly be promoted to Lieutenant? He held that rank with the Kimberley Light Horse and only lost it when they were disbanded.'

Hume remained expressionless. 'That would make three lieutenants and a captain to fifty men. A little top heavy, don't you think?'

'Yes, sir. Perhaps I only need one as well as Donnelly.' Selkirk refused to withdraw from his position.

'You mentioned that you needed a translator. Both your new men speak Boer-Dutch and some native languages. I know one of them personally.' Hume was obviously not inclined to retract his decision either. 'Lieutenant Windrush served under me in the Oxfordshire Regiment.'

'Yes, sir. You said he was experienced. Has he any experience of this type of warfare?' A man with battle experience was always preferable to a recruit, but a man who understood irregular horse tactics was invaluable.

'Both have a little. You will find out more when you meet them again.' Hume's voice remained neutral. He opened the buff folder and lifted the first sheet of paper. 'You may have heard of the peace conferences between General Kitchener and Botha?'

Selkirk nodded. 'Yes, sir. They were held at Middelburg early last year, but nothing came of them.'

'Indeed, but they were not useless. General Kitchener learned a great deal about what the Boers want from this war. Botha asked that Britain pay the debts of the two Republics, that Dutch as well as English be taught in schools and that Britain should pay for Boer farms to be rebuilt.' Hume looked up. 'What do you think of all that then, captain?'

Coming from an agricultural background, Selkirk had never agreed to the British policy of farm burning. He remembered, vividly, the acrid tang of smoke as Boer farms burned on the veldt, and the stomach-turning stench of the thousands of rotted corpses of animals slaughtered by British troops. 'I would say that's fair sir. We destroyed their farms, so we should help rebuild them. Dutch is their language, so of course they can still speak it, and to judge by the Boers that I have met, they don't have two pennies to rub together.'

'So we should pay our enemies?' Hume's voice remained quiet.

'Yes sir. We captured the gold mines of the Rand. We can use the gold. Anyway sir, it will probably be cheaper to pay off the Boers than to continue fighting.' A year ago, Selkirk could not have worked out even such simple economics, now he was prepared to argue his case with a Lieutenant Colonel.

Hume grunted. 'In your opinion, perhaps. However, Botha also demanded that amnesty should be granted to all the Burghers, both from the Republics and the Cape, who fought against us.' He looked directly into Selkirk's eyes. 'That includes the Cape rebels.' He paused for a moment. 'Botha also wants the Boers to have some form of self-determination. What do you think about that, Captain Selkirk?'

'The Boers fought well sir, and it was their country. I'm not sure about the Cape Rebels though.' In common with most British soldiers, Selkirk could admire a brave enemy, but had little time for those he saw as traitors. The farmers of the Cape, whatever their blood and language, enjoyed the advantages of being citizens of the Empire. By biting the hand that protected them, they had helped rock the foundations of that Empire.

'Self determination?'

'Why not? Half the princes in India rule their own lands, and they seem loyal and happy enough. New Zealand too. Why not the Boers?'

'Why not indeed.' Hume sighed. 'God, man. We'll be letting the Irish and Scots go soon. What price Empire then?' For the second time Hume's mask of self-control slipped to reveal the seething reality beneath. He looked at the map, took a deep breath and continued.

'As we both know, these negotiations led to nothing. However, the government of the Netherlands has recently suggested that they broker a peace. As yet, I do not know if our government intends to accept the invitation, or if General Kitchener will meet with Botha again. However, one thing is clear, a peace negotiation is like a game of whist; the side that holds most trumps wins.'

'Yes, sir.' Selkirk had never enjoyed whist. As a private soldier he had played blackjack, that most simple method of parting with hard-earned money and Donnelly had taught him poker while they were in Kimberley. Neither were subtle games, but he understood the rules.

'At the minute we hold most of the trumps, Selkirk. We have the gold of the Rand and the manpower. We have most of the communications of the country and all the main cities. Thanks to the

Reivers,' he briefly focussed on Selkirk's face, 'we have countered the attempts of any foreign powers to intervene in our struggle.'

Abruptly standing, Hume pointed toward the map that stretched across the wall. 'However, the Boers also have a couple of useful cards. They have what they call the 'bitter enders', those Boers who refuse to surrender; the most intractable, stubborn veterans of this war. And they still control some areas of land.' He pointed to Cape Town. 'We are now here,' he explained, as to a child, 'and here is where you are going.' He moved his finger northward, crossing riverbeds and mountain ranges as if they were nothing, until he reached an apparently featureless area in the northern Transvaal. 'You will travel by rail as far as Pietersburg,' he tapped a small dot on the map, 'and ride the rest. This is the Verneuk Valley. When you reach this area you will find a town named Akersdorp. You will report to the officer commanding and present him with this letter.' Reaching into the top drawer of his desk, Hume produced a sealed envelope, which he handed to Selkirk.

'Yes, sir.' Selkirk glanced at the envelope. It was simply marked, Officer Commanding, Akersdorp. 'May I know what it says sir?'

'It introduces you and orders the Officer Commanding to allow you total latitude in how you command your Reivers.' Hume's smile was strained. 'As you see, there is no name on the envelope. That is because we are not exactly sure who commands Akersdorp at present. Some of our units have been pretty roughly handled in the Verneuk Valley. Indeed there are some areas that we no longer enter. Brother Boer is trying to create a power base there, on the frontier between the territory they used to own, and that owned by us and the Portuguese.'

'Yes, sir.' Selkirk could see the complications that even a small area held by the Boers could cause. It would be a fine bargaining tool in any peace conference, or could be the nucleus of a new attempt at Boer independence, perhaps with foreign help. Both the Portuguese and the Germans had an interest in that area of Africa.

'I take it that other units have already tried to chase out the Boers?'

'Four times. We sent in two large columns of mixed horse, artillery and foot. The first swept through in five days and left, declaring the area free of Boers. On the sixth day the Boers attacked the garrison of Akersdorp. The second column stayed longer, and lost a hundred men from disease and sunstroke. One of the casualties was the colonel in command; he remained with the garrison. Indeed he may be in command there, but with no news coming out we cannot be sure.'

Hume glowered at Selkirk. 'After that failure we tried smaller columns; one was ambushed somewhere on the low veldt and some of the men managed to return. The second just vanished. Perhaps it got through but we don't know. Even the blasted natives disappear up there.'

Hume held Selkirk's eye. 'The last man to return was a native runner. He gabbled something about Aasvogels wiping out our patrols. Patent nonsense of course. Aasvogel is the Dutch word for a vulture; frightful brutes but hardly a threat to a patrol of soldiers. No idea what the man was on about. More importantly, he reported that deserters from the garrison have joined the Boers. It seems that they prefer to join the enemy than suffer in Akersdorp. So if you have any doubts about any of your Reivers, send them to their parent regiment.'

'I stand by my Reivers sir.' Selkirk felt himself stiffen at any suggestion of disloyalty by his men.

'No doubt, Selkirk, but will they stand by you when things get a bit sticky?'

'They always do sir.' Selkirk examined the map more closely. 'Do we know how many Boers there are?'

'No. Reports of their numbers vary from a hundred to two hundred.' Hume opened the file again. 'But we do know that they are very good at what they do. They seem to have a grasp of our tactics and they counter us at every turn.' Hume's sudden smile took Selkirk by surprise. 'That's where you come in, of course. Your unconventional methods may just be enough to unsettle brother Piet. Indeed, I'm counting on it.'

Selkirk tried to remain expressionless as he pondered this new situation. He was being sent in with fifty men against an unknown number of the enemy who had already repulsed four British columns, two of them very much larger than the Reivers. There was also the possibility of desertion, the very real threat of disease and apparently a flock of savage vultures.

Hume was watching him carefully. 'We also know that there is at least one woman with the Boers and we think it might be your old friend Helena Van Vuren'

'Again!' Selkirk had faced Helena Van Vuren on numerous occasions from Magersfontein to Pretoria, and had great respect for her tactical skill and fighting ability. He still cringed at the memory of Helena's successful ambush of his Mounted Infantry when they had been left to walk back, naked and ashamed, while the Boers mocked them. He also recalled her successful fighting withdrawal from an unsuccessful attempt to capture General Kitchener. Later they had made an armed truce when the Reivers had defended her farm against Charles Drongan's Ettrick and Cheviot Yeomanry, but her last words had been a warning that if they met again, she would shoot him. Selkirk took her words seriously.

'I see you remember Van Vuren, the Boer Boadicea.'

'Yes.' Selkirk had still not discovered who Boadicea was. Perhaps he would find out in one of the novels he was reading.

'Let's hope that you get a chance to bag her this time.' Like many soldiers, Hume used hunting terminology when he spoke of the war. He looked closely at Selkirk. 'Although I did hear some strange rumours about her on that last trek of yours, when you rode out to collect a man you left wounded on the veldt and returned in pretty poor condition yourself.'

'You can't blame me for rumours sir.' Selkirk was immediately on the defensive. He had not mentioned his encounter with Charles Drongan to anybody, although the Reivers knew the truth, and stories had probably spread through the entire British Army.

'Indeed.' Hume said dryly. His eyes seemed to drive deep into Selkirk's skull, and then he turned away as if in dismissal. 'I want your Reivers to remove the Boers from the Verneuk Valley and reinforce the garrison of Akersdorp until a larger column relieves you.' It was only a few words, but they confirmed Selkirk's future.

'Yes, sir.' Selkirk peered at the map. 'There seems to be an awful lot of nothing around Akersdorp. Why would anybody build a town there in the first place?'

Hume shrugged. 'God knows. Maybe it was a jumping off stage for hunters. I've really no idea.'

'Yes, sir.' Selkirk nodded. 'I'll need maps and salted horses sir, for that's deep in the tsetse fly belt.' He knew that there was a perennial difficulty in obtaining enough horses for the army, but he wanted the best possible for his men.

'I'll see what can be done. I want you ready to leave within a week.' Hume returned to his paper shuffling. 'Oh and Selkirk; your reinforcements will be with you soon. You'd better make sure that they know what they're in for.'

The draft of new men arrived next day, mostly veterans with the sun browned faces and jaunty arrogance of colonials but with a sprinkling of British, complete with the peeling sunburn that earned them the name of Rooineck, or red neck. Selkirk ensured that they were made to feel comfortable, removed Haig and Newman from the newcomers' liquid refreshment and worried over the administrative details necessary in sending fifty men into the field.

They spent the next week preparing for departure, with Pert, Selkirk and Applewood checking each horse before deciding whether it was fit for the rigours of the next campaign. Blackdown, the ex-saddler, was meticulous in examining the equipment, while Sergeant Campbell ensured that every man's carbine was in pristine condition. With the suspicion natural to most NCOs, he stripped and checked the Maxim in person.

It was unfortunate that the Reivers' allocation of horses had not increased proportionally to their number of men, but the British army could never find enough remounts. British buyers scoured half the world for horses, from Argentina to Hungary, New South Wales to Spain. Although they brought in tens of thousands each month, the rigours of campaigning killed two out of every three new mounts. Part-decomposing corpses of horses, sheep and men polluted the veldt, spreading disease such as the enteric fever that was to kill over 13,000 soldiers and invalid 31,000 more before the war ended.

There were only thirty new horses for the Reivers, a mixture of sturdy Walers and poor specimens from the Argentine, so it would not be possible for each man to have a spare horse.

'We might be able to capture some from the Boers,' Donnelly said, doubtfully. He knew how well the Boers protected their animals.

'Maybe.' Selkirk looked up from the sheaf of paperwork with which he struggled. If officers only had to lead their men into battle, the British army would be matchless, for there was not a braver band of officers in the world. However, sheer valour often took second place behind planning and administration, and many British officers were not overly blessed with brains. Selkirk, who had left formal education at the age of eleven, and who had spent most of his childhood avoiding school, lacked even the dubious advantage of understanding the classics. 'Just do what you can, Donnelly.' He returned to his contest with railway timetables and the language of official documents.

'How are the new chums shaping up?'

'They seem a likely enough bunch,' Donnelly said, 'but it's too early to tell yet. I doubt we'll know until we're on the veldt.'

Placing his finger on a column of black print that was meant to convey some meaning, Selkirk looked up. 'Watch them carefully, Donnelly, and try and fit in a little training.'

Well used to the movement of British soldiers, the inhabitants of Cape Town barely glanced up as Selkirk's little unit clattered to the Railway Station to entrain for the north. No doubt there was at least one spy among the spectators, but it was hardly worth reporting the movement of such a small number of men in this war of tens of thousands.

There was the usual bustle as the horses were loaded on to their railway wagons, head to head and flank to flank in the rattling, foetid heat. Many of the men asked to remain with their mounts, but Selkirk, who shared their sympathies, refused permission. He needed his men in fighting condition and soldiers who had spent hours cooped up with a score of horses would be in no condition to campaign. There were the usual incidents that happened when any unit of British soldiers entrained in the dark. About to interfere as Haig exchanged vociferous insults with one of the new men, a Welshman named Thomson, Selkirk thought it best to leave such matters to his sergeants. He watched as Campbell wrestled a bottle of Cape Brandy from Newman, as Fairweather disputed possession of his rifle with a wiry Hottentot who claimed to have won it in a game of cards and as Cobb tested his muscles against a brawny rooineck from Norfolk.

More important was the appearance of their new officers, broad shouldered, confident looking men with steady eyes.

'Excuse me, Captain Selkirk.'

Selkirk acknowledged the salutes.

'Lieutenants Windrush and Cloete reporting sir.' The salute was precise, but Selkirk got the impression that Windrush was inspecting him. His voice had the clipped, foreshortened vowels of South Africa.

At that instant the engine emitted a loud shrieking whistle and a vast amount of steam, which billowed down the gas-lit platform and sent some of the men into false paroxysms of coughing. Windrush remained unmoved, but Cloete seemed interested in watching the reactions of the Reivers.

'I thought you came from Oxfordshire!' Selkirk had to shout to be heard above the commotion of machinery and raucous soldiery.

To add to the noise, a handful of women had arrived. The Reivers had been warned not to tell anybody that they were departing, but some had obviously made attachments during their time in Cape Town and could not bear to slip quietly away. The women were of all sizes and colours, with one pure-bred Zulu maiden glowering at the high-cheeked Malay girl who threw herself toward Blackdown. Despite his reputation as a lady's man, Newman sat in virtuous isolation beside his window.

'No, sir.' Windrush did not have to raise his voice to be heard. 'I'm from Natal. My people came out with the 1820 settlers. They were from Oxfordshire originally, and I was attached to the Oxford Regiment for a few months. After that I was with Colonel Rimington.'

'I see. Well, welcome aboard, Windrush.' Selkirk held out his hand just as the Malay woman and her Zulu rival fell on each other with high shrieks and spitting invective. It was typical of Hume to only tell him half the truth. For a moment Selkirk wondered what else was unsaid about this mission. 'Thank you, sir.' After shaking hands, Windrush pulled a packet of papers from his pocket. 'Colonel Hume sends his regards sir, and asked me to give you these.'

Selkirk nodded, 'we'd better get aboard, Windrush, or the train will leave without us.' He glanced at Cloete, who had not uttered a word the whole time. 'You too, Cloete.'

About half the Reivers were leaning out of the open windows, some saying a passionate good-bye to their lady friends, others watching the increasingly violent encounter between the Malay and the Zulu woman. Blackdown had already turned his attention to a shapely blonde who was apparently attempting to enter the carriage through the half-open window.

Ignoring the confusion on the platform, the guard blew his whistle, produced his flag and the train pulled out into the pre-dawn black of Africa. Selkirk introduced Windrush and Cloete to Donnelly, ordered Campbell to look after the Reivers and ushered his officers into the first class carriage.

'I don't seem to remember your face, Windrush, although I fought alongside Rimington's Tigers back in 1900.' He had served beside the famous colonial mounted unit when Bobs Roberts was beginning his push that ended the first stage of the war.

Windrush shrugged 'I was at Klip Drift sir, and the relief of Mafeking, but I don't remember you either.' He glanced toward Donnelly, who was studying him openly. 'Perhaps our paths just did not cross.'

'So it seems.' Selkirk held out his hand in welcome. 'Well, you come well-recommended, Windrush. And call me Selkirk out of the men's hearing. This is not a regular regiment.'

Windrush's smile transformed his face into that of a mischievous youth. 'Right you are, sir.'

'And how are you, Cloete?' The second of the newcomers was immensely broad across the shoulders, with a mouth that seemed to be set in a permanent sulk. The red band around his collar marked him as a National Scout, one of the Free Burghers who had switched allegiance to fight for the British.

'I am very well, sir, thank you.' The accent was thick but the voice was clear. Probably clearer than his conscience, Selkirk thought.

As if able to read his thoughts, Cloete gave Selkirk's outstretched hand a vindictive squeeze. 'I only want peace in my land.'

Selkirk nodded. 'I can imagine how you must feel. It must be terrible to see a war being fought over the land you carved out of the wilderness.' He raised his voice slightly, in case any of his men were listening at the door of the carriage. 'There are many of your countrymen who agree that the best way forward is to join the Empire. We all know and respect your fighting qualities; the potential of a Boer force fighting within the Empire is limitless.'

Although Selkirk had little time for turncoats and spoke only to preserve the peace within his Reivers, there was some truth in his words. Like all British soldiers, he knew that the British army had a history of recruiting its ex-enemies. The Indian army was largely composed of men whose grandfathers and great-grandfathers had fought against the Empire; Sikhs, Dogras, Gurkhas, Pathans had all been stubborn foes and were now amongst the best troops in the army. Even the Scottish Highlanders had once fought against the Crown. Nevertheless, it seemed a bit early to be recruiting Boers. He looked directly at the broad Burgher, but saw no deceit in the man's face. All the same, Selkirk thought that big Lieutenant Cloete would bear watching; a man his size would be a formidable enemy.

'I agree sir.' Windrush gave his opinion. 'We live in a world of Empires, and there is no room for little countries. It is far better to inspaan with the greatest Empire than to be a mosquito that buzzes and bites until it is swatted.'

'Perhaps we are the swat,' Donnelly said quietly. He surveyed Cloete without rancour. 'But the Boers sure make a dangerous mosquito.'

There was a pause in the conversation, so Selkirk chivvied the officers away. 'Donnelly, you introduce Lieutenants Windrush and Cloete to the men. Make sure that everybody is behaving. And check Haig's waterbottle – and Newman's. These two are not safe with anything liquid.'

Once the trio of lieutenants was gone, Selkirk thankfully shut himself into the first class compartment. The paperwork and stress of preparing for a campaign had left him feeling depressed, and he was glad of some time alone while the train rattled northward. He had hardly thought of Georgina during the last week, but now he imagined her lying in comfort between silken sheets at the Mount Nelson Hotel, cuddling up to James Montgomery, while he again led his Reivers into the unknown.

Strangely, it was easier to remember Georgina as a child at the Ettrick Races than it was to picture her in Africa. Her features seemed to merge with those of Marie, the Griqua woman who had nursed Selkirk in Kimberley and again when he caught enteric fever after drinking water from the Modder River. He missed Marie, who had left for the wild North with Duff the enigmatic hunter. Selkirk always smiled at her memory, for she was undoubtedly one of the most genuine people he had ever met. 'God Bless you Marie,' he said quietly, as his pensive mood continued, 'for you deserve a better man than I could ever be.'

The gaslight allowed him just enough illumination to read the papers that Hume had sent. He learned that Windrush had indeed spent time with Rimington's Tigers, could speak Boer, Zulu and a couple of other native languages and had worked in a bank in Durban before the war. Selkirk had imagined that every Colonial was an expert in hunting and scouting, but of course they had their share of clerks and shopkeepers too. At that moment he could not think what use a bank clerk would be on the veldt, but anybody who had ridden with the Tigers must be good. It would also be useful to have a translator.

Selkirk alternately dozed and stared out of the window as the train rattled north through the beautiful, savage mountain ranges that guarded the tip of Africa. He had travelled this section of the route over two years before when he had been a green private with the Royal Borderers and everybody had hoped to see action before the war ended. He recalled those days when the confidence based on tradition was badly shaken by successive defeats at Spion Kop, Magersfontein and Colenso, but the army had regrouped and relearned. He recalled the great Flank March and the rolling advance under Bobs, when the Boer towns had fallen in quick succession and victory had seemed certain tomorrow, or the next day. Who could have foreseen, then, that the Boer commandos would have fought so long and so hard?

As the train rolled across the semi-desert of the Great Karoo with the vast horizons that Selkirk had come to accept as being part of the African landscape, he caught up on the sleep that he had lacked for the past week. In between dozing he read and studied. His lack of education had proved embarrassing on too many occasions for him to ignore it, so Selkirk had scoured the markets and shops of Cape Town for as many school books as possible. Now he pored over elementary reading books and mathematical formulae that he vaguely remembered from the days when Old Crabby had attempted to fill his head with knowledge by belting the palms of his swollen hands.

In between periods of studying he scanned his pile of letters again, with the writing that was now so familiar, and read the news of the Fethan with a nostalgia that never faded.

He awoke as the train jerked into a siding, eased his cramped body and checked the horses and men, making sure both were fed and watered before the next stage of their journey. Northward and northward across the great plains of the Orange Free State, change trains at Johannesburg and on again, across land that Briton and Boer had fought for, hour after hour, day after day of jolting monotony. He stared out of the window as the winter-brown veldt slid past with the kopjes appearing, rising and fading away with near tiresome regularity.

Selkirk got to know a little about his officers on that journey, but he knew that the real revelations would only come when they were out in the field. He learned that Cloete was taciturn, perhaps slightly contemptuous of the British soldiers with whom he fought. He learned that Windrush was excitable, capable of sudden bursts of enthusiasm and long periods of introspection, but was already popular with the men.

They left the train at a dismal siding just south of Pietersburg in the northern Transvaal and reacquainted themselves with their horses. Men eased stiff and cramped limbs, swore a little and checked the bolts of their rifles for dust and rust, for they all knew that the Boers could attack from anywhere at any time. Although Roberts and Kitchener had ground the main Boer armies into little more than a memory, the remaining commandos were more than capable of destroying any small British force. A unit such as the Reivers, isolated and unsupported, would be an excellent morale–boosting target for the bitter-enders.

After watering the horses, the Reivers ate, then fastened the light saddles that John Blackdown had devised on to their horses. Selkirk fondled the ears of Ben as he fastened the buckles of the girth and checked the saddle for comfort. He slipped a handful of barley sugar into Ben's mouth, did the same for Fleet, his second horse, and ensured that the other Reivers did likewise.

'From here we're on horse, boys.' Donnelly sounded cheerful as the Reivers stretched and scratched. They swore as they realised that the easy times were past. The air was hot and humid, pressing down from a thunderous sky. All around stretched flat dull grass, interspersed by isolated trees and clumps of vegetation.

'Here we go again lads,' Ogilvie checked the bolt of his carbine, 'back to auld claes and porridge.'

'Just like home then, Sawnie.' Thomson, the dapper Welshman who had already argued with Haig, had been displeased to learn that a good number of the Reivers were Scots.

'Where's your home, you Welsh bastard? Inside a sheepskin?' Ogilvie swung the carbine and sighted it on Thomson.

'Enough.' Windrush pushed the men apart; 'we're here to fight the Boers, not each other.'

Selkirk organised them into the familiar order of march, but with double the number of men he could have a stronger protective screen. Retaining thirty men for the main body, he sent five men ahead, five on each flank and five as a rearguard. The Maxim machine gun thudded along with its cart in the centre of the column, together with cases of spare ammunition, spare water, food and basic medical supplies. Half a dozen packhorses carried the rest, for the Reivers rode light.

It was the formation that they had adopted when they rode to Bechuanaland and it was the one that they understood best. They were the Reivers, Selkirk's Reivers, fifty of the finest fighting men that the Empire could produce, ready to settle accounts with Piet for his early successes at Spion Kop and Magersfontein.

As he had expected, some of the original Reivers resented the new men, treating them with a show of superiority, so Selkirk mingled both sets together to ensure that a clique did not form. He gave orders that kept the known troublemakers as distant as possible until they had worked out a pecking order, but with Donnelly and Campbell constantly watching, there was no real need to fret.

The first day's march was hard as the Reivers readjusted to life on the veldt, and by late afternoon men were complaining as they eased themselves from the saddles. The air here seemed humid compared to the crispness of the high veldt or the more maritime climate of South Africa, so men lost more moisture through sweat and seemed to lack energy.

Selkirk called for a camp at the banks of a sluggish brown river and spent three days training the new men how to fight Reiver-style. Simultaneously he assessed their potential. Overall they were good, better than the average British soldier, but woefully below the Boer standard in tracking, riding and marksmanship. However, one or two had potential. There was a Canadian named Bowden whose shooting rivalled that of Macpherson, while Thomson seemed to be adept at tracking. With training, and by following the example of the established Reivers, the new chums would get better. They would have to, for Johnny Boer was a merciless teacher.

Selkirk taught them how to attack a kopje, with the best shots laying down covering fire and the others charging forward, firing and changing position to spoil the defenders' aim. He taught them the rudiments of tracking and made sure that they could care for their weapons in the sandy or damp conditions in which they fought. He told them about personal hygiene, ordered them to water the horses before themselves and ensured that they boiled water before drinking it.

There were the inevitable squabbles as men jockeyed for position, the inevitable newcomer who sneered at Newman for his educated accent and the inevitable aftermath when Haig defended his friend with fist and boot. Selkirk allowed Sergeant Campbell to deal with these situations as he called Donnelly, Cloete and Windrush together and told them all he could of their mission.

'But there's only fifty of us.' Windrush looked around the Reivers. Most of the men were working with the horses while sentries watched over the surrounding countryside.

'We took half this number on our first campaign,' Selkirk said, 'and came back intact.' He grinned, 'that's what the Reivers are for. We out-commando the Boer commandos.'

'I'm intrigued by these Aasvogels you mentioned,' Cloete said in his ponderous fashion. 'The name may mean vulture, but I do not think that your agent was referring to the bird. I suspect there is something else out there.' He gestured to the north with a jerk of his head. 'No doubt we will learn in time.'

They rose before dawn on the fourth morning and moved north and east with extra kegs of water on the cart and their bottles filled. Each man had his blanket behind his saddle, two full bandoleers of ammunition criss-crossed on his chest and his ammunition pouches overflowing. They carried their Lee-Enfield carbines across their laps and scanned the surrounding country. Compared to the beauties of the Cape, this was a barren landscape. The occasional blackened skeletons of a farmhouse spoke with silent eloquence of the ugly turn this war had taken. They passed fields where flies buzzed darkly around the bloated corpses of sheep and cattle. They turned their heads from steadings where once families had lived and laughed, but which now supported only predatory vultures and sad memories.

'They make a desert and call it peace,' Newman said quietly, and although Selkirk did not recognise the alleged quote of Calgacus, he agreed with the sentiments. A farmer by birth and inclination, this wasted land sickened him more than he could say.

'Bastards.'

'That's us you're talking about,' Newman reminded. 'We are responsible for this. The British burned the farms and killed the livestock.'

'Do you think that I don't know that?' Selkirk rounded on him savagely. 'God save us. All these empty farms! Where are the people?'

Cloete looked at him through curiously sympathetic eyes. 'Don't you know where they put the people?'

45

In common with every other soldier in the British army, Selkirk had heard the stories. He had heard about the refugee or concentration camps to which the wives and families of the Boers were driven. For refuge, so the officials said. To keep them from feeding the commandos, said the military hierarchy, while the Boers claimed that they had been herded there to die. Selkirk had heard about the terrible conditions, the disease and the famine that killed scores and hundreds. He did not believe the tales, regarding them as exaggeration or downright lies.

'I've heard the rumours,' he admitted.

'They're more than rumours,' Cloete said. 'The camps exist and they're Hell on Earth. The women and children are dying like flies.' He looked away for a second. 'That's one reason I want this war to end quickly.'

Selkirk could not keep the contempt from his voice. 'You're afraid of being put in a camp?'

Cloete shook his head, seemingly inured to the constant innuendoes of cowardice. 'No. You don't understand. I've seen the camps. I don't want my people to suffer any more. We can't win this war.' He looked deep into Selkirk's face, obviously desperate to be understood. 'If some foreign power, Prussia or the Netherlands, had intervened on our side, we might have had a chance, but they didn't. And now there are too many khaki. And the longer the war lasts, the more women and children will die.'

Selkirk tried to put himself in Cloete's situation. He tried to picture a foreign army dominating the Borders, burning the farms along the Fethan, rounding up the women and thrusting them into a great prison cage. What would he do? Fight? While Jenny and Margaret and Agatha suffered and starved? Or would he make peace, get them released and see what came next.

'How bad are these camps?'

'Some are worse than others,' Cloete was not smiling, 'but none of them are pleasant. Oh, I don't think the British intended to kill the innocent, but many of my people just are not used to that kind of lifestyle. They do not understand about camp hygiene and clean water and using latrines because such things are not necessary in the veldt.'

Selkirk nodded. He remembered the bedroom at Hendrinafontein, where a ram's horn was thrust through the mud wall to serve as a primitive urinal. He recalled Hendrina laughing when Newman asked where the latrine was.

'Wat makeer die wye wereld?' 'What's the matter with the wide world?' In other words, find a suitable place outside. With such an attitude, it was no wonder that disease was rampant and children died in shocking numbers.

Cloete looked away. 'You don't like me, do you?'

'I don't fully trust you,' Selkirk admitted candidly

Cloete nodded. 'I can understand that. I'm not sure if I would understand an Englishman who fought for the Free Republics.' He forced a smile 'Or even a Bergschotten, a mountain Scot like yourself.'

Both men turned away as they passed a field full of slaughtered sheep. Flies rose in black millions from the swollen and rotted corpses. 'Jesus.' Haig blasphemed freely, 'what a way to fight a war!'

Cloete shook his head. 'Even some of the rooineck soldiers seem to agree.' He pointed to the ground. 'There's spoor there, sir. Naked feet. Kaffirs probably, probing to see what they can loot. No danger to us. I can show you one of these camps,' he said, deliberately casual, 'then you can judge if you would rather lose a war or let your family suffer.'

Selkirk recognised the appeal in Cloete's eyes. The man was desperate to be understood; he did not want to be despised as a traitor. 'How far is it?'

'Three hours ride. More time to train your new chums,' the slang phrase sounded strange in Cloete's mouth, 'before we enter hostile territory.'

Their first view was of a giant enclosure, nearly a cage, with tall posts and barbed wire stretching for perhaps three hundred yards on each side of a square. Inside the wire, as regular as the lines of a regiment of British infantry, were row after row of white tents, while in the centre stood a number of wooden huts with corrugated iron roofs, one of which bore a large red cross. The entire compound seemed to seethe with people, some walking in little groups, some standing talking or working, and some running. Most however, just sat listlessly, staring at the sky or at the rolling brown veldt from which they seemed forever barred.

'Most are not fenced,' Cloete explained in an attempt to be fair, 'but this one is. Perhaps for security?' He shrugged, 'maybe the wild tribes?'

'Methods of barbarism indeed,' Newman said, quoting the Liberal leader, Campbell-Bannerman.

Other reivers were more forceful, if less erudite. 'Sweet Jesus.' It was one of the new chums; a gaunt-faced man from Armagh named Elwood who made the comment. 'It's a prison for women and bairns.' He looked round to Selkirk, 'What have they done sir, to be put away?'

Selkirk shook his head, as appalled as any of his men. He had a sudden, vivid recollection of his childhood, running free in the hills above the Fethan, and remembered how much he had hated the chalky confinement of the tiny school. He could not imagine what life must be like for these children secured behind barbed wire all the time, particularly when they were used to the free ranging life of the veldt.

'Is this what we're fighting for sir?' Kirky Macpherson shook his head. 'This isn't what they told us in Kingussie! They said that the Boers had oppressed British people in Johannesburg and had invaded the Cape Colony.'

Selkirk nodded. 'I know. And it was true, Macpherson.'

'They didn't say anything about putting women and children in jail.' Macpherson was normally a very private soldier, content to do his job, read his Bible and ignore the jibes of his less religious comrades. However, he always reacted to any hint of injustice or cruelty, for that, Selkirk realised, was part of the nature of the British soldier. They would fight all day without a murmur of complaint, endure endless hardships for themselves, but rise in indignation at an arbitrary act against someone that they considered weaker or more hard-done-by than they were.

'No, they did not.' Selkirk agreed. He thought of the bitterness of the Amazon Brigade of Pretoria, and the tactical guile of Helena Van Vuren. He was not surprised that the Burgher women wanted to fight, if their children were being placed in camps such as this. 'Maybe the women are safer here than out on the veldt,' he said, 'with all the wild animals and the African tribes.'

Cloete had been staring into the camp, his face unreadable. 'Kitchener has already given orders that no more people are to be admitted to the camps. For humanitarian reasons, he claimed. You don't believe that any more than I do, Captain Selkirk.' He looked at Selkirk, and the mask slipped for a moment, so there was terrible anguish and a smouldering anger that Selkirk could readily understand.

'You see why I want this war to end, Captain Selkirk? Not because I love the British Empire. Not because I want to betray my country, but because I want to save them. They can die in there,' he indicated the camp, 'of disease and hopelessness. Or out there,' another jerk of the head, 'of starvation and exposure. After all, the British have burned their homes.'

Cloete's voice rose. 'You British talk of fair play and sportsmanship, but you don't fight fair. You use women and children as weapons of war.'

An image of the wagons of Paardeberg came to Selkirk, of the burning wreckage where women and children wept as their men surrendered. He remembered the Boers firing on a hospital tent, and raising the white flag to lure the British closer.

'We fight to win, Lieutenant Cloete.' Selkirk knew that he would now watch Cloete even more carefully. 'As do the Boers.'

'Sir.' Selkirk had not seen Campbell approach. The sergeant spoke in a quiet voice so unlike his normal bellow that Selkirk nearly asked if he was sick. 'Sir, may I borrow your field glasses?'

Selkirk watched as Campbell focussed on a distant group within the camp. He saw the sergeant's hands tremble so the field glasses shook, saw him lower his hands, wipe sweat from his eyes and focus again. 'Sir;' Campbell's voice was strained, 'could I ask you to confirm something for me?' He passed over the glasses. 'Over there, between the second and third row of tents, that bunch, with the woman in grey.'

Selkirk twisted the lens so the vague crowd of people snapped into sharp relief. There was a large woman there, round-shouldered and leaning on a stick. At her side was a smaller woman, with a thin face and a kappie that had once been white but was now stained. At her side, dressed in rags that seemed pristine clean, was a young boy.

'Dear God in Heaven.' Selkirk blasphemed, staring at the familiar figures. He knew these people so very well, for the Reivers had sheltered in their farm more than once. The large woman was Hendrina Fourie, with Hansie, her daughter and young Coenraad, her grandson. Instinctively, Selkirk put out a hand to comfort Campbell, for the sergeant had formed a deep relationship with Hansie.

'It won't do, sir,' the tough Glaswegian's voice was shaking as he retrieved the field glasses and raised them to his eyes. 'It won't do at all.'

'They must have been taken while we were in the blockhouses.' These were the Boers whose farmhouse the Reivers had helped defend against Charles Drongan's Yeomanry. Now it seemed that their efforts had been in vain, for Hendrina would never willingly have taken her family to one of these euphemistically termed 'refugee camps.' Fate was cruel to allow the Reivers to see the Fouries in their present predicament. For a second Selkirk glared at Cloete, wondering if the renegade Boer had deliberately engineered this situation. If he worked for Hume, Cloete was probably capable of any deception.

'Can we go and see them sir? Maybe get them out?' Campbell sounded desperate.

Selkirk made a rapid decision. 'No. Where could they go? We couldn't look after them properly, and they could hardly walk back home; Hendrinafontein must be eight hundred miles away. They'll be safer in there for now.'

'They don't look very safe to me!' Campbell's voice rose, as concern for Hansie overcame the discipline of the army. 'It's not right.'

Sympathy fought with duty as Selkirk struggled to decide what was the best course of action. Of course he wanted to help the Boer family that had been so friendly, but would releasing them from a refugee camp be a curse in disguise? Would two women and a child be safe in the veldt? There were worse people than Boer commandos and British columns loose in Africa and a small family like the Fouries would be seen as easy prey.

'I agree that it's hard, sergeant, but there's nothing we can do just now.' As so often in this war, Selkirk hated the decisions that he had to make. 'Come on Campbell, we can't do anything here, let's trek on.'

'I can't leave them.' Campbell sounded desperate.

'We can't help them now.' Selkirk rarely had to impose his authority on his volunteers. 'That's an order, sergeant!'

For a moment Selkirk thought that Campbell was going to refuse a direct order, which could lead to very serious consequences. The sergeant opened his mouth to protest, then abruptly stiffened to attention. 'Yes, sir!' He threw a smart salute, wheeled his horse and resumed his position in command of the rearguard.

Selkirk felt sick. How could he leave the Fouries behind in a place like this?

'Are you beginning to understand, Captain?' Cloete asked.

'Bugger off Cloete. Trek Jous boys!' Selkirk ordered, and made sure that all the Reivers were moving before wheeling away from the sordid horror of the camp. If he had started this war as an enthusiastic novice soldier, now he felt old and dirty. There was nothing clean or glamorous about war.

Selkirk was thoughtful as he rode on. He had already noticed that there was no singing as the Reivers passed the gaunt relics that had once been farms. Veteran soldiers or not, they baulked at spending their nights at the deserted buildings and rode northward with a definite air of depression. He remembered the jaunty confidence when the Royal Borderers had first disembarked for this war and the cheerful professionalism when the Reivers rode to Bechuanaland. This war against civilians was wearing them down. He had to do something to lift their spirits.

'Haig! Sing for us!'

At first there was no response, only a sullen silence that was alien to the Reivers he had come to know, then Haig started the slow, mournful 'Flowers of the Forest' that the Royal Borderers played at funerals. One or two of the other men either hummed savagely or added a phrase or two of the original words. Surprisingly,

Hetherington joined in. Selkirk knew that the Northumbrian had worked on East Learmonth farm near the field of Flodden, but he was not a man to become involved in any protest.

'Wrong song, Haigie! Try again.'

'You cannae order me what song to sing!' Like many of the survivors of Magersfontein, Haig had developed a sense of his rights. He glowered at Selkirk through his narrow, malevolent eyes. 'I know these women, Selks, and it's no' right that they're treated like that.'

'I agree, but we can't help them now. Sing a different song, Haig.'

Haig hawked and spat on the ground beside his horse and reworded his old favourite, The Man Who Broke the Bank at Monte Carlo

'As we rode along the African veldt I heard the ossifers bleat
I can't be bothered to greet
Because I think it's neat
To fight the Boojers and shoot the men
And put their families in a pen
Because that's the way to build old Kitchener's Empire'

As Selkirk wished that he had kept silence, first Newman then others of the Reivers joined in, roaring out their disapproval of the tactics used in this war, knowing that they could do nothing about it but wanting to voice their frustration as loudly as they could. Selkirk felt Cloete and Windrush staring at him, waiting for him to blast his Reivers into silence, but instead he began to sing. Officer or not, he agreed with the sentiments of his men, and if singing helped get the cancer out of their system, then he would help them sing.

By evening the Reivers had roared the mutiny away and were again acting like the professional soldiers that they were. They camped in the hollow between two ridges, with piquets on every side and the horses knee-haltered close to the water. It was a sultry night, with clouds masking the stars and a dark mass of hills threatening to the East, but at least the men seemed more settled. They were still unhappy about treating women and children as if they were convicted criminals, but had accepted the reality of their situation. Selkirk resolved to lecture them in the morning, telling them that the sooner they won the war, the sooner the women could go back home.

He scooped out a hole for his hip and shoulder and lay on his blanket with the sounds of Africa restless in the night and insects humming viciously. When he failed to sleep he tried to compose a speech, until Donnelly loomed up.

'Sir; it's Sergeant Campbell. He's gone. I think that he's deserted.'

Chapter Four Northern Transvaal – March 1902

For a second Selkirk thought that he had misheard, then the anger rose within him and he gave a string of orders. 'He's gone back to that damned camp! Lieutenant Windrush. You're in charge here until I get back. Donnelly, raise Grey and two of the new men.' He lowered his voice, 'people who don't know the Fouries.' Glancing around, Selkirk checked the men. Most were awake and aware what had happened. 'Menzies, bring me Fleet and four fresh horses. Hurry man! And make sure they have food and water.'

They were moving within ten minutes, Selkirk, Donnelly, Grey and two of the newcomers, riding back along the spoor that Campbell had not troubled to conceal and which Donnelly could follow without difficulty. Luckily the clouds had cleared, so they rode by the dim light of moon and stars.

'Donnelly, Campbell's horse will be tired. Take the two new chums and try and head him off. Ride like the wind for that refugee camp and make your way back toward us. Leave Grey to track for me. Move!'

'Sir.' Donnelly saluted and moved. He had seen Selkirk mature from a raw, if brave rooineck to an officer who wore his authority with unassuming ease. A more mean spirited man may have resented Selkirk's promotion over him, but Donnelly was as open as his Arizona homeland. He only wanted this war to finish so he could live in peace once more.

They rode hard for two hours, with Grey reading the signs and Selkirk wondering what he would say when he caught up with Campbell. He had recruited the ex-Argyll into the Reivers when he wanted a dependable regular NCO, and Campbell had been a perfect choice. Now he had deserted, chasing after a woman, and an enemy woman at that.

'The sergeant's horse is tiring sir.' Grey pointed to a faint mark on the grass, 'see how the side of the print is blurred? That's where it slipped. It's done that two or three times in the last mile. I think we'll catch up with him soon.'

'Good. Thanks, Grey.'

This lowveldt was oppressive, with the night sounds of unseen animals eerie in the dark. There were insects too, that unerringly targeted the soft flesh behind Selkirk's ears and puffed up his eyes. Once he heard an ugly, rasping cough that could only have come from some hunting beast, and he reached for his carbine even as the hair on the back of his neck seemed to rise.

'This is as bad as the Outback,' Grey sounded nonchalant, 'but more fertile.' The flash of teeth revealed a rare grin, 'and there are less things that bite.'

With the cloud totally cleared, the African sky seemed high and bright, with the stars seemingly suspended by unseen threads so they balanced in the dark. Constant practice had given Selkirk intimate knowledge of the southern constellations so he used the stars as easily as he handled compass and map. Riding across Africa was simple; dealing with Campbell would not be.

'I think I hear him ahead.' Grey touched a hand to Selkirk's sleeve. 'Stop for a second.' Dismounting, Grey thrust his bayonet into the trunk of a tree and laid his ear against the blade. After a moment he nodded, retrieved the weapon and replaced it. 'It's the vibrations,' he explained, 'you can feel them on the steel. There's a horseman about a mile away, moving away from us. The horse is floundering, tired. That will probably be the sergeant.'

Within ten minutes they had Campbell in sight, riding at a steady trot with his head down and his hat pulled forward over his face. When he heard the hooves behind him he tried to increase his pace, but his horse was blown after a day and half a night's exertion. Selkirk rode alongside him.

'That's far enough, sergeant. You'd best return to the Reivers now.'

Campbell glowered at Selkirk, his expression a mixture of anger and anxiety. 'I can't sir! That's Hansie in that place, I can't leave her there.'

Reaching across, Selkirk grabbed the bridle of Campbell's horse. 'You're not thinking straight man. Where would you go? What would you do?' He was a far better horseman than Campbell and soon had the sergeant's horse under control.

'I don't know!' Strain made Campbell's voice high pitched, 'maybe return to Hendrinafontein, maybe go somewhere else. It doesn't matter, as long as they're out of there.'

'They'd shoot you for desertion, even if you did manage to get her out. And she would be alone on the veldt with a child.' Selkirk lowered his voice. 'Think what you're doing man. Think what dangers you would be exposing her to.' He thought hard. 'That barbed wire is not to keep them in, damn it! It's to protect them!'

Selkirk felt Grey coming from behind, and saw Donnelly and the other Reivers approaching from the front. Campbell seemed to suddenly collapse as the Reivers surrounded him. It was not pleasant to see the tough Glaswegian so distressed, with his tanned face crumpled in grief and definite tears on his face.

'Leave us.' Selkirk ordered, and Donnelly ushered the Reivers away. Dismounting, he helped Campbell off his horse. At one time he would have been shocked to see a man cry, for emotion was alien to men in the Border farm steadings, but Africa had taught him many things. He had seen the horrors of terrible battles, had heard grown men weeping pitiably for their mothers and had learned to respect a man's feelings. In the aftermath of battle, veterans learned to turn their back on sobbing men, or lend a supportive shoulder. Anybody who had visited the shattered laager at Paardeberg, where men held the blackened corpses of their children, and women sat amidst the wreckage of once-prized belongings, knew that emotion was as much part of the make of a man as it was of a woman.

'Colin,' Selkirk found it hard to use Campbell's Christian name, but he had to break the barrier between officer and man. 'I feel the same way about Hansie as you do. I mean I agree that they should not be imprisoned in that place.'

Campbell said nothing. He dashed a hand across his eyes. .

'But this is not the best way to help.' Selkirk was desperately seeking inspiration. He thought of the cheap novelettes that he had read and wondered how the heroes would have coped. Immaculately no doubt, but they were all upper class men with money and education, not jumped-up ploughboys. 'Stay with us just now Colin, the Reivers need you, and write to Hansie. Tell her that you care, tell her that you're thinking about her, that we're all thinking about her. We can send her food, medicines, everything we can.'

'Yes, sir.' Campbell sounded miserable. Selkirk realised that he had no need to be so understanding, he could simply order the man back to duty, threaten him with dire penalties, use the full force of army discipline to thrust him back in line. But he would not. Indeed he probably could not. He lacked both the instinct and the inclination to act like a real officer.

'Come on then. You write to Hansie and I'll write to whoever commands the camp. Maybe we can get them released. I've heard that some of the refugees are allowed out.'

'Do you think so sir?' There was sudden hope in Campbell's face. He had seen Selkirk perform miracles before, when the Reivers were trapped in seemingly hopeless situations. 'Maybe with you being an officer they might let Hansie and wee Coenraad out and Hendrina too, of course. They wouldn't do it for me.' He smiled ruefully at his sergeant's stripes, 'even if you do let me keep the rank.'

'We'll talk about that later,' Selkirk patted Campbell's shoulder, 'but let's see what we can do legally first. If that does not work, maybe we can try other methods.'

'Yes, sir.' Campbell was no more cheerful, but his natural pragmatism enabled him to accept the truth. He straightened his bush hat, saluted and, without warning, held out his hand, 'sorry sir, for acting like that.'

'Don't be stupid man.' Selkirk took the hand with as much relief as anything else. 'Or at least, don't be so stupid again.' He raised his voice. 'Upsaddle! We've got a trek to complete.'

Next day Selkirk took Campbell aside, gave him a private dressing down, demoted him to corporal for the sake of discipline and hoped that the Reivers would not suffer too much from their NCO's bad example. If anything they seemed to respect him more for it. Even Haig, who had never liked the Glaswegian, nodded on his return, and was heard to mutter:

'Jesus, a sergeant with a heart.'

Newman, Haig's near constant companion, had grinned sourly, 'what next, eh? He'll maybe be tucking us up in bed soon and giving us hot milk.'

'Poor old Hendrina though, locked up like that.' Haig shook his head, so the bush hat slipped over his narrow face.

'It wasn't Hendrina he was going to save, it was Hansie.' Newman made an obscene gesture, to which Haig, surprisingly, objected.

'Bugger off, Newy! She's not like that.'

'They are all like that, Haigie.' Newman taunted, ducking from Haig's half-hearted swing, 'except for one.' His face darkened slightly. 'There's only one woman that I've ever met that's been worth tuppence.'

'Who? That sister of yours?'

'Georgina? No! She's as bad as the rest. Sell herself for position and power, that one. No, there's somebody else, but I'm not saying who.'

Frustrated, Haig probed more aggressively. When the playful debate escalated, Corporal Campbell had to intervene to stop them murdering each other. Selkirk watched from a distance. It was not an officer's task to intervene between brawling other ranks, especially not when one was Haig.

To watch them argue like old comrades, it was hard to believe that Haig and Newman came from such widely diverse backgrounds. Selkirk wondered, briefly, who was the one woman for whom Newman had a high opinion. She must be somebody special, for Newman's life seemed to have been one of constant betrayal and disappointment.

'Enough. Corporal, keep these two apart for a while before the noise they make alerts every Boer for miles. We stop for a break in half an hour, and we'll trek on until we reach Akersdorp.' Selkirk glared round his command. 'And I want you all to act like soldiers. We're the Reivers, not some bunch of Aldershot dragoons.'

If any of the Reivers had been looking forward to reaching their destination, they were disappointed when they arrived within sight of the dorp. Akersdorp appeared little more than a scattering of tin shacks and mud built houses on either side of a broad dirt road that stretched to Louis Trichardt and hundreds of miles south to

Pietersburg and Pretoria. North of Akersdorp there was no road save the game trails created by animals. There was a roughly cleared strip of farmland surrounding the buildings and beyond that nothing but the rich scrub of the Lowveld. On the western horizon, the heights of the Soutpanberg glowered threateningly. The houses sulked under the threatening heat and the air seemed dense with flies. Two blockhouses guarded the road from the south.

They halted on a ridge of rough grass and surveyed the settlement. 'That was a long ride to get to nowhere.' Campbell borrowed Donnelly's field glasses and looked around with disfavour. He wiped a mixture of sweat and crawling flies from his face. 'If Johnny Boer wants this place let him have it, I say.'

'It's a thousand miles past the arse-end of bugger-all.' Cobb the Wollongong volunteer had a picturesque turn of phrase. All the Australian troops served on a short six-month basis, but many stayed for a further period. Both Cobb and Gray had elected to remain when their term was over; Selkirk was very glad to retain them. Britain as a whole had been delighted with the response from Australia, where one in every fifty men of fighting age had volunteered, but relations were sometimes strained between the British regulars and the Colonials. Independent minded Australians tended to challenge imposed discipline, while the regulars resented their higher pay and superior attitude. Nobody, however, ever questioned their fighting skills. Selkirk knew that his Australians would have been out of place in a regular battalion such as the Royal Borderers, but they were amongst the best of his Reivers.

'Let's get our job done quick then Cobb, and clear out.' Selkirk glanced behind him, checking the look of his Reivers. The new men had performed well so far, managing to keep pace with the Reivers and retaliating to the not-always-gentle teasing.

They came from every part of the British Isles, with a strong sprinkling of colonials from Australia, New Zealand and Canada, and if they lacked the experience of his old Reivers, they seemed eager enough to learn.

'These Boers that still fight call themselves the "Bitter-enders"' Selkirk said quietly. 'No wonder, if this is all they have left. What a bitter end for a beautiful country.' He eased the stiffness from muscles that had been cramped into the saddle for far too long. 'Let's see what this is all about.'

The Reivers rode in their traditional formation of a loose column protected by a screen of outriders and with scouts further out still. Although they wore British uniform, most of the veterans had added touches of their own, from the tuft of grass thrust through the hatband of Menzies to the corks that bobbed around Grey's face and the twisted rag that kept the sweat from the forehead of Donnelly. Now they all stiffened to attention as Selkirk barked an order, so they rode toward the outer defences of Akersdorp like the soldiers that they were.

'Sir.' Gray lifted a hand and the Reivers slowed, 'look over there.'

Seemingly relaxed, a man overlooked the dorp. He leaned against the bole of a Maroola tree with his broad had tilted over his face and a rifle propped up at his side. He did not stir as Gray approached, seeming content to sit and stare even when the Australian gestured to Selkirk to join him.

'He's dead, sir,' Gray said, unnecessarily.

Skeletal feet thrust from tattered trousers, and skeletal hands were folded over the man's chest. Birds and insects had long since removed every vestige of flesh from the skull that gazed sightlessly northward. Even the rifle was dead, rotted wood attached to metal that had long since rusted.

'They could have buried him.' Gray sounded uneasy.

'Maybe it's a warning.' Applewood suggested. 'Maybe he was set here to warn away the Boers.'

'Warning be buggered!' When Haig touched the corpse with his boot it crumpled on to the ground. The bush hat slipped off and rolled away, showing a few strands of remaining yellow hair. 'Somebody couldn't be bothered burying him, that's all.'

'Aye? They got his boots though.' Campbell pointed out. 'And his ammunition.' Save for the rifle, there was no equipment with the dead man. 'Poor bugger, but he can't harm us, that's for sure.'

'Upsaddle boys, and ride on.' Unable to do anything for the man, Selkirk left him lying at the foot of the tree, exposed to the flies and heat of Africa.

As they approached the dorp, a small group of riders sallied out, stopped to survey the Reivers from a distance and immediately galloped back.

'Not very welcoming.' Donnelly touched the butt of his carbine. 'I think we had better be careful here.'

'Send a scout forward to those blockhouses,' Selkirk said. 'Tell them who we are.'

Applewood, the forward scout, trotted forward, spoke briefly and returned, galloping toward Selkirk in a spray of dust before pulling to a spectacular halt. 'The lieutenant in charge of the blockhouses says that you've to ride forward first, sir, otherwise he'll order his men to fire.'

'Does he indeed?' Selkirk fought his twist of anger. He had tried to school himself never to show emotion in case it damaged the morale of the men. 'I'd better do that then.' Touching his spurs to Ben's flanks, he pushed ahead, leaving Donnelly to bring in the column. Lieutenants Cloete and Windrush may well have held their commissions longer, but as yet they were untried. However capable they had seemed on the journey north, Selkirk would not yet trust them to command his Reivers.

After Cloete's revelations at the camp, he had taken Donnelly quietly aside and asked him to keep an eye on the ex-Boer. Donnelly had reported that Cloete and Windrush tended to avoid each other, but Cloete had done nothing to raise any suspicion of treason. Still not convinced, Selkirk tried to position Cloete where he could be watched.

This war seemed to test the loyalty of men, with Boers switching sides, Campbell trying to desert and the Reivers helping defend a Boer farm from a British attack. It was obvious that experience of war revealed the ugly side of politics, when men had to choose between what was right and what was patriotic. Often the two were radically opposed.

The two blockhouses were set at an angle to each other, allowing interlocking fields of fire. Between the two, and blocking the road, was a massive tree trunk set on wheels and laced with barbed wire. More wire stretched either side of the blockhouses, leading to what looked like sandbagged observation posts that commanded the approaches to either side of Akersdorp.

'Captain Selkirk, Selkirk's Reivers.' Selkirk announced himself to the face that peered from behind the loophole. 'If you'd kindly move the barrier we can ride in.'

'How do we know you're who you say?' At least four rifles pointed at Selkirk, one of which visibly trembled.

Selkirk tried to sound confident. He did not want to be killed by a nervous sentry away up here. 'The helio would have told you that we're coming.' The heliograph was a feature of this war, with the mirrors winking Morse code across the great open spaces to keep parent units in touch with the scattered offspring. By this late stage of the war every nondescript little dorp with a garrison had a heliograph.

There was a pause, during which the rifles remained levelled, then the voice sounded again. 'Who would helio us, sir? There's nobody for miles. We know nothing about you.' Apparently, Akersdorp was considered too unimportant even for a heliograph. No wonder there was so little information seeping south from here.

Selkirk dropped his tone. 'I don't know who you are, but my men and I have travelled all the way from Cape Colony to help you. Unless you raise that barrier and point these rifles in another direction I will personally ensure that you spend the rest of your career supervising latrine cleaning. Now open up!' It was the first time that Selkirk had used his new rank on an unknown soldier and it seemed to work. The rifle-barrels dropped and a squad of soldiers scurried round to unblock the road. Selkirk accepted their salutes with a flick of his hand, ensured that his Reivers were past safely and followed them into the flies and humidity of the little dorp.

'They seemed jumpy,' Lieutenant Windrush reined up alongside him. Nearly as broad as Cloete, he had grown a neat beard on the journey north.

'Too jumpy. We were obviously not Boers.' Selkirk glanced around. 'This whole place seems on edge.'

The town seemed full of nervous men in faded khaki. There was no banter as the Reivers rode past, only sullen stares from soldiers who held their rifles with bayonets fixed and ready. Many of the buildings resembled miniature fortresses rather than dwelling places, with boarded windows and suspicious eyes behind barricaded doors. The few civilians comprised rough looking men in tattered clothes and women whose bright clothing clashed with their heavily painted faces.

'We are in the land of Baal, where harlots walk the streets.' Kirky Macpherson's voice broke the unusual silence of the Reivers.

'Bugger Baal,' Haig said, but even his voice lacked its usual rancour.

Selkirk reported to a young lieutenant with haunted eyes, who directed the Reivers to a piece of level ground between the outermost building of the dorp and the innermost of the defences. 'The colonel's not here just now.' The lieutenant explained, reining in his horse, 'but you should report to him as soon as he returns.' He grinned nervously. 'I'll send a runner to let you know.'

'Where is he now?' Selkirk asked. There was no identification on the lieutenant's uniform, nothing to indicate to which regiment he belonged.

'Out on patrol. He's out most days.' The lieutenant did not seem keen to explain further. 'There's sweet water here for the horses, and trees for firewood.'

'I heard that you were having some problems out here?' Selkirk tried to ignore the buzzing of the flies as he glanced around the campsite. The grass was long and rank, with dense vegetation surrounding what appeared to be a tepid pond. Ten paces away, a double strand of barbed wire marked the outer defences. Beyond that was a scrubby field, then the low veldt, stretching for thousands of miles. He was glad that most of the Reiver's horses were salted against sickness for this was unhealthy country.

'Some.' The lieutenant continued to be elusive. 'The colonel will tell you more.' He eluded Selkirk's eye. 'I'll have to get back now, sir. Things to do.'

'Of course.' Selkirk returned the salute, 'and thank you for your help. What did you say your name was?'

'I didn't say sir. The colonel told us not to tell anybody our names. He says it's bad for security.'

'I see. Well, at least tell me what formation garrisons Akersdorp. What regiment I have the honour of reinforcing.'

'We're from different units, sir. We sort of graduated here from other places. If you'll excuse me?' The lieutenant was already walking his horse away.

'Bad water, sour grass and snakes.' Windrush glowered around the campsite. 'I think we should find a more suitable spot.' He glanced at the retreating lieutenant, 'and he wasn't much help. What sort of place is this, sir?'

'Not one I care to linger in.' Selkirk said quietly. 'Yes, find a better spot.' He raised his voice. 'Donnelly, take Grey and look around the area, just to get the feel of it. Report back in two hours. Hetherington, you and Pert try and speak to some of the garrison, find out who they are and how long they've been here. Ogilvy, you and Applewood locate fodder for the horses.'

There was a better site on the opposite side of the town, with a small spruit for water, and grass that was not infested with insects. As the Reivers tended their horses, with the spare mounts receiving the same attention as their personal animals, Cobb removed the Maxim gun from its cart. He cleaned and oiled it like a mother fussing over her baby, and sited it on a small rise that afforded an all-round field of fire. Strangely, Selkirk felt more secure with that ugly, snout nosed machine glowering down on him.

'I've set Menzies to watch our back, sir,' Campbell said quietly. 'Just in case.' It was significant that Selkirk did not question the decision. Only when their perimeters were secure and sentries in position did the Reivers light fires for coffee and scran. The sound of scratching lucifers always indicated a break, while the scent of coffee wakened the interest of all the men.

By that time the patrols had begun to return with their news. Ogilvy and Applewood reported that they were refused any fodder. 'It's reserved for the Colonel's unit, so they said.' Applewood was incensed that his horses should be denied, while Ogilvy suggested that they return in force and simply seize what they required.

'Perhaps later,' Selkirk said. At least his Reivers had not been affected by the fear that haunted this dorp. He touched the letter in the pouch that hung from his saddle, thankful that he had wide latitude in his command. He did not intend to remain around Akersdorp for long.

Hetherington and Pert had even more depressing news. The men of the garrison had refused to talk, but they seemed to come from virtually every regiment in the army. 'It's a strange mixture sir, but they didn't tell us anything.' Hetherington looked straight at Selkirk, his honest grey eyes troubled. 'One of the men said that the Colonel was a militia man who had become trapped here.'

Selkirk nodded. That tied in with what Colonel Hume had told him.

'Maybe they don't like me being here.' Cloete seemed constantly conscious of his position. 'They might not trust an ex-burgher.'

'I doubt these people trust anybody much, Cloete,' Selkirk told him. 'Not you, not us, and probably not themselves.'

Donnelly and Grey were last in. 'Very quiet sir,' Donnelly said, 'but there are tracks all around the village; horse and man. And sir; there's another dead man just outside the perimeter sir. He wore British uniform.'

'So there's been fighting then?' Selkirk knew that Donnelly had seen many dead men in the last couple of years. One more corpse would not bother him.

'Maybe sir, but this man has been hanged.'

'What?' Selkirk stared at Donnelly. 'Executed you mean?'

'Hard to say, sir. Perhaps that.' He leaned closer, so that only Selkirk could hear him. 'Or perhaps it was suicide sir. The morale here is not good.'

Selkirk nodded. 'Very good, Donnelly. Keep an eye on our men.'

'Captain Selkirk.' The young lieutenant appeared even more worried as he dismounted and threw a hasty salute. 'The colonel has returned. He said that you have to report immediately.' He looked around. 'Sir; this is not the correct campground. The colonel personally selected the one that I showed you.'

'This one's healthier. Don't worry man, we know what we're doing,' Selkirk reassured the lieutenant. 'Lead on, Macduff.' He tried to assess all the various facts that his men had gathered. It seemed that this was a garrison of depressed and defeated men commanded by a militia colonel. He had heard tales of isolated garrisons crumbling in tropical heat, but had never thought to encounter one. The hanged man was worrying too, but perhaps the colonel would enlighten him.

As Selkirk expected, the colonel had commandeered the largest of Akersdorp's houses as his command centre, although it was still little better than a cottage. Two stories high and with Dutch gables that appeared pretentious on its corrugated iron walls, the house sat on one side of the central square, with a surprisingly neat garden behind its white painted fence. Two sentries jumped to attention when Selkirk appeared.

'Very imposing.' Despite his apprehension, Selkirk tried to appear confident when he met a superior officer. Although he had held his commission for nearly two years, he was still acutely aware that he was only a jumped up private soldier with neither social standing nor social graces. 'What is your colonel's name?'

'I'm sorry sir, I am not allowed to divulge that information.' The lieutenant seemed to grow tenser the closer he got to his superior.

'I see.' Selkirk touched the letter inside his pocket. He had never before encountered such security in the British army. Perhaps the colonel was afraid of infiltration by the Boers.

The interior of the house was surprisingly comfortable, with stinkwood floorboards and doors, while the walls were covered with a variety of sporting trophies. More sentries ushered Selkirk into a fairly large room, where a man sat at a desk. He had his back to the window, so Selkirk could see only a silhouette, but the colonel was tall and bulky.

'Captain Selkirk, sir, of Selkirk's Reivers.' Selkirk saluted and stood at attention.

The colonel did not move for at least a minute, then rose slowly to his feet. 'You have taken your time in coming.' It was a statement, not a question, and the voice was that of the Honourable Charles Drongan.

66

Chapter Five : Akersdorp - March 1902

Selkirk remained at attention while Drongan slowly opened and read the letter. 'This document allows you considerable latitude, Selkirk,' Drongan said. He looked down at Selkirk from his superior height. 'I don't agree with that.' Walking slowly back to his desk, he struck a match and applied the flame to one corner of the letter, held it until it was well ablaze before dropping it on the floor.

'Sir!' Selkirk protested, moving forward, until Drongan shouted to him to stand. The instinct of obedience forced Selkirk to obey. Drongan watched the flames for a few minutes, then casually ground them out beneath his feet. 'Now you're mine.' When he looked at Selkirk, he was smiling.

Selkirk remained at attention, fighting his anger and frustration. He was a soldier of the king, a commissioned officer of the British Army. He could do nothing but follow orders. As a colonel, Drongan outranked him, as the son of a lord, he stood immeasurably higher in the social scale, as a man he was bigger and stronger; Drongan held all the aces in a stacked deck. 'So you say, sir.'

'Return to your ragged horsemen, Selkirk.' Drongan dismissed him with a casual flick if his hand. 'I will send you your orders when I want you.'

After three years in the army, it was natural that Selkirk should salute before he left, but he felt sick.

'Charles Drongan.' Donnelly whistled, 'that's bad!' Selkirk had called his officers and NCOs together, sketched in the animosity between himself and Drongan for the sake of the newcomers and then appraised them of the situation.

'But surely, if the man is a British officer, he will be honourable and just?' Cloete seemed unable to grasp the reality.

'It's a personal thing, lieutenant. Charles Drongan and I go back a long way.' Selkirk tried to explain, but Cloete only smiled and shook his head.

'Put it this way, sir,' Corporal Campbell explained. 'It was men like Colonel Drongan who probably thought of putting women into concentration camps.'

'I see.' Cloete nodded. 'Yes. I do see.'

'We could be in for a rough time then.' Campbell stared at the village. 'No wonder all the sentries were scared half to death. Having that for a commanding officer can't be fun.'

Windrush frowned. 'Do you always encourage your men to criticise their superior officer, sir?' He had avoided Campbell since the attempted desertion.

'Corporal Campbell also has personal experience of Colonel Drongan.' Selkirk did not explain further. He doubted that Windrush would understand the Reivers part in defending Hendrinafontein against Drongan's Ettrick and Cheviot Yeomanry. Windrush seemed to have a pathological hatred of the Boers; he refused to talk to Cloete and would probably enjoy burning down a Boer farm.

'I see.' Perhaps because he was a Colonial, Windrush always affected a pose of superiority before the British soldiers. Selkirk was a little disappointed with this attitude; he had fought alongside Rimington's Tigers on a number of occasions and found them to be a professional, cheerful bunch.

Campbell's prophecy was quickly proved correct. Before dawn next morning, Drongan sent them orders to dig new latrines for the garrison, and then to erect barbed wire defences around the blockhouses. The Reivers obeyed, grumbling, as they quickly replaced all the local defaulters in performing every degrading task that Drongan could devise. They were acutely aware that the civilian inhabitants of Akersdorp and the local natives were watching their labours with fascination. Macpherson's painted harlots seemed particularly amused; passing crude comments as the Reivers toiled under the sultry sun.

'Make sure these holes are deep, Reivers. There's a lot of shit in Akersdorp.'

'Aye, and we're well in it!' Thomson grumbled. 'I thought I was joining a fighting unit, not shit shifters.'

They emptied latrines and burned the contents. They cleaned out the trenches. They worked on the road. They cleared scrub from

68

around the dorp, and often Colonel Drongan would pass by, watching, criticising and devising new humiliations. Twice he ordered field punishments and Selkirk could only watch in frustrated anger as members of his Reivers, his personal command, men that he knew as friends, were spreadeagled to the turning wheels of moving carts. As a natural rebel, Haig was one of the unlucky offenders, and he swore in a continual monotone as he was humiliated before the hangdog garrison and the cackling women.

'That's inhumane, sir.'

'Inhumane, Selkirk? It's a recognised field punishment in the British Army.' Drongan watched as Haig spiralled past, suffering. 'As is death by shooting for mutiny. In some special circumstances I can also order men flogged. I've seen many blacks flogged in Africa, Selkirk. There is nothing to stop me flogging a Reiver!'

Twice Selkirk confronted Drongan, only to be beaten back by lawful authority and each time it was his men who suffered by having extra fatigues and less food. Morale dropped day by day as the Reivers toiled in the humid heat and biting flies of Akersdorp. More used to the fickleness of officers, the regulars endured in silence, but the Australians and volunteers spoke openly of desertion or mutiny.

'Now we know why the men here don't say much.' Donnelly scraped filth from his trousers as he knelt by the little spruit that ran by their campsite.

'You notice that there are no officers higher than the rank of lieutenant?' Cobb ran his hand along the barrel of his carbine. 'Except for Captain Selkirk, of course. There are no majors or captains. Only Colonel Drongan and a handful of very young rooineck lieutenants.'

Selkirk nodded. 'I had noticed.' He knew that he should stop his men from criticising their superior, but he agreed with them. He was also interested in what they had to say.

'I think that this is a punishment posting. All the useless officers and the broken men are sent here.' Cobb eased back the bolt and checked the breech of his carbine.

'So why Drongan? And why us?' Donnelly looked at Selkirk. 'Any idea sir?'

'Not yet.' Selkirk shook his head. 'But Colonel Drongan was not posted here. He was in command of a column and got himself stranded.'

'So you were told, sir,' Donnelly said, 'but with all due respect, Colonel Hume is sometimes a little economical with the truth. He only tells you what he thinks you should know and lets you find out the rest.'

'Maybe Colonel Hume and Major Scott have an ulterior motive?' Since Campbell had explained about the concentration camps, Lieutenant Cloete appeared to understand.

'Aye.' Haig lay on his back, staring into the blank blue of the sky. 'Scotty hopes that we'll murder Drongan and do everybody a favour. The man's Doolalli.' He tapped his head significantly. 'The heat's got to him.'

'I am glad that I am not remaining long under his command then.' Cloete was smiling. He alone seemed to have retained his good humour.

Selkirk thought that since he had arrived in Akersdorp he had become very self-assured for a man fighting against his own side. 'Why is that Lieutenant?'

'Have you forgotten my orders? I have to search for recruits for the National Scouts.' Cloete was already walking toward his horse. 'Thank you for bringing me to this pleasant place, Captain Selkirk, but I really think I should leave now.'

'Wait. You can't just wander off like that! This place is surrounded by armed Boers.' Selkirk put out a restraining hand. There was a half moon of dirt under each fingernail, and new calluses caused by pick and spade on his palm. Charles Drongan had insisted that the officers share the burden with their men.

'Exactly so, sir. Armed Boers that are fighting a losing war while their families suffer.' Cloete's smile dropped. 'I am here to tell them the truth about their position. I have documents from General Smuts that even the most hardened bitterender cannot ignore.' Reaching to his collar, he stripped away the red band. 'But I won't be travelling with that badge of infamy. My countrymen have little patience with traitors.'

'They'd shoot you.' Campbell said quietly.

'Very quickly,' Cloete agreed.

'So who are you really?' Selkirk asked. He had long realised that once again Hume had not told him the truth. Cloete was certainly not a recruiter for the National Scouts.

'Lieutenant Cloete. And that's all you need to know.'

Donnelly had been glancing from speaker to speaker 'Will you be with us long?'

'No. I will be leaving early tomorrow.' Cloete looked squarely at Selkirk. 'If you could grant me an escort sir?'

Selkirk smiled wearily. 'That rather depends on Colonel Drongan. He seems to have closed off our options.'

'In that case I will leave without an escort.' Cloete did not ask permission.

'I'll detail a section.' Selkirk attempted to keep some hold on his self-respect. He glanced around his men.

'Newman.' That was a natural choice, for on three separate occasions Drongan had stopped to stare at Newman. If Drongan ever realised that Selkirk had his disgraced younger brother in the ranks of the Reivers, his malevolence would increase beyond all reason. Newman could not keep his head down and his face turned away forever. Time, the sun and experience had inevitably altered Newman's features, but Drongan was bound to recognise him eventually. 'You and Haig escort Lieutenant Cloete out of town tomorrow.'

'Yes, sir.' Newman did not argue. A trip away from Akersdorp, even toward the enemy, would be a godsend to anybody.

'Why us?' Haig complained about any order. It was an ingrained habit that meant nothing.

'Think about it, Haig.' Selkirk glanced toward Newman. 'Or if you can't manage that, ask Newman to explain.'

'Bugger you, Selks!' Haig was not the brightest soldier in the British army, but he understood when he was being insulted.

'That's more like it Haigie.' Selkirk had served beside Haig when they were both privates in the Royal Borderers. He expected nothing but abuse from the scarred little man.

Night sounds were different in Akersdorp than on the high veldt. There were insect noises in abundance and the call of unseen

71

animals to unsettle the men, so that sentries were jumpy, less afraid of a possible Boer attack than of whatever else lay beyond the screen of darkness. Most of the British army were town bred and even at this stage of the war, they were uncertain in the field. Better trained and experienced at living beyond the pale of regular supply columns, the Reivers were more able to cope, but life in Akersdorp was wearing them down.

It was dark when Cloete and his two-man escort left Akersdorp. While all rode with their legs extended in the Boer style, the Reivers carried their carbines ready for instant use, and had muffled their equipment in the old familiar manner. They paused at the outer piquets that Selkirk had set, then vanished softly into the dark

'Lucky bastards.' Thomson said. He seemed to take the constant fatigues as a personal insult.

'Maybe, but God help them,' Campbell voiced a common anxiety, 'for there's something not right out here.' He was normally unemotional but the sight of Hansie in the Concentration Camp had disturbed him, and the atmosphere in Akersdorp had made things worse. 'I just wish we were back on our own patch, sir. Back on the Bechuanaland border.'

'And Hansie?' Selkirk enquired.

'Safe on the farm,' Campbell agreed, 'but not only that. There's something wrong here, sir. There's something else out there besides Boers. I can sense it.'

'Aye.' Selkirk had heard a few of the men saying something similar. Many soldiers on campaign could sense trouble, but this was different. When veterans wasted their sleep in staring into the dark, and borrowed Kirky Macpherson's Bible when they thought nobody was looking, it was time to check that the powder was dry and raise praises to the Lord.

Despite the early hour, most of the Reivers were already awake. Normally they would spend as long as possible in their bed, particularly with Charles Drongan hounding them. Selkirk had never known soldiers more unsettled. 'Let's hope that whatever it is breaks soon, so we can deal with it and get back.' He touched the butt of the Webley revolver he had at his belt. He had never carried a pistol before, as the Boers recognised it as a badge of rank and aimed accordingly, but since coming to Akersdorp, Selkirk had worn his. The feel of the bulky weapon made him feel more secure.

Dawn was as swift and dramatic as always in Africa, with the usual call of 'Stand to' and the bustle as sentries peered anxiously into the bush while morning mist rolled upward from the surrounding landscape. Equally as inevitable was the order from Colonel Drongan for the Reivers to double to latrine duty. Once again, Selkirk protested at this misuse of his men, and once again Drongan sneered in distaste.

'What rank are you, Selkirk?' Drongan ensured that there was an appreciable audience before he commenced the demeaning ritual.

'Captain, sir.'

'By mischance, but we'll let that pass for now.' Drongan was as immaculate as ever, with the creases down the leg of his trousers sharp enough to cut and his tunic tailored to fit his impressive physique. He touched the emblems of rank on his shoulders. 'And what rank am I?'

'Lieutenant-colonel, sir.'

'Lieutenant-colonel.' Drongan repeated the words. 'So you would agree that I outrank you Selkirk?'

'Yes, sir.'

'Yet you still question my orders?' Drongan took three steps away from Selkirk, then turned and bellowed like a parade ground sergeant. 'I make your Reivers do the menial tasks because that is all they are fit for, Selkirk. They are a bunch of scum and colonials, men who whine when asked to work, and who hide on Boer farms when other men fight.' Drongan was screaming himself into a rage. 'You are a pro-Boer, Selkirk, and your Reivers are vermin!'

Selkirk felt himself coming out of the attention position; he felt his shoulders dropping into the boxer's crouch that he had learned on his passage out to Africa, he felt his hands curl into fists.

'Yes, yes Selkirk.' Drongan was beside him, speaking softly so only they could hear. 'That's it; defend your precious Reivers. Hit me, so that I can grind you into the dirt and then charge you with mutiny and have you shot. The last man to mutiny against my orders was hanged.' His breath was hot on Selkirk's face but his eyes were so similar to Georgina's that Selkirk had to step back.

'So you haven't the guts to fight me? You're a coward as well as a traitor. You're a disgrace to that uniform, you jumped-up nobody!' The tirade continued as Drongan attempted to goad Selkirk into a rash attack.

While some of the Reivers watched in astonishment or naked anger, the men of the garrison hardly looked up. Either they were used to their commanding officer, or their spirit was completely broken. Selkirk stood mute. After a few minutes he managed to blank out his mind, as he had done while learning his trade as a Horseman on the Merse, or while a Johnny Raw recruit. He could see Drongan's mouth working, but the words were merely noise, as inconsequential as the buzzing of insects or that curious drumming sound that seemed to be increasing by the minute.

'Horsemen.' Selkirk broke away from his self-imposed trance. 'Those are hoof beats, sir.'

Broken off in mid tirade, Drongan stared at him. 'What? How dare you interrupt me when I am rebuking you, Selkirk.'

'Can't you hear them, sir?' The hoof beats were closer now. So loud that they must number scores, perhaps hundreds. 'Horses!' Selkirk could feel the ground shaking as he spoke. 'Jesus; there must be thousands of them.'

'Well don't just stand there, get your men mounted. Fight them Selkirk, that's what you're paid for!'

Campbell and Donnelly had already begun to muster the Reivers, sending Pert and Applewood to gather the horses from their kraal between the dorp and the campsite, but there was not enough time.

'Christ, man.' Ogilvy pointed to the north, 'That's not Boers, that's beasts!'

It seemed like half the animals in Africa suddenly erupted from the bush, pouring toward the dorp in a frenzied mass of tossing heads and battering hooves. Selkirk could see blurred legs half-hidden in a haze of dust, glaring, terrified eyes, a mass of black and white that seemed to stretch from horizon to horizon. Then there were other animals, deer with straight antlers that jumped and leaped, heavy creatures with crazy, twisted horns, tall animals with humped backs, all intent on pounding Akersdorp and its garrison into the dust.

A young soldier, one of the new recruits, was staring toward the approaching mob. 'They'll flatten us,' he said, 'we haven't got a chance!'

'Reivers! Follow me.' Selkirk hauled himself on to Fleet, his spare horse that Donnelly had pushed toward him. 'We'll turn them away!' He had spent the first twenty years of his life working with animals and knew how easily they could be panicked. If some of these beasts could be turned, the others might just follow.

Those Reivers who had horses trotted behind him, others ran on foot, stumbling toward the danger. One or two of the garrison joined them, but most had abandoned their positions and were fleeing in the opposite direction. Selkirk could feel the fear in Fleet, no doubt transmitted by the advancing horde, and he quietened her before he dismounted. He threw himself behind one of the sandbagged sangers that passed for defence in the rear section of the dorp.

The animals were less than two hundred yards away, galloping forward in a terrifying wall of flailing hooves and heads, with a mantle of dust around each flank. Most seemed to be black and white zebra, but as they got closer he recognised other species. He saw brown and white kudu, antelope that seemed to leap into the air with each bound, even the tall necks of giraffes away in the centre of the fearsome mob.

'Fire at the leading animals! Try and split them so they run round the town rather than over it!'

Selkirk squeezed five rapid shots into the mass, reloaded even as the ejected brass cartridge cases spun to the ground, and fired again. He heard more shots as his Reivers joined him, shouted orders for Donnelly and Campbell to take the flanks and hoped that somebody could hear him through the deafening sound of ten thousand hooves.

Pert was by Selkirk's side, shouting to be heard above the sound of hooves and gunfire and the frantic bellowing of thousands of animals. 'The horses are panicking sir! Shall I get them under control?'

Selkirk nodded, cursing himself for not having considered the possibility. He knew Pert was a good man, a Horseman from the Mearns, but doubted that he could control all the Reivers' mounts. 'Take Ogilvy too!'

'Yes, sir!' And Pert was gone, a khaki man amidst khaki dust, a man who cared more for the horses than the war.

'Cobb! The Maxim!' With more rapidity of fire than a dozen carbines, the Maxim machine gun would be able to carve a hole in the advancing animals.

'Can't sir! It's jammed!' There was desperation in Cobb's voice as he frantically pushed at the breech. 'One of the cartridges has split in this heat.'

Selkirk swore. The thin brass casings of the Maxim were notorious for swelling. He would have to rely on carbines alone.

The animals were falling fast, but there always seemed to be more pressing from the rear, hundred after hundred of bellowing, jumping, galloping bodies with wide, frenzied eyes and matchstick legs that appeared to emerge from a waist high mattress of dust.

Selkirk emptied another magazine and reloaded, fired again, tasting the cordite mingling with dust at the back of his throat, feeling the ache where the carbine thumped against his shoulder. The shooting was creating a barricade of bodies around which some of the beasts were running. A few headed directly for Akersdorp, but most were now running wide, encouraged by the steady fire of the Reivers, some of whom had also taken up positions along the flanks of the town.

When members of the garrison also took part, the stampede was broken. The mass of animals split harmlessly around the town and thundered in opposite directions into the bush. The dust swept over them, settling slowly as men coughed and shook in the realisation of survival.

'That was different.' Donnelly stood up amidst the drifting dust. 'But at least we've plenty fresh meat to eat.'

'Indeed.' Lieutenant Windrush sounded less cheerful. 'But animals don't stampede without a reason, and certainly never toward a town. Something must have made them run like that.'

'Fire perhaps?' Selkirk extracted cartridges from his bandoleer and pushed them into the box magazine beneath his carbine.

'Boers, sir.' Kirky Macpherson said. 'I saw some horsemen on the fringes of the beasts. They were goading them on.'

'Are you sure?'

'Yes, sir.' Macpherson had been a stalker in Badenoch before volunteering for the South African War. His eyesight had been honed while searching for the flicker of a red deer's ear among the Monadhliath Mountains. If he said that he had seen a Boer, there was no question.

'Why? To unsettle us?' Selkirk had little time to speculate as a massive explosion echoed through Akersdorp.

Chapter Six : Akersdorp – March – April 1902

'What was that?' For a second, Selkirk was shocked as the noise reverberated in his head. He stood, numbed, as his Reivers slowly turned to stare across the width of the town toward the road. Selkirk followed the direction of their gaze, noting with mild curiosity the pillar of smoke that seemed to climb slowly toward the already dust-smudged sky. It was the familiar crackle of musketry that brought reality.

'It's an attack. The animals were only a diversion.' Selkirk hauled himself on to Fleet's back. 'Windrush; you remain here with Macpherson and Donnelly in case the Boers come this way too. The rest of you follow me.'

The gunfire was increasing in intensity, punctuated by hoarse yells and an occasional screech of pain. Fleet was still shaking from the reaction of the stampede, so Selkirk wasted a precious minute in calming her down. Then he mounted and, hunched low so that his head and shoulders were level with the neck of the horse, he kicked in his spurs and galloped along the dirt road. There was another explosion, smaller than the first, and a volley of rifle fire that could only have come from British regulars.

Akersdorp was only a small place, with perhaps fifty houses, each with its own patch of scrubby land, Drongan's headquarters and a squat church with a pointed steeple. Within minutes Selkirk saw what had happened. The Boers had stampeded the animals toward one side of the town, then while the British were concentrated there, had attacked the other. They had dynamited the two blockhouses and followed up with an attack by mixed infantry and horsemen. Even as he spurred on Fleet, he admired the organisation that had managed to co-ordinate the two attacks

By the time Selkirk arrived, the entire eastern section of the town was in Boer hands. Men in ragged clothing seemed to be everywhere, sheltered behind the shattered, smoking remains of the two blockhouses and among the houses. Selkirk saw a British soldier stagger from the second blockhouse, his clothes burned from his body and his flesh scorched and smouldering. He screamed wordlessly from a mouth that seemed a pink hole in a charred black face. Sheltering behind the blockhouse, a Boer turned his rifle toward the man and fired twice. It was act of mercy rather than murder.

'Dismount.' Selkirk realised that mounted men made a good target, while infantry could merge with the dust that the stampede had created. He leaped clear of Fleet and slapped her rump to set her running. As he dived behind an abandoned cart, the first shots whined past his head. 'We'll have to do this the hard way!'

The Reivers were dismounting to find cover, from where they replied to the Boers' fusillade. Used to the spaces of the veldt, they were unsure about this street fighting, bunching up for support and exposing more of themselves than they should. Selkirk saw one of the newcomers spin wildly as a Boer bullet smashed into him, heard Menzies swear as a bullet clipped the brim of his hat, then jumped as something slammed into the timber of the cart. Aiming quickly, he fired back, feeling comfort from the familiar kick of the recoil. He worked the bolt and an empty brass case flicked past. Another defender was knocked off his feet by the force of a Boer bullet.

He guessed that the Boers controlled perhaps one third of the town and were advancing house by house, supported by covering fire from the rear. Some houses stretched on either side of the broad road, while others had been built seemingly without any pattern, amidst a maze of lanes and streets that themselves were interspersed with isolated trees. Only Drongan's headquarters and the church were prominent.

Smoke from the blockhouses drifted across the dorp as both sides sought to consolidate their position. He saw one of the young

78

lieutenants draw a sword and charge forward, dying uselessly before he made three paces. Not a single British soldier had followed him. Dust gradually settled on the sword, seeming to highlight the proud name of the maker: Wilkinson.

A group of mounted Boers dashed toward Selkirk's wagon, but when he wounded the first and Grey killed another with a clean shot through the head the remainder wheeled their horses and fled. The shooting continued, now with less effect as men burrowed deeply into cover. Flies buzzed angrily all around.

A bullet smacked against the cart at Selkirk's head, spraying chips of wood and dry paint. He loosed off a shot in reply, worked the bolt and peered into the smoke-hazed dorp. A scattering of bodies on the ground, a man moaning in pain, somewhere a woman was screaming.

'Rollcall!' Selkirk called out. 'Reivers! Shout your names!' He tried to assess casualties as the voices sounded across the battlefield. He had started with fifty men, less the two out escorting Cloete on his tomfool mission, he knew that one man was down and hoped that there were no more. Counting names, he came to forty-five.

'Who's missing?'

'Ahare sir. Shot in the thigh.' Ahare was the Ulsterman who was constantly bickering with McGann, his countryman, until things got tough, when they became inseparable.

'Anybody else?'

'Smith and Maxwell. New chums. Haven't seen them at all.' Corporal Campbell was feeding the information; he knew the number and position of his men at all times.

The firing stopped completely as both sides sought to consolidate their position. Selkirk raised his head cautiously, searching for targets. He estimated that there were about fifty Boers, perhaps more, and they controlled a tight knot of buildings around the main road to the town. If he could drive them out, it would be a major blow to their morale. If they could hold on, the British position would be untenable. He glanced around; Grey and Campbell were close by, with two of the new men beyond them.

'Campbell.' Selkirk tried to whisper with enough force to convey his message, but quietly so the Boers could not hear. 'I'm going for their left flank. When I move, give me covering fire.'

The nearest house was twenty yards away, but a thick-boled tree stood beside the road within five yards of Selkirk's position. Nerving himself, Selkirk yelled 'now!' and jumped forward. Campbell opened fire immediately, supported by Grey and one of the new Reivers. Keeping low, so the settling dust could conceal him, Selkirk waited for the Boer bullets to hiss and kick around him.

The Boers seemed slower to react than normal, so that only two shots flicked past Selkirk before he dived behind the tree. The trunk was massive, with the branches above appearing more like roots, as if the whole plant had grown upside down.

Selkirk lay still, calculating the distance to the house, knowing that the Boers were aware of his position and could probably guess his intentions. There was another lull, then a number of shots. Bullets ripped through the tree, passing right through the massive trunk as if it were paper and screaming past his head.

'Jesus!' Selkirk tried to burrow into the ground as he realised that the tree afforded no protection at all. He would have to move somewhere safer very quickly. With fifteen yards of open ground to cross, he would be lucky. There was another shot, and a bullet zipped through the tree and bore into the ground at Selkirk's head; another, and the bullet tore a furrow from the dirt at his left hand. Some marksman was deliberately targetting him.

'Time to go, Drew, my boy.' Selkirk knew he could not cover fifteen yards. He would have to withdraw. The next bullet blasted wood splinters into his face, so he blinked, cursing.

'Get out of that, sir! That tree's no more protection than a whore's promise!' Campbell's words were urgent. 'Covering fire, lads. Make the bastards keep their heads down.'

There seemed to be more Reivers present, for at least a dozen carbines opened up. Selkirk waited for a second, then, keeping low, ran in a zigzag. He knew that it would be sense to return to the cart, but he was too stubborn to go back. His pride forced him onward toward the houses. Bullets kicked up dirt all around him, and as he dived behind the timber and mud house, something slammed into his foot, spinning him in a semi circle so he landed face up and legs asprawl on the hard ground. His head made sickening contact with a pile of newly cut fence posts.

'Jesus! I'm hit!' He lay still for a moment, trying to control the panic and waiting for the pain that he knew would come. There was none; only a faint throb in his left leg and numbness in his left foot. Fearful of what he would see, he looked down, to see that a bullet had ripped the heel off his boot. He nearly giggled in relief when he saw there was no other damage. Something exploded in the smoking ruin of the second blockhouse and a fusillade of bullets howled around the dorp.

'Sir! Are you all right?'

'Aye. Keep firing.' Realising that he still held his carbine, Selkirk rolled to the corner of the building. A ricochet whined past his head. He could clearly see the gleam of metal as it slammed into a post.

There were two Boers within forty yards, both nestled behind a building as they alternated in shooting at the British. They seemed very relaxed, one even sucking at his pipe when he rolled back into cover. Quite deliberately, Selkirk sighted on the pipe-smoker's head and squeezed the trigger. The man died instantly, without even realising that he had been shot. His companion looked around in alarm, and Selkirk shot him in the chest.

'Khaki!' The word that had warned of British soldiers for the past two years reverberated across Akersdorp, passed from man to man as the Boers became aware of this new threat on their flank. Selkirk sensed movement from the Boers as they readjusted their positions. He tried a couple of shots to tempt them out into the open, but these men must have been veterans. They remained concealed.

However, if he could not see them, neither could they move forward. Threatened from front and flank, their advance was effectively halted. It was stalemate.

Firing broke out again, sputtered for a few minutes and ended as both sides realised that there were no targets. The sun rose slowly toward its zenith, baking the dorp and its sweating, suffering inhabitants; insects plagued the men, who lay unable to swat or scratch in case the enemy saw the movement and fired. Smoke from the blockhouses continued to mask the town.

It was the smoke that gave Selkirk the idea. If he could not drive the Boers from the town, he might be able to smoke them out. He patted his pockets, but had no matches.

'Campbell!'

'Sir!'

'Lucifers? Do you have any matches?'

'Yes, sir.' Campbell rarely sounded surprised but he did allow his voice to rise a little. 'And baccy sir.'

'Throw them over. Only the matches.'

The box landed short and lay, blue and white, on the brown grass of Africa. Selkirk hooked it closer with the butt of his carbine, wincing when a bullet ricocheted from the ground close by. Gathering an armful of dry grass, he wrapped it around one of the fence posts that were piled behind the house, making a rough torch. He could feel Campbell watching him as he struck a match, shaded it with his cupped hands and applied the tiny flame to the grass. Guessing that something was happening, the Boers put down fire, so that a deliberate stream of bullets thumped into the dust around him.

'Covering fire!' he yelled, and dashing out into the open, swung the now blazing torch toward the nearest of the Boer held houses. He winced as a bullet ripped through the leg of his trousers, gasped in pure fear as another tugged at his bush hat. It seemed a miracle that he was not hit.

As the Reivers fired, Selkirk ducked back to his shelter and watched the torch arc lazily through the air, turning end over end until it landed on the roof of the nearest house. He had chosen that one specifically because it was thatched, unlike most, which were roofed with corrugated iron. Almost at once flames began to spark from the sun-dried grass, and the Reivers cheered and redoubled their efforts.

The Boers were still firing, their bullets now coming in clusters of eight. 'Use the cart for cover!' Bunching his muscles, Selkirk waited until the pattern of eight ended, then pushed himself out. Weaving, and ducking, feeling bitter fear at the back of his throat, Selkirk ran back toward the cart and, sheltering behind the scarred wood, tried to push the clumsy vehicle toward the second of the Boer houses. It was heavier than he had expected, with the wheels rusted by long disuse. He felt the muscles in his back and arms strain, but the cart remained static.

'A hand here! Quick now.'

He saw some of his Reivers emerging to join him, but at the same time was aware of an outburst of firing at the farther end of the town.

'They're attacking from both sides,' Campbell said. Firing as he ran, he moved across the open to Selkirk's side. 'Let's hope that Lieutenant Windrush and Donnelly can hold them.' Leaning beside Selkirk, he pushed forward the cart so the tall, spoked wheels began to grind over the ground. Bullets crashed against the stout wood, sending vicious splinters whining through the air. Somewhere a Boer shouted, his voice high pitched. More of the Reivers ran to help, with two of the garrison.

After ten yards the cart picked up momentum and began to roll of its own volition, so Selkirk was able to crouch in its shelter and fire at the Boer positions. He heard a gasp as one of his men was hit, but had no time to look around as the wagon thundered through the flimsy mud wall of a house and continued onward, finally halting well into the interior. Selkirk threw himself beneath the wheels and rolled out the far side, snap shooting as he glimpsed a retreating man.

'They're running!'

The Reivers followed, fanning out as they moved, boots sliding on the leaf mould, thumping on sun-hardened ground. One section of men gave covering fire to the next in the manner that the British army had learned after the initial disasters of this war. The Boer had taught them how to fight, and now the Boers were paying the price.

It was unusual for Boers to hold a position once their flanks were turned, for they did not fight for territory. However, one group of Boers seemed more stubborn than normal, firing into the advancing British. A soldier yelled and fell, holding his leg. Selkirk fired two quick shots, then cursed furiously as his carbine jammed. A rifle cracked, the bullet jerking the carbine from his hands and sending it spinning on to the ground. The shock numbed his right arm.

One of the Boers rose from cover and Selkirk saw the barrel of his rifle foreshorten as it aimed at him. Swearing, he threw himself into a fold of the ground, aware that at that range, any Boer could not fail to hit. The barrel faltered, and a clear voice laughed,

'It's Lieutenant Ogler and the vitschudden commando!'

Helena Van Vuren lifted her hat in salute, so her brown hair tumbled around her ears. 'Just you lie there, Ogler, or I'll shoot you.' She laughed again, waved cheerfully, and ducked away. The green cockade in her hat bobbed amidst the dust for a second then vanished.

Selkirk clambered up, feeling very foolish, but none of his men seemed to have noticed. No wonder the attack had been so well planned, if Helena Van Vuren was concerned. He shook his head. God, but that woman was good at her job.

There were bodies on the ground, British soldiers killed during the initial assault and bearded Boers that the Reivers had hit. One man was writhing, moaning as he held both hands to his belly, from where his intestines slithered in a horrifying kaleidoscope of white and pink. Bullets crackled and whined across Akersdorp, but the danger was passed now and the Reivers were simply mopping up stray Boers.

'I think we've won, sir.' Sitting in the shelter of the blazing house, Campbell was reloading his carbine. He grinned over to Selkirk, his face streaked with vertical lines where sweat had carved through the grime of dust and smoke.

There was a flurry of movement and the Reivers leaped for cover as the Boer fire suddenly intensified. Volleys of bullets thudded against the houses and ricocheted from the ground.

'Maybe not yet.' Selkirk swivelled. He should have known that Helena was not so easily defeated.

'That came from outside the town.' Campbell sounded calmly professional. He had rolled from his position to a fold of ground and glared toward the shattered blockhouses. 'I think that it's to cover their retreat.'

Selkirk was at the corner of the house nearest the road. Taking a deep breath, he cautiously put forward his head, and saw the backs of a dozen men as they withdrew from the town. 'Shoot them, boys.' There was nothing personal about his order. He knew that the Boers were brave men defending their country in the best way that they could, but he also knew that the spread of the British Empire was for the benefit of all humanity. More importantly, the more Boers that he killed today, the less there would be to threaten his Reivers tomorrow.

He led the way, weaving toward the blockhouses, from the sheltering walls of which he aimed and fired at the bobbing, ducking men who ran into the bush. Even as the firing at this side of town decreased, there was an upsurge elsewhere.

'They've broken through!' There was panic in the voice. 'The Boers have broken through! They're all around us!'

'Jesus but she's good!' Selkirk shook his head with admiration. Helen Van Vuren had reorganised her attack and thrust at a different section of the town. 'Campbell! Stay here with three men in case they come back. The rest, follow me.' Realising that his carbine was useless, Selkirk unfastened his holster and pulled out his revolver. He had only fired it a few times in his life, and never against a live enemy. Now he would see how good he was.

Feeling rather foolish with such a small weapon, Selkirk led his men back into the centre of the town. He had fought the Boers in a dozen battles spread across half of South Africa, and he knew them for a courageous, skilful enemy. He had never known them to be so tenacious before, working out a complex attack plan and coming from alternate sides to confuse the British. Selkirk wondered just where Helena had learned her tactical skills.

There was firing all across the town, with small pockets of British, both garrison troops and Reivers, sitting tight as they tried to repel the attack. The Boers seemed to be everywhere, mounted and on foot, working their way from house to house as they systematically dealt with each centre of resistance.

Selkirk counted his men. He had eight Reivers and five men of the garrison; hardly enough to mount a major counter-attack. He coughed as acrid smoke from a burning building blew back in his face, winced as sudden pain stabbed from his foot. Glancing down, he saw that the heel of his boot was completely off now, and he must have been limping for the past ten minutes. Perhaps for longer, for time seemed strangely foreshortened when he was fighting.

There was a further outbreak of firing ahead and a rush backward by khaki clad soldiers. The mouth and eyes of the leading man were wide with terror. He had dropped his rifle and his sun helmet was dangling loose. A single shot sounded, the man staggered, wailed high pitched and stopped. He stared straight at Selkirk. 'Help me, sir. Please.' Blood exploded from his mouth and he fell forward, his fingers scrabbling at the dirt

'Reivers! Hold them.' Selkirk flattened himself behind the wall of a house and loosed three shots toward the Boers. He swore as two Reivers were among the British that abandoned their positions and ran towards him. 'To me, Reivers!'

The Boers appeared to be everywhere, advancing from the front and both flanks. Selkirk swore again as he saw British soldiers giving up, standing with their arms erect in the humiliation of surrender. 'Bayonets! Fix bayonets! Drive them out Reivers!' Then he called the old familiar cry that had been heard for centuries all along the Scottish – English border. 'Fethan! Fight for the Fethan!' He rose, feeling the kick in his numbed arm as he fired the revolver.

But it was a different Borderer that rallied the men. In the confusion and slaughter, Selkirk had forgotten all about Charles Drongan, but now the colonel appeared, incredibly wearing the full scarlet regimentals of his Ettrick and Cheviot Yeomanry and holding a rifle, on which the bayonet gleamed evilly.

'To me, men!' Seemingly immune to the bullets of the enemy, Drongan allowed himself to be seen by both Boer and Briton. Raising his rifle aloft, he moved slowly toward the centre of the Boer positions. Recognising his authority, the dazed men of the garrison emerged from their shelters to join him. 'Come on my lads!' Drongan levelled his rifle and charged, cheering. Caught up in his madness, a dozen men of the garrison followed, bayonets glinting evilly.

'Jesus help us.' For a second Selkirk could only watch, then he threw himself forward at the Boers. 'Reivers! Follow the colonel. Drive out the Boers!'

Whether they were surprised at the ferocity of the attack, or could not believe the suicidal idiocy, the Boers began to withdraw. As the bayonet men got close, even the most stubborn Boer fled. Not a single man remained when the British took their positions.

'Chase them all the way to the Limpopo, men.' Drongan loped across the ground, wielding his rifle like a spear. Many of the British who had already surrendered dropped their hands and lifted their rifles to rejoin the fight, following Drongan as he raced between the houses. There was a scattering of shots as some of the Boers turned at bay, but Drongan continued, his red coat a visible emblem.

'Reivers!' Selkirk shouted, chasing in Drongan's wake, as he had done so often on the racecourse at Ettrick. He saw Donnelly emerge from the ruins of a hut, saw Windrush sitting on the ground, wrapping a bandage around a bloody arm and wondered how many more of his men had been hurt.

There was a thunder of hooves and a press of mounted Boers galloped past the dorp, driving a mass of horses before them. Selkirk swore as he recognised Fleet among them, but then he was outside the dorp and into the bush, with the Boer infantry still running but the horsemen turning to fight. Out in the open, a mounted man would easily defeat a man on foot. Selkirk hesitated, but Drongan charged on, still yelling.

Selkirk swore as he saw a green cockade bouncing among the mounted Boers. He saw Helena turn, her face shrouded in the dust, then she stilled her horse and lifted her rifle. Ignoring Selkirk, she aimed at Charles Drongan, the man who had burned her home and tried to rape her.

The first bullet caught Drongan high in the chest, spinning him round so that the second only tore through the outside of his leg. The Honourable Charles Drongan fell, cursing, and the impetus disappeared from the British counter attack.

Even as the British hesitated, Selkirk drove them on. He knew that he could not catch the mounted Boers, but he also knew that a garrison stuck without horses in an obscure outpost of Africa had little chance of survival. As best they would be besieged, and he had no desire to experience another Kimberley. At worst they would suffer starvation, mutiny and a lingering death as military attention focussed on more central areas of the war.

Selkirk glanced around. Donnelly was behind him, with Kirky Macpherson at his side. 'You two – fire at the horsemen. I want to stop them driving away our mounts.' He knew that Donnelly and Macpherson were among the best shots in the Reivers. He wanted to order them not to kill Helena. Once again, as so often in this war, duty clashed with personal feelings. He watched as they settled into a comfortable firing position, saw Macpherson's rifle point toward Helena and deliberately stepped across his line of sight.

'Careful, sir. I nearly shot you there.' Macpherson lifted his rifle, just as Helena turned toward Selkirk. Their eyes met for a second, and then she kicked in her spurs and galloped into the dust.

Donnelly and Macpherson fired simultaneously, and the closest horseman fell at once.

'Keep at it,' Selkirk ordered, hating himself for saving the life of one of his country's most dangerous enemies, while thanking God that Helena was safe. He ran forward across the open ground. He knew that every Boer in range would target him and swerved as best he could. Twice he staggered as bullets smacked into the ground at his feet, but each time he recovered. Although he could not distinguish individual shots, he knew that Donnelly and Macpherson were still firing, for the Boer riders were ducking and their control was looser.

As Selkirk had hoped, some horses had run free. He threw himself across the nearest, a rangy, sharp-backed Waler whose frightened eyes rolled backward when he leaned forward to quieten it. Blowing into the distended nostrils and rubbing the horse's ear, Selkirk quietened it down, then pushed forward toward the Boers.

Two broke off their herding duties to challenge him, the closest swinging his rifle from the hip as if it were a pistol. Selkirk knew that it was almost impossible to fire accurately from a galloping horse, particularly when the target was moving, so he fired his revolver, missed, returned the weapon to its holster and spurred savagely, hoping that one of his Reivers could get a clear shot. He did not hear the crack of the rifle, but the furthest Boer jerked back in the saddle and fell backward, with one foot remaining in the stirrup. The horse dragged him, bouncing bloodily, along the ground. The second Boer turned instinctively to help and then Selkirk was past, whooping and waving his hat.

The captured horses had split into three groups, with the larger in front and the smallest in the centre. They galloped in panic, hooves thundering as Selkirk circled around the last two groups in an attempt to drive them back toward Akersdorp. Sweat streaked the dusty flanks as they pounded onward, eyes wild and nostrils distended. Waving his hat, Selkirk turned the first animal, then shouted to catch Ben's attention. The horse pricked up his ears at the familiar voice, butted aside his neighbour and powered toward Selkirk. Some of the others followed, and then Selkirk was guiding thirty horses back, choking in the dust as he weaved and yelled around the herd.

'I lost twenty! I'll have to go back for them!' He allowed Pert and Ogilvy to care for the recovered animals. 'We can't afford to lose them.'

'We can't afford to lose you either.' Donnelly placed a hand on his bridle. 'You're the garrison commander now that Colonel Drongan is wounded.'

'What?' Although he was well aware that Drongan had been hit, Selkirk had not realised that he was now the senior officer. He stared at Donnelly, making rapid decisions. 'Right. Take two men, Fairweather and Applewood if you can find them, and go after the horses. See how many you can round up but don't get involved with the Boers. Has anybody seen Lieutenant Windrush?'

'Here sir.' Windrush's uniform was torn across the breast and there was a smear of blood around his mouth. The bandage on his forearm was already sodden with blood.

'You take over here. Watch for any Boer counter attacks and give covering fire to Donnelly's men. I'll see to the Colonel.'

An officer had moved Drongan to the shade of a tree and had spread a tunic over him. The Colonel stared up at Selkirk, his mouth working in pain. Selkirk looked back. This was his enemy, the man whose false accusations had forced him into the army, the man who had threatened his family with eviction, the man who had destroyed the farm at Hendrinafontein and shamed the British army with plunder and rape. This was also the man who had beaten him up and who had treated his Reivers with contempt. 'Let's have a look at you, sir.'

Drongan's scarlet uniform was sodden with blood. He gasped with pain as Selkirk cut away the cloth. One bullet had entered his upper chest, too high for lungs or heart but leaving a nasty hole. It had smashed the left shoulder blade as it exited, leaving splinters of bone spread over the wound. The second bullet had torn a gouge across the outside of Drongan's thigh leaving an ugly but not dangerous wound.

'Where is the hospital, lieutenant?'

The lieutenant shook his head. 'We have none, sir.'

'None?'

'No, sir. The colonel thought that it would pamper the men.'

'I see.' Selkirk would have to treat the wounds as best he could. 'Fetch me some bandages then, and whatever medical equipment we have. And fresh water.'

'Damn you, Selkirk! Leave me alone. I forbid you to touch me.' Drongan twisted in pain as Selkirk cut away his shirt to examine the wound more closely.

'Yes, sir. I'm trying to save your life.' Selkirk washed out the wound as thoroughly as he could, ignoring the noises that Drongan made and the raw blood that flowed over his hands. Pressing a pad of linen to the gaping hole, he leaned the Colonel forward. 'This may hurt a little.'

Working as quickly as he could and trying to ignore Drongan's writhing, he extracted the most visible splinters of bone before pushing more cloth firmly over the wound. 'Hold him,' he said and bandaged the struggling man as best he could. When Drongan fainted, Selkirk finished the task and then treated the leg.

He was acutely aware that there was a queue of men waiting for his orders. The entire garrison now depended on him, and he had to make a score of decisions very shortly. At the same time, he knew that if Drongan died, he would always wonder if it had been deliberate. For his own sake, he must do his best for this man that he hated so much.

'Sir.' The young lieutenant looked agitated, 'the men have not eaten yet. Shall I feed them?'

'What? Of course feed them. You don't need orders for that, surely?'

'Yes, sir. The colonel always had to give the orders sir.' The lieutenant glanced from Selkirk to Drongan.

Selkirk took a deep breath. 'What's your name man?' He suddenly realised how demoralising it must have been for this young man, he could not have been more than eighteen, to live with a tyrant such as Charles Drongan. Selkirk would have to restore the man's confidence and mould him into a useful officer of the king.

'Lieutenant Simon sir,' the lieutenant stiffened to attention. 'From the Norfolk Yeomanry.'

'Well, Simon. Colonel Drongan is out of action, and probably will be for some time. I leave it to you to feed the men whenever you think it best. You make the decision and you give the orders in future. All right?'

A mixture of fear, apprehension and pleasure crossed Simon's face. 'Yes, sir. Shall I go now sir?'

'Yes, Simon. Feed them now.'

Selkirk knew that the rudimentary treatment he had given Drongan was not enough. The man should be in hospital. That meant transporting him to Louis Trichardt.

Selkirk sent for Windrush. The lieutenant looked pale, in obvious pain from the wound in his arm. He swayed as Selkirk gave him orders. 'Windrush: I want you to fit up wagons and send the wounded away to Louis Trichardt. If you can, give Colonel Drongan a wagon to himself.'

Windrush glanced toward the still unconscious Drongan. 'Will he live, sir?'

'Perhaps. If we get him to hospital in time.'

Windrush nodded. He did not look pleased at the news.

Selkirk gazed around his shattered town, noting the still burning houses and the emergence of shaken civilians. 'How many other wounded are there?'

'I don't know sir. I was organising the defences, as you ordered.'

'Find out.'

There were eight British and three Boer wounded to fit into two wagons. Selkirk refused to allow an escort for the small convoy, for he knew that the Boers would not attack such a target. However he did detail a corporal and two men to act as medical orderlies. He heard Campbell giving a stern warning to the men to take good care of the casualties, particularly Andy Charlton, the Reiver who had already been wounded at Magersfontein.

As the wagons rolled out of Akersdorp, Selkirk passed his written report to the corporal with orders to hand it to whoever was in command at Louis Trichardt. With nobody close enough to heliograph, he could not signal out his news. Instead he posted guards around the perimeter and gathered together the combined garrison and Reivers.

'Many of you garrison of Akersdorp don't know me,' Selkirk had heard enough morale-rousing speeches to adopt the accepted formula, 'but I am beginning to know you. My Reivers are among the finest troops that the Empire has to offer, and today you fought alongside them, shoulder to shoulder against the Boer.' He paused for dramatic effect, watching the play of expression across the face of the listening men.

Most looked tired, some were plainly despondent, a few nearly broken. None of them met his eyes, but looked away as he scanned them.

'I was proud of you all. As you know, Colonel Drongan was wounded in your gallant defence, your victorious defence. I have sent him to Louis Trichardt and I will become garrison commander for a while.'

There was little reaction. One bastard officer was much like another. Selkirk suspected that these men had been so browbeaten that they had no spirit left.

'We will draw up new defences for the town, and from today will adopt a more aggressive approach. You will no longer have to wait for the Boers to attack; we will take the war to them. We will dominate this section of Africa!'

There was no applause, but one or two of the men looked up with a different expression in their eyes. It was Blackdown, the saddler and ex-poacher from the West Country, who called out for three cheers for Captain Selkirk, and the Reivers who made most noise. Selkirk waited for the men to quieten down.

'Thank you men, but you are wrong. The cheers should not be for me, but for you.' Even as he spoke, he felt immensely pompous. What right had he, an ex-ploughboy, to take command of a garrison and give speeches to men who had probably been soldiering far longer than he? Yet he also knew that he was right. These men needed hope, it was his duty to supply it. 'So one last cheer for yourselves, for the men of Akersdorp!' In a theatrical gesture that he abhorred, Selkirk raised his bush hat high in the air as the Reivers again led the cheering, but this time more of the garrison joined in.

Calling his officers to him, Selkirk watched the men return to their positions. Perhaps some thought of him as Captain Selkirk DSO, but he knew the truth. He was Drew Selkirk of the Fethan and he would swap all his rank for one hour of the cool peace of the Fethan Valley, and all his authority for a scent of the Border air.

Chapter Seven : Akersdorp And The Veldt, May 1902

'Horseman approaching, sir. I think that it's Haig.' Re-established as a sergeant, Campbell saluted as he made the report.

'Alone?' Selkirk looked up from the map that he had been studying in place of the forms that were half covered in his large, ill-formed writing. He already hated the paperwork that accumulated on his desk, particularly as his reading and writing skills were not fully developed. He had not realised that a garrison commander's life consisted mainly of poring over reports and lists. Duty rosters, lists of sick, accounts of fodder for horse and food for men; he spent most of his time holding a pen rather than a rifle.

They had been a week working on the defences of Akersdorp and already Selkirk could feel a new spirit about the place. Men were marching with a more purposeful air and the aura of fear had been lifted, although there was still an underlying tension that he could not explain. Hopefully he could relieve that by careful treatment of the men. His first task was to make Akersdorp secure, then he intended to take the war to the Boers, which was what the Reivers did best.

Investigation had proved that the Boers had blown up the blockhouses with dynamite. The explosion had killed all the men in the first position but surprisingly, had only wounded three in the second. Selkirk ordered a wide protective ditch dug in front of the blockhouses, then ordered a search of the town for barbed wire. In the peaceful days before the war, Akersdorp had served the hunters who had decimated the elephants in the low veldt of the north. Barbed wire had not been a priority, but with the foraging instincts inherent in all good sergeants, Campbell had sniffed out half a dozen rolls languishing in the outhouse of the church.

There had been much cursing and a few torn hands as the soldiers strung the wire in front of the ditches, but now no Boer could approach close enough to throw dynamite. More soldiers became labourers as they rebuilt the blockhouses, while others extended the ditch so it slowly stretched around the perimeter of the town. Selkirk ordered the scrub cleared for a radius of quarter of a mile and established Maxim gun positions at strategic spots, with interlocking fields of fire. Few of the garrison had known the Maxims were in the town, for Colonel Drongan had not believed in such weapons. His ideal had been the arme blanche.

Only when the perimeters were secure did Selkirk allow his Reivers to begin patrolling the surrounding area. He wanted every man to know the main landmarks and demanded that they draw an accurate map for his own use. Desperate to escape from the tedium of administration, he led two patrols himself, but on both occasions his return to piled-up paper depressed him so much that he did not lead a third.

Campbell was still waiting for a reply. Selkirk realised that he must have been standing for a good five minutes.

'Bring him directly to me, Campbell.'

'Yes, sir.' The salute was too brisk to be correct and the manner in which Campbell stamped his feet as he left told of concealed resentment. Sometimes Selkirk wondered if he was too lax with his men. He grinned at the thought. Only the King's Commission gave him any right to order Campbell around. In a sane world, the Clydeside sergeant was far superior to him in every way.

Haig looked as ugly and insubordinate as ever as he stood in a semi-slouch in front of Selkirk's desk. His uniform was torn and stained, he had at least three days' stubble on his face and there was a fresh wound across the back of his hand. The carbine he gripped was clean and oiled.

'Report, Haig.'

'The lieutenant led us through the bush sir, until we met a group of men. Nice enough lads, but a bit suspicious of us.' Haig sniffed, as though he possessed the most immediately friendly character in the world.

'Boers?'

Haig screwed up his face as he tried to think. 'Maybe. Some were; I'm not sure about others. They didn't look the same, sort of.'

'And then?'

'The lieutenant said to leave him there, so we did. We got ambushed on the way back. Newy got shot.'

He spoke in such a casual manner that Selkirk only nodded. 'I see. Is he badly hurt?'

'Badly enough.' Haig looked directly into Selkirk's eyes, his voice suddenly flat. 'He's deid.'

Selkirk could not read any expression in the small man's face. He knew that Haig was a granite-hard survivor but Newman had been his friend. Newman, the black sheep who had slipped from Society to land in the Barrack Square, had found Haig an ideal companion in drink and trouble, and had grown close in the skirmishes around the Bechuanaland border. Now Haig hardly blinked as he reported his death.

'You got back though.'

'Aye. I got back.' Dipping into his pocket, Haig produced a small linen bag, which he opened and emptied on the desk. 'This is all Newy's stuff, sir.'

There was not much to show for a man's life. A few coins, a piece of card with Newman's name inscribed on top, a handkerchief with the initials JD embroidered at one corner. Selkirk held the handkerchief for a moment, wondering if he should tell the Drongan family that one of their menfolk had paid the ultimate price for the sake of Empire and freedom. J.D., James Drongan; that had been Newman's real name before he followed the path of so many other outcasts and lost himself in the ranks of the army. Now he was dead, killed in an obscure skirmish in an unwanted corner of Africa.

'I liked Newman.' Selkirk said. 'I'll miss him.'

'So will I.' There was still no expression on Haig's face. He stood as inscrutable as the sphinx whose existence Selkirk had recently learned about.

Selkirk sighed. That was another good man gone in this bloody war. It was also another loss to the Drongan family. This war was proving expensive for them, one son killed, another gravely wounded and a daughter married. Selkirk tried not to think of Georgina in the arms of James Montgomery. 'Very well. Dismiss Haig.' He looked up, 'I'm glad that you made it back though.'

'What?' Haig glowered across the desk. 'Bugger off Selks.'

Selkirk glanced around the forms that were piled precariously on his desk. 'I wish I could Haigie, I really wish I could.'

'Why don't you then?' Leaning forward, Haig touched the insignia of rank that Selkirk wore on his shoulders. 'Don't these things mean that you're in command? Well take command then. Tell somebody else to do the bloody paperwork.' He came closer, examining the top form on the desk. 'After all, they can't do a much worse job than you. That's just a bloody mess.'

Selkirk looked at the childish scrawl that disfigured the neat buff paper. Haig was right. He was no good in an office. He needed a personal clerk. 'Send in Sergeant Campbell will you Haigie? And Haigie – thanks.'

Haig's face twisted in what might have passed for a smile in another man. 'Bugger off. Somebody's got to keep you recruity officers right.'

Sergeant Campbell did not know of any suitably qualified men in the Reivers, and a check of the garrison was equally unsuccessful. It was only when he asked the officers that Selkirk found his victim. He had forgotten that Lieutenant Windrush had been a banker before the war, and was as adept at handling forms and figures as Selkirk was with horses. Windrush accepted the position in the office with something approaching relish, asked permission to rewrite the already completed forms and had the place organised within a day. Even with his arm in a sling, he looked far more comfortable in the office that Selkirk ever had.

'I'll leave you in charge then, Windrush.' Selkirk withdrew as gracefully as his haste would allow and took a deep breath of freedom as soon as he crossed the threshold of the house. If promotion meant working with inkwells and paper, then he had enough of it. He was a man of the open air, not a starch-shirted clerk, and as soon as he got back on to a horse the better.

Although Selkirk had seen a lot of his friends die in this war, he had never got used to it, and knowing the past history of Newman made it worse. He needed to find somewhere quiet for a while, somewhere that he could think and put things in perspective. Unfortunately that was a near impossibility for the commander of a garrison. There was always somebody demanding his attention. Life in command seemed a constant series of distractions.

'If anybody wants me, I'm inspecting the perimeter.' Selkirk strode quickly away before Windrush enquired further.

His patrols had discovered many footprints around Akersdorp. Boers had obviously made some, but of others Selkirk was less certain. Gray brought his attention to a spot where a large body of men had kept the village under observation for some time. Mingled with the soft prints of veldshoen were the distinctive pattern of British army boots and a number of tracks made by bare feet.

'Don't understand that, sir. These are British soldiers, sure as death, and these are natives.'

'Maybe Boers using captured British boots?' Selkirk hazarded.

'No. The spacing is all wrong. These are infantry strides, not cavalry. I don't understand at all. And these natives too. I know the Boers have black servants, but they would not bring them so close to us, sir.'

'Very good. Thank you, Gray. Keep looking.' Selkirk hid his worries, but he could feel that there was something very wrong here. He had thought that with the removal of Charles Drongan, things in Akersdorp would improve. However, the whole atmosphere surrounding the dorp was bad. Macpherson put it into simple words.

'There's a rottenness here sir, like somebody's put a curse on the place.' He had fingered his Bible. 'Some of the boys have asked me to read to them, and they've never done that before.' The smile was triumphant, 'maybe the Lord is just working in his usual mysterious ways.'

Maybe He was, but Selkirk suspected that Colonel Hume was also involved. However mysterious the ways of the Lord, the Hume was capable of some pretty devious measures himself. Not for the first time, Selkirk wondered exactly why he had been sent here.

There had been three minor attacks on the town during the last week, enough to keep the garrison on their toes without causing casualties on either side. With his experience at Kimberley, Selkirk did not expect the Boers to be very active in their attacks; they were not known for accepting casualties in pursuit of military objectives.

Nonetheless, with Helena leading the enemy, anything could happen. Selkirk did not intend to just sit tight and await events.

Colonel Hume had originally sent the Reivers here to locate the Boers and keep them busy until the main columns arrived. Now that he had a grasp of local affairs, Selkirk knew that the idea was impractical. There were no main columns up here, nothing but the rag-tag and bobtail of the garrison, which had been recruited from the rejects and wounded of half the units in the army and reinforced with the remnants of Charles Drongan's column. They might suffice to defend a town, but Selkirk certainly would not trust them as a mobile column.

With Charles Drongan providentially removed, Selkirk could work out how to defeat these Boers. It was really quite obvious; he commanded some of the best horsemen in the British army, men who were wasted skulking behind the sandbagged walls of an insignificant dorp at the wrong side of nowhere. He would trace the Boers to their base and destroy them there. After that, he had a personal matter to put right.

Knowing how unhealthy this northern low veldt was for horses, Selkirk checked them personally, with Ogilvy, Fairweather and Pert there to add their advice. All the original Reivers' horses had been salted for thickhead disease, but they had mixed with the less healthy animals from Akersdorp and some had gone down with unspecified complaints. Selkirk ordered the sick weeded out and kept in quarantine, and watched the remainder anxiously for any sign of weakness. He was already dangerously short of mounts; he liked to have at least one spare horse for every man, but was reduced to three horses between two riders.

'How is our present strength?' Selkirk had called Donnelly, Windrush and his sergeants into the large house he had taken over from Drongan.

'Thirty fit Reivers sir; three were killed in the assault and the rest sick or wounded.'

'And how many fit horses?'

'Fifty one sir, including the animals for the wagon.' Donnelly glanced at the piece of paper he carried. 'But there are twelve in the sick corral that may be well enough to travel.'

'Not enough,' Selkirk shook his head, 'but it will have to suffice. Lieutenant Windrush, I know that you came along as a translator, but I want you to be garrison commander while I lead the Reivers.' He waited for the protest but Windrush seemed to stoically accept his fate.

'Very good. Donnelly, you and I have a plan to work out. Sergeant Campbell, I want you to select twenty-five Reivers, including ourselves. The rest will remain in Akersdorp to reinforce the garrison.'

'They won't like that sir.' Campbell warned.

'Nor do I, but we don't have sufficient horses. Be diplomatic when you tell them.'

Selkirk grinned; he knew that Campbell's idea of diplomacy was an order bellowed with the full force of lungs strengthened by years of shouting above the noise of shipyard rivetters. There would be disappointed faces among those Reivers who were left behind, but they were disciplined soldiers and would have to accept their fate.

In the event there were twenty-seven Reivers that rode out of a quiet Akersdorp that morning. Eighteen were veterans of the expedition to Bechuanaland. The rest were relative newcomers, but they all rode jauntily, glad to escape the confines of the town and be back in the saddle again. When somebody began to whistle *Border Reivers*, most of the others joined in, but only Selkirk wondered whether the atmosphere lightened because they were mobile again, or because they had left Akersdorp behind.

Every man carried his personal weapon, usually a Lee-Enfield or Lee-Metford carbine, but Macpherson and Grey preferred the longer range of the Lee-Enfield rifle. There was also the Maxim gun, known to the men as 'Cobb's lover.' Selkirk had been impressed by the way dynamite had destroyed the blockhouses and had brought some along. As Donnelly was a mining engineer he knew about explosives and might find a use for the stuff.

Once they were a mile from the town, Selkirk organised his men into the familiar fighting formation. There were outriders on each flank, a rearguard two hundred yards behind and scouts up ahead. As always, the spare mounts and the Maxim gun, with spare ammunition and water, were carried on the cart in the centre of the men.

Selkirk had collated the reports of the various patrols he had sent out during the previous two weeks. None of them had seen a single Boer, but there seemed to be a pattern to the hoof prints that they had found. On initial investigation, every Boer patrol seemed to have approached from a different direction, but persistent tracking had followed them to a general source. Donnelly had led a three-man patrol to that area and had spent four days in chasing each print, which had all ultimately originated from the north and west. Now he guided the Reivers in that direction, with each man more wary with every mile they passed.

Before Selkirk had left Britain, his idea of Africa had been of thick jungle populated with naked tribesmen and ferocious animals. In common with many of the Royal Borderers, he had been surprised at the topography in which he had campaigned. Now, he was entering a land he would have recognised more as the Africa of his beliefs. It was a country of thick bush and soft ground, of sudden downpours of rain and the scurried movement of exotic animals. Twice the Reivers disturbed elephant, which lumbered away at an impressive speed, and three times they heard a barking cough that Donnelly believed was a leopard.

'All we need are lions now,' Haig grumbled, but Selkirk could see that the little man was nearly at ease out here. Haig was habitually tense, ready to take offence at any slight, real or imagined. The only time he was really relaxed was in battle.

'Look.' Gray, the man from the New South Wales outback, pointed to a muddy patch of ground where some large animal had left his imprint. 'See that pad mark? That might be a lion.'

'Jesus.' Haig worked the bolt of his carbine so that there was a round in the chamber.

'That won't help.' Gray was a laconic man, good in a fight, excellent in the field but, compared to the British soldier, singularly lacking in humour. 'You need a bigger bullet than that for a lion, mate. You'll just get it annoyed.'

'I'll bloody annoy it all right.' Haig slipped the bayonet from its scabbard and clicked it in place. Selkirk had allowed his men to carry whatever style of bayonet they preferred, and where most used the shorter 12-inch, Haig opted for the long eighteen inch. Combined with the small man's aggression, carbine and bayonet made a formidable weapon.

'What are you going to do mate, prick it to death?' Gray's laugh was taunting and Selkirk nodded to Campbell to ride between the two before murder was done. Although Haig had not visibly reacted to the loss of Newman, he had been more morose than normal since he had arrived back from that event.

Selkirk used the information brought back by his patrols to supplement the army-supplied map as he led his Reivers deeper into the bush. This was a new type of land to him, where wide spaces of rough ground were surrounded by impenetrable bush, where millions of insects tormented the Reivers in the morning and evening, yet there was a lull of silence in the searing heat of noon. He changed his outriders every two hours as he probed slowly on, ensuring that every man had experience of working alone, but nobody was left isolated.

It was strange, but out here in the low veldt, men from the towns were proving as adept as the bushmen from Australia or Donnelly from Arizona. Men like Haig, or Bryant, a self-confessed Larrikin from the Rocks of Sydney, were as likely to find tracks in the bush, and were often quicker to react to sounds than the countrymen or plainsmen.

In the evening, as they drank their coffee and ate paste-covered biscuits under Africa's brilliant stars, Selkirk discussed the day's events with his NCOs and men. He remembered and despised the absolute barrier that had been in place between officers and other ranks in the Royal Borderers. He knew that experienced soldiers could contribute much to any plan, and listened to everybody's opinions as he gathered information.

On the third evening of the trek, as they camped on an ironstone ridge, beneath the smooth curving boughs of a wild sour date palm, and with the low veldt spread out in gloom and glory all around, Selkirk spread out his map. The men gathered round him, coffee in hand as they watched him pencil in all the observations that men had made during the day.

'There were hoof prints here, here and here,' he marked the place on the map, and traced their likely route. 'As you can see, they all seem to be heading in the same direction.'

'How many prints?' Donnelly wondered. 'I only found two or three.'

'You found three separate sets, Gray found half a dozen and Burke saw another two.' Burke was one of the new men, a dapper Irishman from Connaught whose wit and charm kept the column lively during the march.

'Not very many then.' Donnelly said. 'There were quite a few Boers in the attack on Akersdorp. I wonder where they have all gone?'

'As long as they have not circled round us to attack the town again.' Campbell voiced Selkirk's fear.

There was a lull in the conversation as men imagined another sustained assault on the little dorp. None of them had ever known the Boers to press home an attack with such tenacity.

'We keep going.' Selkirk decided. He had found a telescope in Drongan's headquarters, and now unstrapped it from his saddle. It was Macpherson who had taught him to locate an object with the field glasses, but use the telescope for greater magnification. Now he focussed on what appeared to be a smudge of smoke about ten miles into the bush.

'Donnelly, what do you make of that?'

One by one the men struggled to peer through the fading light. 'Smoke, I think. Or maybe a low cloud.'

'That's what I thought.' Selkirk recovered the telescope and peered into the eyepiece but the light was nearly gone. 'So do we investigate tomorrow, or keep to our route?'

The discussion was lively, with the men equally divided in their opinions. Selkirk listened to each, and made his decision. 'All right; we continue as we are, but send out outriders in that direction. As you say, Macpherson, it could be smoke from a native village, or it could be the Boers.'

'I haven't seen many natives around here,' Donnelly said, 'but what I have seen I haven't liked. Only the prints of men. No women, no children, no dogs. That's bad medicine, sir.' He drained his

103

coffee and tossed the dregs on to the ground. 'In my father's day, that would mean a war party.'

They dropped down an escarpment in the morning, encouraging the horses to push through dense bushes that left dozens of thorns embedded in their legs. Once they were on lower ground the heat increased and the outriders reported seeing the spoor of more game. There were lions around, and new types of deer, with the occasional brightly coloured snake that both fascinated and repelled Selkirk. Twice the Reivers halted as warthogs charged from concealment in a thicket, and as often the men halted to feast on prickly pears.

They passed a dense group of tall mupani trees and rested at a small spring around which were grooves made by wagon wheels. 'Old,' Donnelly dismissed them at once. 'See how the dirt has crumbled at the edges, and how dense the vegetation is at the bottom? These were made maybe two, maybe three years back.' He glanced around at the clearing with its stretch of long grass and the flicker of colour as butterflies hovered, waiting to savour salt sweat or salt urine of man and horse. 'Maybe some ivory hunter passed this way before the war.'

Selkirk found it hard to visualise a time before the war. His life seemed to always have been lived around the buck-up crack of a Mauser, with khaki-clad figures dodging and ducking and the ever-present prospect of agony, mutilation or death. He accepted Donnelly's word and scanned the surrounding bush with his field glasses. There was a hint of movement as an antelope vanished into the vegetation, but nothing else.

'Maybe there are no Boers out here. Maybe they have doubled back to attack Akersdorp.' Campaigning out in the bush was much different to riding on the high veldt. He missed the space and the clean air; here everything seemed closed in, almost claustrophobic. He felt very much at a disadvantage.

'Sir!' The call came from Ogilvy, one of his Angus Horsemen. 'Over here.' He pointed downward. There was a set of fresh footprints on the ground.

'Barefeet.' Gray was on his knees, examining the prints closely. 'Too small for a man, a child perhaps, or a woman. And see how broad they are? The black fellas in the bush all had broad feet; white feet are narrower, because we train ours inside shoes.'

'So much for your war parties, sir,' Bowen grinned to Donnelly. As the only men from North America in the Reivers, the two had grown close.

'A native woman then?' Selkirk wondered. He knelt at Gray's side. The right foot print was clear, but the left was slightly smudged and the small toe appeared to be crooked, as if it had been broken at some time and badly set. His first thought had been for Helena Van Vuren, but she was no bare footed native.

'She's probably watching us right now!' Gray gave a twisted grin. 'Just so long as she hasn't got a couple of hundred of her friends with her. Donnelly's war party indeed. Remember these lads in Bechuanaland?'

Selkirk had vivid memories of the fighting regiment of Chief Lentshwe. The Kgatla men had looked more than capable of mopping up a handful of stray British soldiers. He had no doubt that the local tribes, the Shangane or the Matabele or Batongas or Barotsi, or whatever they were, would be just as handy. 'Aye. Let's keep moving and stay alert.' His only consolation was that any tribesmen would be as likely to dislike the Boers as the British. Hopefully they would remain neutral and allow British and Boers to settle their disputes without interference.

The Reivers passed groves of ebony trees, whose broad boughs afforded welcome shade from the sun. Selkirk marvelled at the quality of the wood, then slid the Reivers around a gentle slope dotted with giant wild fig trees. Monkeys chattered from the tall branches and bright-plumaged birds exploded skyward in sudden panic. Not far ahead, at the foot of a hill that was dominated by a single, massive boabab tree there were the unmistakable signs of camp fires.

'There's the smoke from last night.' Gray knelt at the side of the nearest blackened circle. He stirred the ashes thoughtfully. 'And here's something else.' He lifted the blackened remains of something metal.

'Breech block of a Lee-Metford sir.' Trust Campbell to recognise any part of any weapon at a single glance. 'White men then. Boer or hunter?'

Gray glanced around the ground. 'At least thirty people, maybe more, by the areas of flattened grass. Hoof prints too.'

'Sir.' Macpherson lifted something from the ground. He brought it to Selkirk for inspection. 'Cartridge case. There's more over here.'

Selkirk held the brass case in his hand. '303. Could be British then. The Boers are more careful with their cartridges.' He glanced around, 'Donnelly, away up that hill with the field glasses. See what you can see. Gray – find out where these men went.'

There were too many men to be a hunting party. This must have been a detachment of the Boer force that he had been sent to locate. At this stage of the war it was common for the Boers to use captured British weapons and ammunition as their original Mausers were worn out, lost or simply out of ammunition. It was not so common for Boers to lose cartridges at a campsite. They were normally as careful of ammunition as British soldiers were careless. Possibly there were British deserters riding with the commando.

'Macpherson; go over this ground carefully. See if you can find anything else.'

It was oppressive in the heat, with flies plaguing the men and horses, but Selkirk waited as patiently as he could while Macpherson searched around the campsite. The highlander located another two cartridges, two discarded tins and a piece of khaki cloth that might have been from a uniform jacket. There were also prints from a score of horses and uncountable men. Some of the men had been barefoot.

'Which direction, Macpherson?'

'That way, sir.' Macpherson pointed north and east.

Selkirk pushed them on to the brown and limpid Luvuvhu River. The trees that lined the steep banks drooped under the sun while monkeys and birds watched these strange horsemen walk past. They crossed at a drift situated above a sudden descent into rapids, with the roots of wild fig trees half in and half out of the water. There were more hoofprints, with parallel grooves that could only have been made by a wagon, and the prints of booted feet.

They moved on, past what must have once been a native village but was now only a collection of abandoned beehive huts surrounded by a thornbush hedge. Some of the huts had boasted stone walls, which were now little more than small mounds.

'The Boers call these places kliphoks,' he said quietly. 'It seems that once there were many more stone-built villages in the interior, but the inhabitants were wiped out by war or disease.'

'Is that so? I didn't think Africans could build in stone.' Selkirk touched the walls. In shape and size they were little different to the shielings that Border families had once used while summer pasturing.

The Reivers snatched at unripe maize that hung languidly in weed-choked fields as Gray pointed to another group of hoof prints and more brass cartridge cases.

'They're very careless.' Donnelly gave his opinion. 'Whoever they are, they're leaving a trail that even a Limey could follow.'

'Either they're very sure that we won't come looking for them, or they're luring us into something very nasty.' Selkirk checked the bolt of his carbine for the fourth time that day. He glanced around his Reivers. Everyone was riding warily, watching the bushland on either side, checking behind them every dozen yards, looking at the tops of trees for hidden marksmen or watchers. The sense of unease that had possessed him ever since he rode into Akersdorp redoubled.

'They're not far ahead now.' Years of campaigning had sharpened Selkirk's perception of danger. He could sense that the Boers were nearby. Perhaps it was a combination of experience and small signs, or perhaps there was something more fundamental, an instinct inherited from his Border ancestors who had played cat and mouse with the English. He halted his men and, signalling to Donnelly pushed forward with great care.

They were in an area of sparse trees but a great deal of secondary growth. Every bush seemed to be defended by long hooked thorns and a thousand varieties of biting insects, while snakes flickered through the long grass underfoot. Every so often a herd of gemsbok or hartebeest would run in front of them, and once they stopped as a group of ostriches galloped madly away.

'Some bloody country this. Even the birds have to run.' Haig sighted along his carbine but did not fire. Selkirk guided Ben between the bushes, keeping a firm grip of his carbine and hoping that he would see the enemy before they saw him.

Out on the high veldt it had been possible to smell the Boers, either by the acrid drift of their campfire smoke, or through the stink of their latrines or the friendly scent of cattle and horses. Here there were myriad scents, of animal and rotting vegetation, so it was harder to sniff out the enemy. He listened for the murmur of voices, or the soft whinny of a horse, or the click of metal on metal, but Donnelly saw it first.

Donnelly's hand raised in front of him, fist clenched, and Selkirk stopped. Moving slowly, they dismounted and knee-haltered the horses so they could not stray.

'A flash, sun on metal.' Donnelly's explanation was enough.

Crouching low, they moved on, Donnelly in the lead, Selkirk three yards behind and slightly to the side. Twice they halted at the threat of faint sounds from ahead, and once Selkirk jumped when a troop of young monkeys erupted from a tree to scamper across the ground in a chattering horde.

They smelled the coffee simultaneously and halted exactly where they were. They moved a dozen slow steps forward before stopping in the shelter of a patch of dense bush whose broad red flowers afforded splendid camouflage. There was a ring of huts ahead, around which a score of men moved with a careless lack of concealment that told of total confidence. Knee-haltered horses grazed the long grass and a dozen native servants worked around cooking fires or repaired damaged equipment.

The Boers wore a mixture of attire, from some dressed entirely in British khaki to the tall, bearded man in the remains of a morning suit and top hat. There were more voices, and another group rode in from the north, sun darkened, bearded men who looked wiry and fit, carrying Lee-Enfield rifles or battered Mausers that might have seen action at Ladysmith or the Modder.

Selkirk signalled to Donnelly to withdraw, and they worked their way back to their horses, then to the patiently waiting Reivers. They gathered around him, wondering.

'There are at least thirty Boers, and probably more,' Selkirk explained. 'We might catch them all, but I suspect that they would split up and regroup. Then they would have the advantage, for they know the country and we don't.'

'Sir. There were more than thirty that attacked Akersdorp.' Fairweather looked pale and tired.

'You're right. I reckon they've more than one camp. If we rode straight in, they would be able to calculate our strength. So we won't do that.' Selkirk knew that most British officers would ride straight in, surround the camp and attack in a pincer movement. Rather than follow traditional British army tactics, Selkirk reverted to his Border guile. 'Maybe we should let them come to us.'

He moved the Reivers back to the abandoned native village, appointed sentinels and called together his NCOs to explain his strategy.

'We'll make this our base. I want it fortified with trenches and tripwires, and a second strongpoint a hundred yards outside, so that we can catch them in crossfire. Campbell, I want you to take charge here. I'll take ten men out before dawn and try and locate the Boers. With luck I can bring them to you. Any questions?'

There were none. The Reivers were used to Selkirk's unconventional tactics and set about making the deserted village into a trap.

Not surprisingly it was Bryant who was first to complain. 'These bloody buildings are full of bloody snakes.'

'That's all right Bryant. They'll keep the rats down.' Donnelly had experience of native huts. 'They'll not bother you any.'

There were other forms of wildlife too, from the ever-present mosquitoes to the flies that hung in a black cloud above the central cattle kraal, which Selkirk had hoped to use for the horses. Neither was as bad as the fleas that hopped and skipped in the huts, so that Selkirk eventually ordered a withdrawal. He refused to subject his Reivers to such an ordeal.

They camped instead a hundred yards from the village, where there was sweet water and wild fig trees while the sounds of low veldt Africa mocked their retreat. Flexibility was necessary in a commander of irregular horse, so Selkirk adapted his plan overnight, working out the details with Donnelly and Campbell.

'Perhaps the village was not my best idea,' he conceded, 'but we can adapt it. We'll stage our ambush nearby, and hope that the Boers will use the village for shelter.'

'Of course they will.' Donnelly agreed, 'although I can't see how that will help us. Do you expect the snakes and fleas to chase them out?'

'Much worse.' Selkirk said. 'Do you remember our explosive wagon?'

Donnelly nodded. While they had been campaigning along the Bechuanaland border, the Reivers had driven a wagon full of explosive toward a Boer position around a waterhole. The result had been devastating.

'We'll do something similar here. We have the dynamite. Listen.' Selkirk outlined his plan, accepting the refinements that Donnelly and Campbell added. In most situations the British regular soldier was a brave fighting man but he was not always blessed with imagination. He was trained to obey orders and march unthinkingly to the battle. Irregular warfare required a different type of mentality.

As well as toughness and resilience, Selkirk's Reivers needed an independence of mind; they had to be able to adapt to new situations. Not every recruit survived. Many were physically not up to the challenge but many more were mentally unsuitable. Regulars, with years of unyielding discipline behind them, were often unable to find that flexibility of mind necessary to make an irregular horseman. On the other hand, few new recruits could accept the discipline. Selkirk's force was a blend of Australians, regulars and Yeomanry. Often the Australians were best in the bush, but found it hard to accept the discipline, while the regulars seemed to lack initiative. The Yeomanry were as good as any, being willing to learn from the Australians and often of a higher intelligence than the regulars were.

Although he would never have admitted it, Selkirk's leadership style of firmness and personal bravery, mingled with his own experience, made the Reivers the fighting force that they were. During his time as an infantryman with the Royal Borderers, Selkirk realised that there was an immense gulf between the officers and men. While the men resented the officers' detached, often aloof manner, the officers scorned the men as unthinking creatures that could do nothing without directions. Selkirk had experienced both attitudes, and refused to command the Reivers as a regular infantry unit. He invited the other ranks to participate, but in return expected his men to think for themselves. Every Reiver had an important part in this war.

They listened to Selkirk's plan, added their own refinements and argued out the details well into the night. Selkirk considered everybody's ideas but in the end he made the final decisions. While the men slept, he lay in his bedroll, trying to ignore the biting insects as he mentally checked every facet of his strategy. The basic tenet was simple; send out a patrol as bait and let the Boers follow them back into an ambush. It was nothing new; the Border reivers had perfected the technique back in the sixteenth century. Only the weapons had changed.

It was nearly dawn when he slept, but although he had double-checked every angle of his idea, there was something nagging at the back of his mind. He had missed something, somewhere. The uneasy thought kept him company through his troubled dreams.

Chapter Eight :Northern Transvaal - May 1902

For once Selkirk did not lead the Reivers' patrol himself, for his place was with the main body. He disliked sending men into danger, but with Donnelly in charge, he knew that the ten-man patrol was in good hands. Although he hated to admit it, Donnelly was probably better at this sort of work than he was. The men rode out just before dawn, a loose formation of riders, every man with his equipment padded so it did not rattle, and with every piece of metal painted brown to ensure there was no reflection from the sun.

Selkirk watched them go, noting the near casual ease with which they rode. He had created this force, he had trained them into the ways of irregular fighting and now he could no longer ride with them. For a moment he wondered if he would be missed, decided that it was unlikely and turned his attention to the task in hand.

He divided his remaining men into two unequal bodies, with the smaller party centred on the Maxim gun, and settled down to await events. He had done all that he could do and now it depended on Donnelly and the Boers. If they reacted as they should do, as they had always done in the past, then his ambush would work and they would be one small step closer to victory for the Empire. More importantly, it would be another step towards going home.

The morning passed slowly, with Selkirk gauging Donnelly's progress by his watch. He made the men eat breakfast, watched as a small herd of eland walked cautiously past his defences and hoped that they would not spring any of the trip wires. He slapped at the hordes of mosquitoes that made life a misery. Already there were four men sick with malaria, and Selkirk expected others to follow. At this rate, his Reivers would be unable to function as a fighting force within a month, and far too many brave men would have been wasted. The Nobleman once told him that disease always felled more men than enemy bullets. He had scoffed at the time, but not now. The army's main enemy in Africa had been enteric fever, with Boer Mausers far less deadly.

'Sir.' Macpherson's soft whisper summoned him. The Badenoch man had been checking every aspect of his position, examining the surrounding trees and ground as if he were stalking for deer. 'Over there in that thorn bush.'

Placing his field glasses to his eye, Selkirk followed Macpherson's gesture. There was something suspended from the bush, something white and red and slowly moving. He focussed the lens, moving very slowly, for any sudden movement could alert a careful enemy.

'It's like a man, a naked man.' Selkirk passed the glasses to Macpherson, who began to pray.

'It was once sir. Not now.'

'Is he coming toward us? He's certainly moving.' Selkirk could see a strange writhing, as though the man was struggling against something.

'No, sir. He's dead.' Macpherson handed back the glasses.

'Cover me.' Feeling vulnerable as soon as he left the defences, Selkirk moved forward. He had not got six feet before he realised what he had seen. A dense cloud of insects rose from the corpse on which they had been feasting. It had been the movement of the insects that had given the appearance of movement to a body that was very dead indeed.

The man had been castrated and blinded, either before or after death, and his body had been opened so that certain of his organs could be removed. It must have happened recently, for Selkirk could see the viscera trailing still wet and bloody among the thorns.

'What sort of people are we dealing with here sir?' Macpherson sounded shaken.

'I don't know Kirky, but make sure you keep a good look out.' The thought of that tortured corpse unsettled Selkirk for the rest of the day. Used to fighting the Boers, Selkirk was uneasy at facing whatever creatures inhabited this African bush. All his boyhood stories of cannibals and jungle savages returned, so that he started at every small sound and snapped at his Reivers. The men accepted his mood philosophically, but only Haig appeared unconcerned at the mutilated corpse.

As the heat increased, the men began to lose concentration. One or two preferred to hunt for shade rather than probing their

113

surroundings for movement. Selkirk walked around the positions, snarling. Some seemed unaffected; Haig and Bryant were too bloody-minded to allow any discomfort to concern them, Hetherington and Blackdown were far too responsible soldiers to relax, while Macpherson had been used to lying for hour after hour in the heather of Badenoch. The fidgeting of the others was likely to give away their positions to the Boer.

'Staggered rest periods, lads,' Selkirk passed the order. 'Every alternate man take ten minutes off, then change. After that we'll have thirty minutes on, thirty off until Lieutenant Donnelly returns.'

He could sense the relief as half the men withdrew from their positions. He allowed them to play cards, but not to speak, and was not surprised to see many rolling into shade to fall asleep. Constant tension seemed to exhaust men.

It was Macpherson who signalled to him with a raised fist. 'Sir,' he whispered. 'Somebody's coming.'

'Where?'

'Listen.' Macpherson placed his ear to the ground. 'Can't you hear the horses?'

Selkirk had seen Donnelly listen in the same manner, but although he concentrated, he could hear nothing but distant vibrations that anything could have caused.

'At least thirty horses coming this way fast.' Macpherson glanced up. 'They're in two distinct groups, one larger than the other.'

'Sounds like our boys are coming home.' Selkirk agreed. At one time he would have asked Macpherson if he was sure, but he had learned to trust his men. 'How far away are they?'

'Ten minutes. Maybe a wee bit more.' It was a sure sign of Macpherson's excitement that he omitted the 'sir' when he spoke.

'Stand to. Pass the word.' Selkirk was gratified at the new alertness of his men. He ran over to the smaller position and told them what was happening. With Campbell in charge here, everything was as efficient as one of his Clyde build engines. Cobb, his Maxim gunner, grinned as he thumbed the levers of his weapon. 'Here we go then.'

'Aye, but mind you let our boys past first.' Selkirk had heard of tragic affairs where British soldiers had fired on their colleagues in the heat of battle. He wanted no such incidents with the men under his command.

'Yes, sir.' Cobb said. He sighted along the water-cooled barrel of the Maxim and shifted his position slightly.

There was an explosion of birds rising from the trees, then a sudden hush, as if nature recoiled from the impending clash of men. The drumming of distant hooves became distinctly audible. One of the Reivers yawned to break the tension, another began to giggle until Selkirk glowered him into silence. Lifting his field glasses, he focused on the gap between two trees through which he expected Donnelly's patrol to thunder. There was the sound of a rifle, then another, and Bryant licked his lips. Haig lowered himself down, cuddling the stock of his Lee Enfield into his shoulder. He had never learned the knack of keeping one eye open but lazy, so closed his left eye tightly, as if the force extended by his eyelid would help him defeat the Boers.

'Wait for it, lads,' Selkirk whispered, although he knew that the Boers could never hear him above the pounding of their horses' hooves, 'and make sure that Donnelly's patrol is safe first.'

'Who the hell's that?' Blackdown the poacher pointed to the edge of the cleared killing zone, from where two riders had appeared. They rode leisurely across the line of British rifles, unconcerned that they were entering a battleground.

'Jesus. That's Selkirk's tart.' Hetherington changed his tone slightly, 'that's your woman sir! Not the rich bint – lady, sir. The other one.'

Selkirk swung the glasses on to the riders. One wore the stained khaki uniform of a British soldier, with a broad bush hat that concealed his face, while the other wore a man's trousers and jacket, with a broad brimmed hat, but there was no mistaking the long hair that hung down her back. As if in confirmation, the woman glanced briefly toward the British positions.

'Marie.' Selkirk breathed the name as the riders rode nonchalantly toward the native village with its collection of booby traps and explosives. He sensed, rather than saw, the first of the patrol burst between the two trees, and noted without surprise that Donnelly was at the rear, where there was most danger. He saw Marie turn toward the approaching riders and instinctively kick in her heels to get out of their way.

Marie! Of course it was Marie! Selkirk suddenly knew what had been nagging at him for the past few days. He had unconsciously recognised that woman's footprint in the mud. He had seen Marie's broken left toe half a hundred times, and had laughed at her explanation of falling from a tree when she had been hunting for honey. But what was Marie doing down here when she should be safely up north with Thomas Duff the hunter?

The Reivers were riding hard, one or two firing over their shoulders as they headed toward Selkirk's position. The leading rider swerved to avoid Marie and her companion, but Selkirk was already moving. Although he knew that he risked compromising the ambush, he could not let Marie ride into the village. He was astride Ben and into the clearing even as the first of the Reivers galloped past on horses that were streaked with sweat.

'Marie!' Riding against the press of horsemen, Selkirk ranged alongside the Griqua woman, who looked at him with wide eyes.

'Selkirk. What are you doing here?'

'Saving your bloody life!' Reaching out, Selkirk grasped the bridle of her horse with his left hand and began to ease the animal away. It was a hard-mouthed creature, with wild, terrified eyes, and wrestled back furiously. 'Marie! Kick your feet free.' Selkirk shouted in her ear, 'Don't go into the village.'

The Reivers were nearly past now; only Donnelly remained, glancing anxiously at Selkirk and over toward the trees, where what looked like half the remaining Free Burghers in Africa were approaching at terrifying speed.

There were more rifle shots and Marie's horse staggered. For the first time since he had met her, Marie panicked, screaming in sheer fear as her horse pitched forward, trapping her beneath it. 'Selkirk! Help!'

Her companion began to move to help, but his horse slipped and he fell, rolling on the ground uselessly.

'Jesus. Selks! Leave her!' Donnelly remained at Selkirk's side. He fired his carbine at the Boers, 'you'll just sacrifice yourself!'

'So will you.' Selkirk glanced at the Boers and at Marie, who was trying to wriggle free of the thrashing horse. 'Go, Donnelly. Take command of the Reivers!'

'Damn you Selkirk, you stubborn bastard! I'm not leaving.'

'Take command, Donnelly. That's an order!' Without waiting to see if Donnelly obeyed, Selkirk dismounted. The horse lay on top of Marie's left leg, trapping her. 'Lie still,' Selkirk shouted, then gasped as a bullet whipped past him to smack into the horse. As the animal whinnied and writhed, Selkirk hauled Marie free. Mounting Ben, he reached down grabbed Marie's arm and hauled her face down over the crupper. He swore loudly, spurring furiously as bullets flicked past him.

'Maak dood die verdomde khaki!' 'Kill the damned khaki!'

The voice was harsh behind him as the Boers advanced, forty, maybe fifty strong, shooting and shouting as they came. Selkirk knew that Ben carried a double load and was built for endurance rather than speed, but he also knew that he was fresh, while the Boer horses had been riding at the canter, if not the gallop, for some distance. He also knew that Ben had a stout heart and would perform to the last ounce of his strength.

'On Ben! On for Fethan!'

'Keep your bloody heid doon, Selks!' Only Haig would shout that in the middle of a battle. Selkirk ducked as the British firing started.

By dashing out to rescue Marie he had endangered not only the success of the ambush but also the lives of every one of his men. He knew that, and they knew that. However they also knew that he would have done the same for any one of them, and although Selkirk hardly cared to admit it, many of them would have risked their lives for him. They understood his actions, and now proved his faith in them by opening a controlled fire on the advancing Boers.

Covering Marie as best he could, Selkirk galloped toward the Reivers' positions. He saw the tilted hats and levelled rifles then urged the doubly laden Ben to leap over a trip wire. There were shouts from behind as the Boers realised that they had blundered into an ambush. Now he had to guide them toward the deserted village.

Sergeant Campbell was waiting for his signal before opening fire. Selkirk bundled Marie to the ground and yelled at her to keep out of trouble before taking stock of the situation. Because he had picked up Marie, the Reivers had delayed firing for a fraction too long, so the Boers were closer than he had planned. Once they had recovered from their initial surprise they charged in with renewed ferocity, firing from the hip.

Every second Reiver fired back. Enough firepower to slow the charge but not sufficient to turn it back. Selkirk saw only one man fall from his horse. He stood up, well aware that it was nearly impossible for a man on a galloping horse to hit anything at which he fired, but nervous nevertheless. He lifted one hand in the air and waited, feeling more foolish than afraid. The sound of gunfire had become so much a part of his life that he could nearly ignore it, but he could hear the muttered comments from his men.

'Come on you boojer bastards. Come on you boojer bastards.'

'Call yourself bitter enders? Well, here's the bitter end.'

'Oh Jesus don't let me be killed. Please don't let me be killed.'

'Aim low! Aim low, pay them back for Magersfontein.'

'Get doon you daft bastard, Selks! Get your heid doon!'

'Selkirk, my other British soldier! Be careful.'

The leading Boers were about thirty yards away now, close enough for Selkirk to make out the expression on their faces. There was the usual mixture of grey-bearded men and thin-faced youths, some with battered civilian clothes, now worn and patched beyond recognition, others in full British khaki. Twenty-five yards, with the horses frothing, their hooves thudding hollowly on the soft ground. They seemed full of confidence, cheering as they approached the deliberately slender British line.

'Now Campbell! Now!' Selkirk dropped his hand. He remembered a phrase that he had read in some history book and repeated it, relishing the words of a real general. 'Now Reivers! Now's your time!'

The opening volleys of the battle of Magersfontein remained as the worst nightmare of Selkirk's experience, when thousands of concealed Boers had opened fire on the Highland Brigade and the Royal Borderers. He remembered the shock and the awe and the horror of that day, and wondered if any of the Boers present had been on the opposing side. If so, they now experienced something similar as Cobb's Maxim gun and the remainder of the Reivers opened up.

The Boers were caught in a crossfire that cut down fully a third of their numbers within thirty seconds and continued to whittle them even as panic set in. All the bravery, all the fury evaporated before that merciless onslaught, as brave men turned to flee and young boys screamed in fear. There seemed to be no ordered retreat, just a frenzied dash to the nearest sanctuary, which was the temptingly close native village. Selkirk watched them run, some hatless, others without rifles, through the gap he had made in the thorn-bush barrier, then, hating himself for a murderer, he heard the first of the explosions.

Each hut had been carefully rigged with tripwires that led to charges of dynamite. If the Boers entered a hut, they were as good as dead. There was a second explosion, then a third, and then silence except for the terrible sound of a wounded horse and the hoarse, terrible cry of a grown man calling for his mother. This was a massacre, not a battle. Even as he gave the order, Selkirk felt the nausea rising in his throat.

'Cobb! Put fifty rounds into the village. Flush them out.'

The Maxim gun hammered briefly, hurtling fifty .303 rounds into the village. There was another prolonged scream, then a harsh voice shouted, 'for the love of God, enough! We surrender!'

'It could be a trick, sir.' Haig had also been present at Paardeberg, when the Boers had raised the white flag, only to fire on the British troops as they advanced to take the laager.

'Perhaps.' Selkirk raised his voice. 'Come on out, one at a time, without your weapons and with your hands above your head.'

He glanced back, to where Marie huddled close to the ground with her hands shielding her face. 'Look after her, Haigie.' He jerked a thumb to where Marie's companion huddled on the ground, face covered by his hat. 'And that one. I want a word with him.'

There was silence in the bush, broken only by the screaming of the wounded horse and high-pitched sobs from a badly injured man.

119

Kirky was mouthing prayers in Gaelic and English, while pressing fresh cartridges into to his magazine.

The first Boer emerged with one hand high and the other hanging limply by his side. Others followed until there were twelve men standing in front of the village. Most nursed minor wounds or flesh blackened by burns.

'And the rest of you.' Selkirk shouted.

'That's all of us that can walk.' The Boer with the wounded arm claimed. He was small for a Boer, with battered black trousers under a khaki jacket. 'You've killed us all.'

Selkirk slid clear of the Reiver's position. 'Hetherington! Blackdown! You're with me.' Keeping his carbine levelled at the Boers, he moved slowly forward. 'Stand clear from the entrance.' The Boers obeyed, staring as if in shock as Selkirk approached.

'Watch them.' Selkirk looked inside the native village. After more than two years of war he was virtually inured to horror, but the sight of men and horses lying in shredded lumps of meat sickened him. He entered cautiously, ensuring that he did not trigger any remaining trip wires and very conscious that there might be a vengeful Boer lying in wait with a rifle.

The only Boers were either dead or horribly injured. The village was a shambles of mutilated bodies, blasted to pieces by dynamite or shredded by Cobb's Maxim gun. Selkirk's quick check assured him that he could do nothing for the wounded. They pleaded with him through agonised eyes, but he could not bring himself to kill helpless men. He left hurriedly, sickened by the suffering that he had caused.

'Right lads, get these Boers away from here.' Selkirk was aware of the horror in his eyes, but he was a King's Officer, he had to do his duty. He kept his voice deliberately harsh. 'And call for Marie. She's best at helping wounded men.'

As always after a battle, he felt overwhelming tiredness mingled with contempt for himself. The self-loathing seemed to grow stronger each time, as his store of memories became congested with images of dead and dying men. He was not a natural soldier and as soon as his six years' service was complete, he would leave the army without a backward glance.

Why did people glorify this chaos of agony and mutilation? Why did people dress hell in gaudy uniforms and play pretty tunes for men to march to slaughter? Selkirk closed his eyes; if all the politicians in the world, all the kings and queens and petty tyrants, could be brought to just one battlefield, then all wars might end. If the people that ruled the armies could only see the maimed men, the blind and crippled, the men whose minds were shattered by fear and horror, then perhaps this monstrosity could be banished from the world and all the decent people, of whatever country, could live together.

It would never happen, of course. Men would always join the colours to impress their women, and women would always look up to a brave man. That was human nature, just as much as it was natural for a politician to want to control the destiny and finances of others, be they Boer, Briton or Zulu.

The Boers sat in a disconsolate group, menaced by the levelled rifles of half a dozen Reivers. Of the seventeen survivors, five would not live long, one had a broken arm and the remainder had relatively minor burns or scratches. Three of the men were obviously officers, possibly field cornets, but the others appeared to be just ordinary, hard riding Boers. Most wore a mixture of civilian clothes and khaki, now scorched and tattered.

'Sergeant Campbell. Have these men watched.' Selkirk hoped that he sounded like a sadistic Rooineck officer. 'If they try to escape, shoot them.'

'Yes, sir.' Campbell jerked a callused thumb to the men, 'you two come with me. Bryant! Burke!' he selected two of the Reivers, 'watch them. If they escape, you'll take their place.'

Selkirk had frequently heard Bryant complain about the uselessness of the British soldiers, so he would probably enjoy his new duty, but Burke was different. Although he came from a nation with no cause to love the English, Selkirk had never heard him voice any dislike for anybody. Still, Campbell knew his men.

'Marie!' Selkirk realised that the wounded men remained unattended and suffering. 'Where's Marie? And the man that was with her?'

'She's gone sir.' Haig sounded unabashed. 'She must have slipped away during the fighting. I didn't see the fellae.'

'Slipped away where?' Selkirk looked around angrily. 'I thought I ordered you to look after her.'

'Yes, sir,' Haig admitted readily, 'but I was busy shooting the Boers. I can't look in two directions at once.' He paused, significantly. 'Not even for one of your women, Selks.'

Selkirk glared at the small man. Haig's face was expressionless, but Selkirk felt that he was being mocked. Haig was entirely capable of looking after Marie if he had wanted to and equally capable of helping her escape if it suited his purpose. 'Did you see where she went?'

'No. Like I said, I was shooting Boers. When I turned to check on her, she was gone. I reckon that she just slipped away back to the bush. Maybe she was happier there.'

About to blast Haig for an incompetent fool, Selkirk paused. He did not own Marie, who had already left him twice, and the Griqua was probably far better equipped to survive in Africa than any of his men were. No doubt she had another man out there, either Thomas Duff the hunter or her companion of today, whoever he had been. Selkirk wished her well.

'Good luck to her then, but as you let her go, you can take her place. Look after the wounded Boers, Haigie. Treat them like you would treat your own brother.'

'Yes, sir.' Haig's grin was as evil as anything that Selkirk had ever seen in his life. 'I knifed him sir, after we argued.'

'Well treat them like they were your sweetheart then.'

A search of the battlefield revealed forty dead or dying Boers. Selkirk did what he could to make the wounded comfortable, had the prisoners bury their companions and made arrangements to return to Akersdorp.

'Right Reivers, let's trek.' He heard the weariness in his voice and hoped it would not be transferred to his men. He needed them at their best, for although they had just won a sizeable skirmish, there was no telling how many Boers remained at large. At best, he had inflicted a mortal blow against the Boer commando. At worst, he had weakened it. Now he had to attend to some personal business.

Chapter Nine: Northern Transvaal - May 1902

Ever since Lieutenant Cloete had showed them the refugee camp, the Reivers had been restless. Certainly they had fought well enough when the occasion offered, but Selkirk recognised that they lacked something of the verve they had possessed in Bechuanaland. They were quieter, nearly sulky, and that was never good. The reason was obvious; the sight of Hendrina, Hansie and young Coenraad suffering had upset them. These were tough men, most of them were veterans of some of the ugly battles of the early part of the war, all had seen the vicious little skirmishes of the guerrilla campaign, yet they all felt for the two Boer women who had looked after them so well.

Campbell, of course, had been the worst affected, but Selkirk had heard the evening murmurs and the grumbles around the horse lines. Hendrina was one of them, to an extent, an adopted Reiver, and their sympathies were entirely with Campbell for trying to desert, rather than with the British authorities for interning a woman who would certainly harbour the enemy if given the opportunity. Selkirk felt torn between two duties; his responsibility to hunt and destroy the Boer enemy, and his feelings for a woman who had proved a true friend.

There was at least one other factor. If he could do something for Hendrina and Hansie, he would restore the morale of the Reivers, which in turn would make the unit a more effective fighting force. Then he would be better able to scour the bush for the remaining Boers. Even although this most recent expedition had been a success, he had kept his Reivers on a tight rein in case their morale had been weakened. Now it was time to restore it.

Selkirk refused to think of Helena Van Vuren.

'Sergeant Campbell.' As soon as the idea had germinated, Selkirk was determined to carry it out. He was not a man to agonise on his decisions.

'Sir!' Campbell had been checking the ammunition for the Maxim. The gun had jammed twice recently and Cobb was concerned about the feeding mechanism for the belt.

'A word, if you please.' Selkirk tried to look as authoritarian as a real officer would, but he knew by the sudden gleam in Campbell's eye that he had failed. The sergeant realised immediately that his officer was planning something. 'We have wrongs to right, Colin.'

Campbell caught on at once. 'That we have, sir.'

'When can you be ready?'

'Now, sir.' Campbell dropped the ammunition belt and reached for his carbine.

Organising the Reivers was easy. Selkirk picked half a dozen men who had known Hendrina and could be trusted to follow his orders to the letter. As well as Campbell, he chose Haig, who had formed a strangely close bond with Hendrina, and Blackdown. The ex-poacher's muscle would come in handy, while Selkirk knew that he would welcome the chance to bend a few rules. He also took Pert, the horseman from Angus whose saturnine features hinted at ancestry from the old wild races beyond history. Pert was a steady soldier and as expert a horseman as Selkirk. Gray the Australian was always ready to twist authority's tail, and McGann the Ulsterman was as wild as the heather and as reliable as granite.

Six men. Selkirk wished that Newman could come too, for he knew Hendrina better than any of them. Haig had taken the death of his friend remarkably well, but there again, Haig was a long service veteran who had seen his colleagues die from the barren rocks of the North West Frontier to the vast deserts of the Sudan. Selkirk had heard Haig's tales of finding the corpses of Borderers whom the Afridi women had first castrated and blinded, then propped open their mouths and urinated into their mouths until they drowned. Newman was only one of a long list of friends that Haig had lost in the service of Empire.

These were veterans who knew exactly what to do and how to do it. Although Lieutenant Windrush was nominally in charge of the garrison, Selkirk gave Donnelly specific orders to look after the Reivers. 'Don't do anything aggressive until I return. Keep within

Akersdorp except for limited patrolling, and don't provoke Piet,' Selkirk grinned, 'as if I need to tell you. You trained me after all.'

Donnelly shook his head; his Arizona drawl was as calm and reassuring as ever. 'So now you blame me? I should come with you to hold your hand, Drew.'

Outside the Borders, only Donnelly had ever called him by his Christian name, and then only when he was worried.

'I need you here, Donnelly. I need you to look after things when I'm gone. Windrush is probably competent enough, but he's not a Reiver. Not yet anyway. Look after him.' Selkirk hesitated, unsure what to say to this man with whom he had shared so much, 'and look after yourself as well.'

They moved quickly, seven Reivers with fourteen horses, a fast moving force of men well used to African conditions and who had a single object on their mind. Selkirk, Campbell and Donnelly had discussed the best methods of releasing Hendrina's family, and decided that a combination of direct action and subterfuge would fit their purposes. At one time they had favoured Campbell's idea of a quick raid through the wire, but Donnelly had pointed out that nervous guards might open fire, and the thought of stray bullets among the huddled women and children was appalling.

Lightly equipped and with spare horses, it took only a week to cover the distance, and while Haig grumbled incessantly and Gray's nasal accent complained about 'bloody useless Pommy officers and their bloody silly notions of bloody silly soldiering', Selkirk was more concerned about Campbell. The nearer they came to the camp, the more nervous the normally taciturn Clydesider became, so that he jumped at the call of a night bird and rode with his finger constantly curled around the trigger of his carbine.

'Relax sergeant.' Selkirk advised, to be rewarded with a tight smile and a jerked nod.

'I'll be fine, sir.'

The camp seemed even more sordid close up, and Campbell pointed significantly to the large graveyard outside the wire, where mounds of fresh earth told of continued mortality within. One grave boasted a pathetic handful of wild flowers, wilting in the heat.

Selkirk had expected to see a military guard but there were civilians at the gate, and it was a man in a neat grey suit that approached him as he entered.

'Please state your name and business.' The man was tall, with a ridiculous monocle gleaming in one eye. He spoke brusquely through a mouth as thin as charity, as if he was addressing a new client at a bank rather than a soldier of the King.

'Captain James Montgomery,' Selkirk said cheerfully, 'of the Ettrick and Cheviot Yeomanry.' If anybody was to be blamed for this work, then he could think of nobody more suitable than the hectoring, cheroot-smoking landowner that had stolen away Georgina. 'And we come on the Queen's business.'

'What?' Tall as he was, the man in grey still had to lean back to address Selkirk on his horse. 'Queen Victoria has been dead this last year, Captain.'

'Indeed? Then it must be unfinished business then.' Selkirk matched the pop-eyed stare of the man in grey. He signalled with his hand and his Reivers filed past, with Campbell leading them toward the spot where he had last seen Hansie. 'We are going to question two of your inmates.'

'You have permission I suppose?' The man in grey held out his hand, obviously expecting an official document. Selkirk shook the hand so vigorously that the man winced and tried to withdraw.

'Colonel Drongan sent me in person, Mr?'

'Mr Thatcher. Horace Thatcher, BA.'

Selkirk released the hand of Horace Thatcher, BA. 'Delighted to meet you, Mr Thatcher. Now, I have to ask if these people have given you any trouble?'

Horace Thatcher screwed up his face as if contemplating a major problem. 'They are the most ignorant type of people, Captain Montgomery, indeed some are hardly worthy of the name. Dirty, diseased, unruly,' he shook his head, 'I despair sometimes, Captain.'

Selkirk glanced around the camp, seeing pinched faces and children's bodies swollen with malnutrition. He saw mothers desperate with anxiety and fathers hunched in despair and defeat. He saw eight-year-old children with the eyes of old men, and aged women with the light of madness in their eyes. As he looked, he remembered the free farms of the veldt, where Boers had carved out a living from the wilderness, combating a harsh environment and hostile tribes. He remembered the open-handed hospitality the Reivers had received at Hendrinafontein and the love and laughter of that farm.

'Despair, Mr Thatcher? I can believe that you are no stranger to that.' Selkirk leaned closer. 'However, there is one thing that I should tell you. We have reason to believe that there are Boer agents operating in this camp. They have contacts outside with Helena Van Vuren, the Boer Boadicea.' Selkirk paused for effect. He could see the beginning of consternation in Thatcher's face. 'Of course they will tell her how kind you are to these good people, how you always make sure that they receive their full allocation of food and medicine, things like that.'

Thatcher nodded; he had paled, then turned an interesting shade of pink. 'This Van Vuren, is she as bad as people say?'

'Bad?' Selkirk looked away. 'She's worse than bad. I've been trying to hunt her for years. Sent six agents after her. She shot three of them in person. The others she just mutilated and left to die,' he swallowed hard, 'she likes to play with prisoners, so I'm told.'

'Well, she's no reason to come here. I always take the best care of my refugees.' Thatcher must have been aware of the crowd that had gathered around. Mostly women and children, they seemed to be listening intently as they looked from Thatcher to Selkirk.

'As long as they are given all the food that's due to them, and have adequate medical facilities, I'm sure that Van Vuren will leave you in peace.' Selkirk saw his Reivers returning with the Fourie family. While Hansie and Coenraad shared the back of a horse, Haig and McGann were helping Hendrina. Gray acted as rearguard, sweeping the entire camp with his carbine. Selkirk had worried that the old woman might be too large to sit on a horse, but she had lost so much weight that the animal supported her without difficulty.

'We are taking these people away with us,' Selkirk adopted a high hand. 'They are known to be Boer agents.'

Thatcher adjusted his monocle with a hand that visibly shook. 'All of them? Even the child?' He indicated Coenraad, who stared listlessly back through huge eyes.

'Especially him.' Selkirk dropped his voice. 'He ran with messages.'

'But what are you going to do with them?'

Selkirk shrugged. 'Shoot them of course.'

'But Van Vuren!' Thatcher appeared on the edge of tears, 'she'll think that I had something to do with it.'

Ignoring him, Selkirk nodded to Campbell. 'Any problems Sergeant MacDonald?'

Well used to Selkirk's subterfuge, Campbell saluted. 'None at all, sir. We located the spies as you ordered.'

'Then take them out of here.' Selkirk felt a wave of anger at the lines of hardship that had been carved so deeply in the faces of these people that he knew as friends. He felt the hot fury surging over him, taking over his self-control and reached for the pistol at his belt, until Hendrina reached across and touched his arm. Her eyes were deep and dark and haunted, but still contained the compassion that he had come to expect.

'You can't shoot them here.' For a moment Selkirk thought that Thatcher was pleading for the lives of the Fouries, then he realised the commandant was fearful of retaliation. The disgust that he felt nearly pushed his anger over the edge and again his fingers scrabbled at the butt of his pistol.

'Meneer,' Hendrina's voice sounded as if it belonged to somebody else. What had once been deep and melodious was now a husky croak. 'It was not his fault. Let me stay in this place and help.'

'What?' Selkirk looked deep into the eyes of Hendrina and saw the sorrow beneath the suffering, the deep depths of pity and pain and anguish that he knew were not for herself but for those around her.

'Sergeant! Get these people out of here. Ride hard and fast and don't listen to anything that they say.' He heard the harshness in his voice as he forcibly transferred his anger from Thatcher to the situation in which they all found themselves.

'Please, please let me stay,' Hendrina begged, 'there are people who need me here.'

'Ride, sergeant.' Selkirk kicked sharply with his heels and Ben, who was not used to that sort of treatment, protested by rolling back his eyes and lips. Thatcher recoiled from the Captain who had suddenly shown the true savagery of his nature.

They left the camp at speed, with Haig cursing foully under his breath and Campbell forbearing to support Hansie until they were out of sight of the barbed wire fence. Only when they were a good two miles from the camp did Selkirk order a halt, choosing a sheltered spot beside a spruit overhung by trees lively with birds.

'Haig, get a fire going and we'll feed these people.' Selkirk helped Hendrina dismount. He caught her as she staggered. Campbell was doing the same for Hansie while the remaining Reivers tactfully removed themselves to act as sentries. Haig was alternately swearing at 'them bastards that treat wummen like that' and winking at Coenraad.

They had brought hard biscuits, which they smeared with army issue meat paste, and biltong, which Coenraad chewed as if it were a stick of liquorice. Selkirk fought back his emotion when he saw the women trying to eat delicately, so he suggested that he take the Reivers for a short patrol until the Fouries had a chance to recover.

'May I stay here, sir?' Campbell had one arm tightly wrapped around Hansie.

'What do the women think?' Selkirk waited for Hendrina to take charge, but she appeared to have lost her vitality. She sat with her back propped against a tree, silently weeping as she stared into the bright bubbling water of the spruit.

'Ja, Lieutenant. Let him stay.' It was Hansie who made the decision. She had aged in the camp, with silver strands of hair showing among the blonde and deeper lines around her eyes. Her eyes appeared sunk into a hollow dark tube as she looked to Selkirk. 'Why did this happen to us?'

Selkirk had no answer. He shook his head slowly. 'I do not know, Hansie.' In his youth, Selkirk had admired the scarlet clad soldiers of the Royal Borderers when they swaggered and laughed their way through the Ettrick Fair. He had admired them for the romance and glory that they portrayed and wondered what it was like to guard the frontiers of Empire. He had also listened to his grandmother's tales of life on the old Border, when Scot fought with English and bold riders clashed with sword and lance along the sweet valleys of Ettrick.

Nobody had told him about the pain and misery of war. He had never envisaged the fear that the 'buck-up' snap of a Mauser could create or the horror of seeing what remained of a man after a shell had shredded him. There were no words to describe his feelings when he had first slid his bayonet into a screaming Boer, or to depict the sounds and stench of a thousand men left wounded or dead in the African sun.

Worst of all was when the war came to civilians. Selkirk could still taste the bitter soot of burning farms and see the fear in the eyes of women whose family was made homeless and whose possessions were destroyed. Was that the true price of Empire, the small change casually discarded by the men who wanted the map painted red or green or whatever other colour their national pride preferred?

'Why us, meneer?' Hansie looked over to her son, who was sitting beside Haig, eating everything that the small soldier gave him. 'We are only little people. What value is our land to the mighty British Empire?' Her voice rose slightly. 'You have so much, we have so little, yet you want to take even that?'

As her anger took hold, Hansie shook away the comforting arm of Campbell. 'I will not be helped by a rooineck! I will not let you touch me, Colin Khaki!' She pushed herself to her feet and pointed a finger at Selkirk. 'It is your fault that our country lies in rags and all the children are dying in their hundreds!' Her voice dropped a little, 'hundreds and hundreds of little children, sick and suffering, so thin and then so swollen as they die.'

'Hansie,' Campbell placed his hand on her arm again. This time she did not push him away.

'Then the diarrhoea takes over and the fever and they die crying.' Hansie was trembling. 'Crying for their mother and crying for the pain, crying for the diarrhoea to stop and crying to go home. Have you ever heard a hundred crying children, meneer? Or a thousand? Or ten thousand? Have you?' Her finger still accused Selkirk. 'Ten thousand children dying at once because you rooinecks wanted their country. There is a curse on this country now, a curse of suffering.'

Selkirk nodded. There was nothing that he could say.

130

'But you will never take our land, Lieutenant Rooineck. You may cover it with khaki and plant as many flags as you like. You may make us all speak English and drink cups of tea and sing God Save the Queen. You may call us part of your Empire, rooineck, but you will never take our land. Do you know why not?'

'Tell me.'

'Because it is salted with our dead. .We are part of the soil now. As long as there is one Boer woman left, we will breed men to fight you. As long as there is one Boer breath, we will use it to curse you. As long as there is one Boer thought, we will think of freedom. Ons land; our land!'

Campbell caught Hansie as she fell. 'Best leave us for a while sir. I'll make sure the women and Coenraad are all right.'

'Excuse me sir.' Pert sounded urgent as he slipped down from his position as sentinel. 'I thought I saw movement over there.' He indicated a patch of slightly denser bush about quarter of a mile to the south.

'Animal or human?' Selkirk slid to the ground and levelled his field glasses. He could see nothing unusual, just the branches of a tree, swaying in the faint breeze.

'Not sure sir, that's why I told you.'

'See what you think Gray.'

The Australian studied the trees intently. 'Can't see anything at all sir. Do you want me to go and have a look?'

On an impulse, Selkirk shook his head. 'No. I'll go myself. You stay here and guard the women. They've been through enough.'

'Best if I go, sir.' Like many of the Australians in the Reivers, Gray often let his democratic instincts overcome his military discipline. 'I'm better than you in the bush.'

'That was an order, Gray.' Hansie's outburst, coupled with the scenes at the camp, had upset Selkirk more than he cared to admit. He needed to do something active rather than skulk in a hole while others faced danger.

'And Gray; in case I don't return, tell Sergeant Campbell to get the rest of the patrol and the civilians back to Akersdorp. Do you understand? Don't come looking for me.' Selkirk put a great deal of emphasis on his words. He did not want his precious Reivers blundering about the bush to be picked off one by one by the enemy. 'I'm relying on you to get them back, Gray.'

'Yes sir, but I still think that I should go.'

'That was also an order, Gray.'

This entire section of countryside was flat, dotted with clumps of dense bush and isolated trees. It seemed to brood beneath a sulky sun with even the grass dull and heavy. Leaving Ben in the care of Gray, Selkirk slid on to his stomach and moved sideways for a good two hundred yards before edging toward the patch of bushland.

As soon as he left Gray, Selkirk began to regret his decision. He felt the sweat start from his pores and exploring insects tickle the soft flesh behind his ears and around his eyes. The grass was harsh, so that the edges of each blade rasped against his hands and rustled against his uniform. He crawled forward, hoping that there were no snakes or poisonous spiders nesting out here, swearing softly as he stared ahead. There was nothing there. He was wasting his time. As he was about to stand up, something hard dug into Selkirk's hand.

The brass cartridge case gleamed guiltily from its position among the grass. Selkirk lifted it. It was a nine-millimetre Mauser cartridge, the kind used by the Boers in the early stages of the war, before a scarcity of ammunition forced them to adopt British equipment. Perhaps there were still a few veterans who had hoarded their supply, but Selkirk suspected that this particular specimen had lain in the grass for some time.

Even as he prepared to drop the cartridge, the wind carried a whisper of sound to him. Only a couple of words, but they were spoken in Dutch. Selkirk froze into immobility as he attempted to locate the source of the voices. They were from the nearest clump of trees, but he was not close enough to hear what was being said. He kept low, peering through the slow-waving blades of grass toward the Boers. If he had not spent time with that Mauser cartridge, he would have stood up and given away his position.

Selkirk swore again. It seemed that Pert had been correct. He had hoped to find nothing out here, but if there were Boers nearby, then his little patrol would be quickly overrun. Good soldiers though they were, a handful of Reivers could not stand against a commando of Boer bitter-enders.

132

Moving with more urgency, Selkirk continued toward his original objective. Now he ignored the rasp of sharp grasses and forgot about snakes. Every few yards he cautiously lifted his head and studied the trees. Pert had been correct; he had seen movement, and there were Boers.

The drift of conversation came to him, the guttural accents of Afrikaans, a short laugh and a distinctive curse. Selkirk tried to hear what was being said, but the words escaped him. He had a choice now; either he could continue with his patrol until he ascertained the fighting strength and capacity of the Boers, or he could withdraw and get his people quietly away. Selkirk shook his head. There was no choice. He had to go forward. He was in a position to learn information that might be invaluable.

Selkirk covered the last fifty yards at a painful belly crawl that sapped his stamina and left him soaked in perspiration. Twice his carbine snagged on clumps of grass so he had to wrestle it free, and once he froze when a Boer stepped casually from the shelter to urinate against the bole of a tree. The man looked ragged and lean, but his bandoleer was full and the Lee-Enfield strapped across his back was well cared for.

Insects clouded around his head as Selkirk finally manoeuvred himself into a fold of ground from where he could observe the Boers. He saw only six men, one of whom wore a bandage around his arm, but all carried rifles. There were at least twelve horses knee haltered behind the trees. Selkirk cursed; he had hoped for only a couple of refugees, perhaps an isolated family whose farm had been burned. Now he knew their numbers he realised that it would be best to return to his Reivers and slip quietly away.

Sighting along his carbine, Selkirk knew that he could drop two before they knew that he was there, but that left four angry Boers, and there might well be more. This group might only be a patrol from a larger commando.

He rested for a few minutes before beginning his withdrawal.

'Wie gaan?' 'Who goes?'

Selkirk froze. The voice had come from behind him, echoing across the tufted grassland.

'Wie gaan?' This time the ominous snick of a rifle bolt accompanied the question. 'Wies daar?' 'Who's there?' The words seemed to echo in the heavy air.

Selkirk had to think quickly. He knew there were at least six men in front. He did not know how many were at his back. Somehow he had to warn his Reivers about these hostile Boers so they could get back to Akersdorp. That meant making noise and delaying the Boers as long as possible.

Rolling on to his back, Selkirk fired a single shot, then rolled away before the reply came. He was on his feet and running before he heard the ugly crash of a Lee-Enfield. The bullet zipped past, furrowing a path through the long grass. Birds were scattering from the trees as the first group of Boers shouted startled questions.

'Khaki! I saw him!' The words were urgent, spoken by a young man. Selkirk ran, hoping to draw the Boers away from his men. Another rifle cracked, this time with the distinctive 'buck-up' crack of the Mauser.

Selkirk heard the Boers shouting to each other as they hunted him, the words guttural, menacing in the sullen heat. Breaking cover, he ran again, twisting like a Border hare when the hounds were loosed. It was only a matter of time before they shot him, but the longer he kept them occupied and the further he took them from the spruit, the more chance his Reivers had.

There was another of these deceptive boabab trees ahead, its thick trunk no protection against the bullets that flicked past him, so he feinted toward it, then altered direction, much like a rugby forward on the fields of Fethan. A bullet thudded into the tree, passed right through with an explosion of bark and paper-soft wood and vanished somewhere in the distance.

Selkirk ran, twisting and ducking as the blood pounded in his head and the fear dried his mouth. He knew that the Boers were amongst the best shots in the world, but he also knew that it was nearly impossible for a man on horseback to hit a moving target. About eighty yards ahead, a curving line of bush marked the course of a spruit. If he reached that, he could move in either direction, perhaps keep hidden until nightfall then slide away in the dark.

Thorn bushes fringed the trees, ripping into Selkirk's uniform and clutching angrily at his carbine. He heard the hoof beats of horses thudding behind him, heard the disappointed shouts as he disappeared into the trees. Bullets cracked and whizzed overhead, sending leaves cascading downward. Selkirk stumbled, cursed as he felt the heel of his boot come away. He had repaired it himself after the assault on Akersdorp, and now his lack of skill became apparent.

Selkirk kept low, ducked beneath a thick branch and slithered toward the spruit. Water, greeny-brown and muddy, lapped toward him and insects hovered hungrily. The shouting faded.

Which way? Overhung by trailing branches, the spruit wound in lazy curves in either direction, with the bank a waist high tangle of vegetation. For a second Selkirk was back in the Fethan, guddling trout and evading the gamekeeper. Except the gamekeeper would not have shot him and there were no poisonous snakes in the water. The thought of snakes made Selkirk's scalp creep.

The hunters would expect him to run, to gain distance by following the spruit. They would expect him to try and move round their flanks. In which case it would be best if he kept still and let them do the hunting. Every hour gained was precious for his Reivers. Alerted by the shooting, by now Campbell would have the men on horseback, cantering toward Akersdorp while the Boers wasted their time around the spruit.

Still hesitant in case he disturbed a snake, Selkirk concealed his tracks by stepping into the middle of the spruit and took thirty slow steps upstream. The water was no deeper than mid calf, warm and opaque. He thought of snakes again, but kept moving while the sweat seeped from his scalp. Each time he lifted his foot, he listened for the sound of the pursuers, but heard nothing but the melodious whine of insects. The dense bush acted as a mask, dissipating all sound from the outside world.

There was a slightly less dense clump of bush to Selkirk's right, with a single tree that had fallen on to its side to expose a tangle of roots. Selkirk squeezed between the root system, felt the panic rise as something scurried across his legs, and gasped relief when he saw that it was only a rat.

Under here, he had no view, no field of fire, but any searcher would have to come up very close to find him. Lying back, Selkirk tried to relax as he waited for the day to close. Insects clouded around him, feeding frenziedly on his sweat, but he dared not move. He had often admired the patience with which Gray, Macpherson and Donnelly could wait to kill their prey, and knew that the Boers were every bit as skilled hunters. They would be out there, somewhere, waiting for movement, waiting for a glimpse of human flesh or khaki. He just had to endure the tormenting insects and wait for night. The sound of the river seemed to diminish into a soothing melody. He could nearly be beside the Fethan, waiting to guddle a trout.

Selkirk awoke with a start. Instinctively he eased the cramp in his back and limbs before he remembered where he was. It was dark, with the night calls of Africa, eerie amidst the trees. Selkirk put a hand to his face, feeling the innumerable lumps where insects had bitten, then reached inside his tunic pocket. The single dry biscuit that he had with him made a poor meal, but washed down with water from his water bottle, it would have to do. Remembering the results of drinking from the Modder, Selkirk was not tempted by the water of the spruit.

A huge moon was already waning when Selkirk cautiously emerged on to the shadowed rim of the spruit. A long look revealed no Boers, so using the stars as a guide, he began to move northward. He kept low, trying to make his silhouette as near as possible to that of an animal. Once he stopped, appalled at the massive roar of a hunting lion, and twice he waited, feeling the fear dry his mouth as some animal padded past.

Out here, on foot and with only his carbine for company, he felt naked. It was a long way back to Akersdorp. He took each step with extreme caution, probing the dark all the time. After an hour Selkirk began to relax. He was well outside the radius where the Boers would be expected to search. After two hours he straightened up and moved more freely, lengthening his stride into the lope that had taken him over so many heather miles on the Border hills.

By dawn he was a good twelve miles from the spruit and beginning to feel more confident. All he needed to do was keep walking and he would reach Akersdorp.

'Kiek daar!' 'Look there!' The shout took him by surprise. A group of half a dozen horsemen had emerged from a fold of ground. One was pointing toward him.

Selkirk ran at once, heading for the nearest belt of trees. He heard the horsemen behind him, their hooves sounding hollow as they herded him, shouting, laughing, completely in charge of the situation.

As Selkirk neared the trees, three men on foot, what the Boers knew as voetgangers, emerged.

'Khaki! Skiet kerels!' 'Shoot boys!' A fusillade of shots crashed out, none of them anywhere near Selkirk, who ducked and ran frantically for cover. With horsemen behind and voetgangers in front, he had only seconds to decide.

'Damn! Damn! Damn!' Selkirk cursed his luck. He had come so far, only to run into these men. A man on foot could never outrun horsemen in such open country. He could either surrender, or turn and fight for as long as possible. Selkirk ran directly toward the men on foot, then weaved to one side and threw himself into the copse.

Once under cover of the trees, he changed direction, ducked low and slipped out at right angles to his original route. He slid close to the ground and hoped that the Boers would ride past.

The Boer voices sounded again, querying where he had gone. One man pointed to the left but the others disagreed.

'Ne! Daar after!' 'No! Over there!' That was the voice of a young man with obviously excellent eyesight. A rifle cracked and the bullet howled perilously close to where Selkirk huddled. He was in a slight hollow, with a wait-a-bit thornbush at his side and a good field of fire. Lying prone, he sighted along the barrel of his carbine. Three Boers were moving slowly toward him, one on foot and two on horseback. Incongruously, one horseman sported a battered top hat that had once matched the dignified white beard that swept down his chest, the other wore a wide terai hat and carried a Mauser. The man with the top hat seemed to be in charge. Selkirk placed the foresight squarely in the vee of his backsight, centred it on the man's forehead and squeezed the trigger.

The recoil slammed into his shoulder, but the Boer jerked backward and fell off his horse. The top hat slipped off his head and flopped into the grass.

'Nee! Paulus! Oom Paulus!' The man on foot instinctively moved toward his fallen companion and Selkirk fired quickly and missed.

'Kiek daar!' The man in the Terai hat jerked a finger to the thorn bush. Pointing the Mauser one-handed, he loosed three shots and began to gallop forward, with the hooves of his Basuto strangely subdued on the long grass. Still prone on the ground, Selkirk worked the bolt to push a new cartridge into his carbine, and aimed at the man's throat.

The Boer was shouting, waving his Mauser like a club as he closed. Although seventy summers had tanned and wrinkled his face, his eyes were lively as those of a boy. The clothes he wore had once been smart but now they were little more than rags held together by clumsy stitching and an impressive array of patches.

Selkirk took first pressure on the trigger and froze as the cold metal of a rifle barrel pressed into his temple.

'Hand up, meneer. You have done your killing for the day.'

For an instant Selkirk contemplated resistance, but then he stood up and handed his carbine into the open hand of Helena Van Vuren.

Chapter Ten :Northern Transvaal,May – June 1902

'So, Lieutenant Ogler,' Helena looked more closely at Selkirk's badges of rank, 'no, Captain Ogler, you are my prisoner again.' Her eyes were as blue as ever, but were deeply sunk into an exhausted face. Her cheekbones thrust out as sharp as the blade of a knife. 'Where are your men, Captain Selkirk?'

'Ek weet nee, Mrs Van Vuren,' 'I do not know, Mrs Van Vuren.' Selkirk shook his head. 'I lost them yesterday and was wandering in the bush.' He smiled as disarmingly as he knew how. 'If your men had not found me I might have died of hunger.'

'So you shot them?' Helena shook her head so her broad bush hat bounced from side to side. From her neck down she wore patched British khaki.

'They would have shot me,' Selkirk explained.

'They still might.' Some of the Boers had gathered to inspect their prize, staring at the British officer whom they had captured. They were a ragged looking bunch, some wearing British khaki, others the remains of homespun suits. One was dressed in what appeared like sacking, with holes cut for his arms and legs. All looked gaunt, hungry, but their weapons were bright and clean. Of them all, only the man in the terai hat glowered at him.

Helena stood over the body of Paulus, the man that Selkirk had shot. She sighed. 'Another good man gone in this war. When will it end? When will the rooinecks leave our land?' She looked up, suddenly looking very old and weary. 'Will you please arrange for a burial, Johannes?'

A short man dressed in black nodded. 'Ja Veldcornet Van Vuren.' He sighed deeply as he looked toward Selkirk.

'So now you have me, what are you going to do with me?' Selkirk knew that every minute he delayed the Boers gave his men time to escape. He hoped to keep them talking as long as possible.

139

Helena, however, was also an experienced commander. 'The Captain will not be alone. Denys, take five men and track his movements. See where he came from, but be careful. These are slim skelms, dangerous rascals. They are not like the usual rooinecks. Joubert, take the others and form a defensive perimeter. Captain Selkirk's men may try to snatch him back. Benjamin – remove the Captain's equipment. Search him for any documents he might be carrying.'

The men obeyed immediately, with Denys, the man in the terai hat, giving Selkirk one last glare before gathering his men. The man dressed in sackcloth deftly unfastened Selkirk's bandoleer and Sam Browne belt before ruffling through his pockets. Selkirk noticed the running veldt sores on Benjamin's wrists, and innumerable scratches along his bare legs. He wore veldtshoen, shoes of untanned leather similar to the brogues once worn by Scottish Highlanders. 'There is one letter, Helena.'

Helena withdrew a few paces and levelled her rifle at Selkirk. She had his carbine at her feet. 'Throw it to me Benjamin.' She scanned it quickly, nearly smiling, 'That sister of yours certainly keeps in touch, doesn't she?'

'That's a personal letter,' Selkirk complained, but without heat.

Helena threw the letter back. 'All right Benjamin, you can join the others now.'

'Do you know this man, Veldcornet?' Benjamin asked; he pointed his rifle unwaveringly at Selkirk's face.

'This is Captain Andrew Selkirk of the Reivers.' Her sudden smile transformed her face. 'He was also in the vitschudden commando.'

'The vitschudden commando?' one of the older Boers had overheard. He moved closer, smiling. 'I have heard of that. You told me that it was a mooi sight.'

'It was,' Helena agreed solemnly. 'Especially this man here. I left my mark on him.' Her giggle was more girlish than Selkirk remembered, 'but get about your business now, and don't let Johannes hear about all this.'

'Will you be safe with the rooineck?' Benjamin looked about fifteen years old, with huge, haunted eyes, yet he held his rifle like the veteran he probably was.

'I am sure I can handle him.' Helena said, solemnly. 'I have questions to ask of him.' She waited until Benjamin left, then sat cross-legged with her back to the bole of a slender tree. Tipping back the brim of her hat, she drank from a water bottle, all the time examining Selkirk's face.

'Now Andrew, you can tell me how you come to be here.'

The use of his Christian name surprised him, but Selkirk shook his head. He shifted his position slightly so he was in the shade of Helena's tree. 'May I have some of your water Helena? Young Benjamin has taken away mine.'

'Of course.' Helena's eyes had dilated only slightly. She tossed over his waterbottle and watched as he drank. 'How many men are with you?'

Selkirk removed the bottle from his lips and wiped his mouth. 'As your men will soon report, one hundred and twenty men, with three maxim guns. We are the scouting party for a major column that is coming to drive through this area and remove all the hostile Boers.' He met her eyes. 'And tell me, what does vitschudden mean? As in vitschudden commando?'

'I see.' Helena ignored the question as she nodded gravely. 'About ten men then.' Her sudden smile reminded Selkirk of her mother. 'And working without support. I am beginning to understand your methods, Andrew Selkirk of the stripping commando.'

'Stripping?' Selkirk shifted uncomfortably at the memory of the last time Helena had captured him. He also recalled that she had called it a mooi sight, a beautiful sight, and decided to keep to war matters.

'So you think ten men, Helena, but are you willing to risk the lives of your men on your understanding?' Selkirk forced his mind to operate. Helena had about fifteen men with her. That was more than enough to wipe out his small band of Reivers. He had to put doubt in her mind so she would not pursue his men. If in doubt, go on the offensive. 'Indeed, Helena, it would be best if you left this area as quickly as possible before Colonel Drongan finds you.'

'Ah yes. The man I shot,' Helena countered with a nod, 'and whom you sent to hospital. Perhaps he has returned for revenge on me? Or on you, perhaps?' Helena was smiling again, gently mocking. She tipped forward her hat so it shadowed her face. 'I have not forgotten the events at Hendrinafontein, Andrew.' She leaned forward, 'I will never forget the debt we owe you, Andrew, but we are still enemies. As we were in the day of the vitschudden commando.'

'I would wish it were otherwise.' The shadow of her hat seemed to mask some of the fatigue, so that Helena looked younger. Selkirk noticed the fine bone structure of her face, with the line of her jaw as determined as her character.

'So would I, meneer, but it is not.' Helena's expression suddenly darkened, as if she realised where she was. She lifted the rifle again. 'So Captain Selkirk, if you will not tell me how many men you have, you will at least tell me why you are here, so far from Akersdorp?'

'Of course I will, just as soon as you tell me why you are here.' Selkirk brushed away the flies that were feasting on the sweat on his face.

Helena looked downward. When she looked up, her jaw looked more stubborn and determined than ever. 'I think I can tell you that, Andrew. We go to rescue my mother, my sister in law and my nephew.'

Selkirk felt something restrict his breathing. Could Helena have found out about the Reiver's abduction of the Fouries from the camp so soon? If anybody could, it would be her. She must have read his mind. To have worked out his movements from the previous night and then trap him so neatly.

'Rescue them, Helena? From where?' He tried to sound innocent, but Helena looked up sharply.

'They are in a concentration camp, Captain Selkirk. After you left the farm last year, I returned to the war. A column of your rooineck, horse foot and guns rode directly from Pretoria to Hendrinafontein. A thousand men and horses to destroy one small farm with two women and a small child! Is that how your great Queen built her Empire?' Helena's eyes were as expressive as her choice of words. Both revealed the anger and compassion that contended for her soul.

'I doubt that either the late queen or the present king were consulted,' Selkirk said dryly. 'So where do you believe that Hendrina is now?'

'I do not believe, Captain Ogler. I know that they are held in one of your concentration camps.' When Helena tipped back her hat, only her tears muted the blue fire of her eyes.

Selkirk nodded. There was disappointment mixed with relief that she had not learned of the Reiver's raid. Some part of him would have liked Helena to have omniscient powers. 'So you are going to attack this camp, kill all the guards and break out the prisoners? And what then, Helena? Will you let them loose on the veldt, to starve or be eaten by wild animals?' Knowing that Hendrina was safe, Selkirk could enjoy testing Helena, watching her temper rise as she met his challenge.

She snapped back at him, dropping her rifle as she gesticulated with her hands, allowing her anger to take control. 'Better free on the veldt than dying in some fever camp.' She prodded his chest with a long finger. Selkirk noticed that her nail was short, dirty and broken. 'What right have you rooinecks got to confine people like that?'

'No right at all,' Selkirk told her.

'It's inhuman. You are destroying a nation just to increase your vrot Empire! You say that we mistreat our blacks. That is a lie. You are skelms. All of you! You verneuk us with words like a farmer uses a spantou to tie his cow before he milks it.' Helena's breath was hot and sweet in his face; her finger prodding with every word as she deliberately mixed Dutch and English in her tirade.

'All you have to do is surrender,' Selkirk added sugar to the fire, 'and the war will end. It is only because of the hard liners such as yourself that your family, and thousands of other families, are suffering.' He felt his own temper rising now. 'Don't forget that you attacked us first. You treated the Uitlanders like dirt. Your men returned to their farms with a promise to stop fighting, then promptly picked up their rifles again. Your farms acted as storehouses and bases for the commandos.'

'Oh?' Helena stepped back with her hands on her hips. 'And what would you have us do, Captain Selkirk? Surrender? Would your verdomte Reivers surrender? Would you surrender, Drew Selkirk of the Fethan?'

The words were strangely powerful coming from Helena. About to launch into a tirade about violation of the white flag and misuse of British uniforms, Selkirk decided to change tack completely. 'Only to you, Helena.' He tried to prevent his smile, but she caught it.

'You're laughing at me!' Selkirk did not understand the next few words but guessed that they were supremely offensive.

'What terrible language from such a well bred woman.' He shook his head, enjoying the contest despite his situation.

Helena shook her head as the anger dissipated from her face. 'Andrew, you must understand; this is our land, ons land. We made it from the wilderness. It holds our dead and our hopes. We will never give it up.'

'So your sister in law told me.' Selkirk recognised the terrible sincerity of her words. Reaching forward, he touched her arm. It was thin and muscular beneath his hand. She did not withdraw. 'They are safe now.'

'Safe now?' The sudden terror in Helena's face shocked him. 'What do you mean? Are they dead?'

It was compassion that made Selkirk embrace her. 'No! Not at all. They are with my Reivers, Helena. Sergeant Campbell is taking care of Hansie and Coenraad, while Haigie has Hendrina. Believe me, they're safe and well.'

Helena remained within the circle of Selkirk's arms. 'Oh thank God. Thank God.' He felt her shudder as she controlled her emotions. 'When, Andrew? And how?'

'Just yesterday. We requested their release from Mr Thatcher, BA.' It felt very natural to hold Helena safely while the African sun poured its warmth upon them and a brightly coloured bird blessed them with its song.

They remained like that for some minutes, until Helena stirred and gently broke his grasp. 'This is hardly fitting for a prisoner,' she chided. Her voice had a throatiness that he had never heard before. 'Sit on the ground so that I can point my rifle at you.'

Selkirk returned to his position under the tree. Helena wiped away a tear from her face and recovered her rifle.

'Don't think for a minute that I will let you go, Captain Ogler. You are still my enemy.'

'Indeed,' Selkirk agreed. Judging that his men would have had enough time to travel a fair distance, he related how they had rescued the Fouries, watching the interplay of expression on Helena's face as she listened. She smiled at all the right places, nodded understandingly at Hendrina's desire to return to the camp to help the less fortunate, and smiled at Hansie's display of temper.

'We seem to share some ideas, Captain Selkirk. But why would a unit of rooineck skelms wish to rescue a few stray Boers?' She was teasing him now, more relaxed than before. 'Could it be that they hold some vital information? Or was it that Corporal Campbell makes the decisions in the Reivers now.'

'Veldcornet! Helena!' The shout broke the ambience as Denys returned, sliding off his horse with a rustle of cloth and leather. Four of his riders followed, two immediately covering Selkirk with their rifles. 'We have found their spoor. This rooineck has only six men with him, Helena, and also two women and a child. They left last night, while we hunted for this man.' He threw Selkirk a significant look.

'Not a hundred and twenty then,' Helena teased, but the mood was broken now. She reassumed her role as field cornet of a Boer commando. 'The captain has done part of our work for us, Denys. He has removed Hendrina, Hansie and Coenraad from the camp.'

'Good.' Denys glanced at Selkirk with a little more warmth. 'But then there is bad news, Helena.' Denys gestured with his rifle, 'news that I do not think the rooineck should hear. I do not know how much he understands.'

'He is going nowhere. Speak.' Helena commanded.

'The enemy is being trailed by the Aasvogels.' He touched his rifle. 'We found their spoor. Sixty of them, blacks and whites.'

'Aasvogels! Dear God in his heaven!' Helena looked as though somebody had struck her. 'Then we are all in trouble.'

Chapter Eleven :Northern Transvaal - June 1902

'Aasvogel? That means vulture, doesn't it? But what's the significance? What does it mean?' Selkirk tried to listen but one of the Boers thrust him back with the muzzle of his rifle. 'Tell me! That's my men out there. And Hendrina.'

As Denys lifted his rifle as if to strike Selkirk, Helena intervened. 'No! I have fought this man before, he is an enemy, but an honourable man. She knelt at his side. 'Denys tells me that there are about sixty renegades following your men. These are the worst elements of the war, deserters from your army and burgh-right erven – that is, poor white trash from the slums of our cities, foreigners who hope to profit from the war, black savages who have left their tribes.' She shook her head 'these are bad people, Captain Selkirk, terrible people, thieves and murderers and worse!'

'Jesus.' Selkirk tried to sit up, but Denys pushed him back. 'You must let me go to them. I have to warn my men.' The snick of rifle bolts being drawn reminded him of his position. Suddenly he remembered the tracks that his men had discovered, the mutilated body that the ambush party had discovered and the atmosphere of foreboding. 'And the women! Christ, man, what will these people, these Aasvogels, do to the women?'

'They will rape them,' Denys said, brutally, 'and then kill them. The boy too. And maybe your rooineck soldiers, if they are young and pretty.'

Selkirk saw his horror mirrored in Helena's eyes. 'How many men have you, Helena?'

'Fifteen. And you have six.' Her look was searching. 'Do you have more men that I do not know about?' She hesitated for only a second. 'This is outside the war, Andrew. This is more important.'

'Not between here and Akersdorp. You?'

'Not here. We have a camp in the north, but we will not be able to bring down men in time.' She spoke in sharp, clipped sentences.

'We raided your camp.' Selkirk gave her brief details. 'I am sorry.'

Helena closed her eyes. 'Verdamme! You have cost us dear, Captain Selkirk.'

'And you us, Field Cornet Van Vuren. We call you the Boer Boadicea because of your exploits.'

'And we call you a damned rooineck pest.'

For a second they glared at each other in mutual irritation and admiration, then returned to business.

'We must join forces.' Helena stated. 'A truce. Do you agree?'

'I agree.' Selkirk held out his hand. Helena accepted it without hesitation.

'Will you give your word of honour that you will not try and escape as long as the truce lasts? And afterwards, you will return to us as a prisoner?'

That was galling. Selkirk did not relish the idea of being a prisoner, but he thought of Hansie, who had endured so much already, in the power of some vicious deserter. The images were horrifying. 'You have my word.'

'Then upsaddle.' Helena tossed him the carbine that had been lying neglected between them. 'Somebody find this rooineck a horse. Upsaddle! Upsaddle kerels!' Helena gave rapid orders that had her Boers mounted and moving with an efficiency that would have done credit to the Reivers at their best. The short man in the dark coat brought Selkirk a roan mare, told him to watch for its tendency to buck at odd moments and added, strangely, 'you'll be fine with us son, we're all Jock Tamson's bairns here.' It was a statement that Selkirk's grandmother had often used.

Before Selkirk could reply the man had moved on to somebody else. They moved rapidly, with Denys taking the lead on the tracks that he and his men had created. Sixteen men and one woman on a mission of death and mercy, with thin horses and threadbare clothing and the sun drying their sweat the instant it appeared on their faces.

It felt strange to be riding with a Boer commando, to hear the guttural Taal being spoken by men fighting on his side, and to respond to a friendly wink from a man who wore a claw tailed coat and carried a captured British Lee-Metford rifle. These men rode as casually as if they were inspecting the herds on their own farms, without outriders or a rearguard, yet they seemed to miss nothing as they followed the Reivers' trail without breaking their steady canter. Denys did not even dismount to show Helena the spoor of the renegades. She looked down, nodded her agreement and kicked her horse into motion. They moved with even more urgency, riding through rolling countryside interspersed with dense clumps of bush until the sun reached its zenith, when Helena called a halt.

'We must eat,' she commanded, 'or we will be too weak to fight.'

Selkirk could only share with the rest, drinking the hot coffee without savour and chewing the biltong as quickly as he could. He watched Helena roast pieces of meat on a fork made from fencing wire. She arranged the meat in an alternating pattern, first fat meat, then lean, then fat again.

'We call this a bont span,' she told him, 'because it resembles a team of oxen that are not of the same colour.'

They also made cakes of flour cooked in boiling fat, which Helena said were known as stormjagers, or storm hunters because they could be cooked very quickly. 'We also know them as maagbommen,' she added, dryly, 'that means stomach bombs. You'll soon find out why.'

'Enjoy the coffee Captain?' Johannes, the man in the black coat asked. 'You should; we took it from one of your wagons.' His smile belied the poverty-thin trousers that gapped at the knees every time he moved. 'It makes a change from our normal coffee, a mixture of ground up corn, maize, dried peaches and sweet potatoes. Not quite what you drink in Edinburgh.'

Remembering the man's previous Scottish expression, Selkirk asked who he was. 'Jock Tamson's bairns? Where did you get that from?'

Johannes gave a slow, peaceful smile. 'I am the minister for this commando, but everybody just calls me Johannes.' The smile broadened. 'At least to my face. I don't know what they say ahint my back!'

'You're Scottish,' Selkirk accused.

Johannes shook his head. 'Pure Transvaal Dutch, Captain, but I was trained at your Free Kirk College in Scotland. A lot of us terrible Boers were!' His laughter was unfeigned. 'You should see your face, son.'

'Upsaddle!' Helena ordered. She shook the last dregs from her coffee cup on to the ground. 'Come on kerels! Trek vous.'

They trekked again, slightly slower now that they were closer to their enemy, and twice Denys signalled for the commando to halt so that he could check the tracks. The second time he called Helena over. She signalled Selkirk to join them as she crouched on the ground, examining the spoor.

'More men have joined the Aasvogels. See?' Denys pointed to mass of hoofprints on the ground. 'These are the marks left by the original group, and these joined them here. About ten more horsemen.'

'That makes seventy then.' Selkirk looked ahead. Africa stretched before them, baking in the heat, dull green with menace. A yellow-throated longclaw hopped on to the top of a thornbush, mocking them with its call.

'Yes,' Denys agreed, 'but the rooinecks know that they are being followed. They are moving faster, with two men riding behind the rest and the women in the middle.'

'They have changed direction too,' Selkirk said. 'We're heading east of north now, not north, toward Akersdorp.'

'The rooinecks are being driven like cattle.' Denys pointed to faint tracks beneath a tree. 'See that? The Aasvogels established a post here, and sent a patrol in the direction that your men are heading. It was a trick, but your patrol has altered its route to avoid them.'

'It's a trap.' Selkirk and Helena decided together. Their eyes met for a second, then they again concentrated on the matter in hand.

'Denys is right. They are being driven into something. Perhaps an ambush?' Helena looked to Selkirk for confirmation.

'I'd say so.'

'We must move faster then.' Helena stood up. 'You are concerned about your men. I am worried about my family.'

'We all are.' They spoke in clipped sentences, wasting neither words nor energy as they followed the spoor. Twice they rode so close that their legs touched, but neither made a comment. Nor did they pull further away.

By mid afternoon they could see drifting dust in front of them and Helena pushed them harder, so that even the hardy Boer ponies were wilting with exhaustion. The Boer who wore the stitched sacks as clothing was drooping in the saddle, until Helena rode beside him. Selkirk saw how her smile of encouragement perked the boy up. He straightened his back. 'For you tante Helena, I will do it.'

It was late evening when the first gunshot reached them. It was followed by a rolling fusillade that caused Selkirk's mare to roll back her eyes and paw the ground. Helena held up her hand so her commando gathered around her. Bearded men checked the breech of their rifles and waited for this woman, their Veldcornet, to give her commands. There was only the sound of anxious breathing and the occasional snort of a horse.

'We can do two things,' Helena told them. Now that the battle seemed imminent she was smiling, her eyes bright as she strove to encourage her men. 'We can harass these bandits, scour their flanks, make them think that we are a larger force, or we can ride straight through and reinforce the rooinecks.'

'I do not want to fight beside the rooinecks.' Denys said at once. He glowered at Selkirk. 'They are no friends to my people.'

'I agree,' a slender man named Joubert said. He fingered the scar that had cost him one eye and which furrowed his left cheek. 'We fight alone. We wish to rescue our women, but the rooinecks can care for themselves.'

The other Boers gave their opinions, all of which Helena listened to, for although she was in command, the Boers had a much more democratic approach to war than would be accepted in the British army. Even the young boy in the sack spoke.

'And the rooineck?' Johannes the minister asked, 'what would he like to do?'

'I would prefer to be with my men. It is where I belong.' Selkirk paused for a second. 'It is also where the women are, and the more guns around them, the better.' He felt Helena's eyes on him.

'You are right, rooineck. You belong with your own kind.' Denys agreed at once. He touched the barrel of his Lee-Enfield, obviously indicating where he thought all rooinecks should be.

150

Helena placed a small hand on his arm. Her touch seemed to burn through the cloth of his uniform jacket. 'Don't forget that I have your word, Captain Selkirk. You are still my prisoner.'

'I won't forget.' Selkirk told her. 'Will you give me some covering fire while I ride through the bandits' lines?'

'Of course.' That wonderful smile was back. 'We don't want to lose our prize prisoner. Imagine having the gallant Captain Ogler as a bargaining counter. And imagine Akersdorp trying to defend itself with only Lieutenants Donnelly and Windrush in charge.' Helena was teasing Selkirk with her knowledge of the British dispositions. 'We shall take it in a week.' Sudden clouds darkened her eyes. 'Take care of them, Andrew, until I get there.'

Their fingers touched briefly, then they were riding forward, Boer and Briton together, forward toward the sound of the guns.

At first there was only the bush and the crackling of musketry, then the shapes of men, on horse and afoot, startled faces in the shrubbery, somebody shouting, a sharp crack as somebody fired and then more men. Scores of men and a face that Selkirk recognised. The man wore what had once been the uniform of a British officer, but battered by wear so it was the colour of mud. He stood with his shoulders stubbornly square and looked at Selkirk with one corner of his mouth lifted in a sneer.

The memory came back to Selkirk, the chained prisoners at Cape Town, the men who had shot their prisoners, the sympathy of his Reivers for their sentence. That had been Nat Blunt, sentenced to death for murdering prisoners. He must have escaped, to join these Aasvogels up here in the north, where a fugitive could slip from British into Portuguese or German territory at will.

Then Selkirk was past, firing his carbine into a group of bandits, black and white and mixed, seeing one man fall, hearing another curse. Predatory faces appeared in the dusk; a spear flickered through the air, falling short as Selkirk kicked speed to his horse.

There was clear space in front, dotted with bodies, the shifting shape of a wounded horse, the tall mound of an ant hill, then he felt his roan stagger as a bullet found its mark and the ground rose to meet him. He landed with a soft thump, felt the skin burn from his face, but kept hold of his carbine and rolled to safety. He heard people cheering, heard loud yells.

'Reivers! Selkirk's Reivers!'

Bullets hammered at his side, each one raising a fountain of dirt and grass, then Haig's ugly face was in front and someone was at his side, pulling at his arm.

'Get up! Get up! You must get up.'

Selkirk grinned, enjoying the sensation of peace as he listened to the birds singing from the trees of the Fethan. Tam was calling to him, laughing as he paddled barefoot in the cool water. But then Tam's voice roughened, the Border cadences altered to guttural Edinburgh.

'Move Selks, you useless bastard. Jildi! You Johnny Raw bugger. Jildi!' With Haig kicking him, Selkirk lurched to his feet, knowing that there was one person holding on to each arm but not fully sensible of his condition until he was bundled over the bole of a felled tree and rolled in the dirt.

Chapter Twelve :Northern Transvaal – June 1902

'Evening, Missus Van Vureniss!' Haig's grin made his face even uglier than normal. 'Have you changed sides then?'

Helena shook her head. 'Not me; it's a temporary truce, Private Haig. Captain Selkirk knows all about it.'

'Does he? Pity these buggers out there don't!' Pulling Helena to the ground, Haig emptied five quick shots at the surrounding trees. 'They've pinned us down right good and proper.' He raised his voice into a jeering roar. 'Is that the best you can do, you bastards? It's the Reivers you're fighting, not the bloody Mount Nelson Dragoons.' He grinned to Helena, 'Are they friends of yours miss?'

'No. They're Aasvogels, vultures. Renegades, Haig, bad people.'

Gray threw a hatful of cold water in Selkirk's face. 'Welcome back, sir. We thought you were dead. Thought it better to get the women back to safety.'

'Quite right Gray.' Selkirk blinked away the pain that was beginning to pass over him in waves. He glanced quickly around their position.

The Reivers were along the bank of a small spruit, with holes gouged into the muddy banks for trenches and the horses tied fetlock deep in the water. To their right was a grove of fever trees, bowing their slender branches in companionship with every slight puff of air, while the dark green phalavurha shrub presented its rough green leaves toward the enemy. The Reivers had removed their saddles from the horses and piled them into an improvised breastwork, behind which they stood. As Selkirk would have expected, Sergeant Campbell had them well in order, with McGann looking to their rear and the others facing the main force of the enemy. Helena and Johannes lay at his side in the midst of their enemy. He could not see the Fourie family.

'I thought you were staying with your commando, Helena?'

'My horse bolted,' she explained, 'and when I saw you fall, I was closest.' Touching Selkirk's arm, 'I'll be back in a second, don't kill all the Aasvogels until I return. Mother! Hansie! Coenraad! Where are you?'

They emerged from the fragile shelter of one of the dug outs, white-faced and obviously shaken by their ordeal. Hendrina held out her arms and pulled Helena close to her.

'These are not Boers out there,' Selkirk explained who the enemy was while the Reivers listened. Campbell nodded. 'I thought this lot acted differently. Seventy men you say? And there are now nine of us, including Helena.'

'Eight,' Selkirk corrected, 'Johannes is a man of God. He will not fight.' He grinned, 'but there is a commando of Boers out there fighting on our side, so we're not alone!''

'What a stupid, bloody war!' Haig gave his considered opinion. 'We're fighting with the boojers against British deserters and a mish mash of badmashes?' He spat into the river. 'Aye, and we're meant to trust them, too? I remember the white flag at Paardeberg, even if you don't Selks. How we all walked forward trustingly and were shot to pieces.'

'That was a mistake!' Helena insisted. She had made her family safe and had joined the conversation. 'Nobody meant that to happen.'

'No? And the Iniskilling dragoons that turned out to be English killing dragoons?' Haig had a long memory for injuries, probably because so many had been done to him in his life. 'Was that a mistake too?'

'No. That was military strategy!' Helena blazed back at him, 'like your disguising yourself as Boers in Bechuanaland.'

Selkirk started; he had no idea that Helena knew about that episode.

'Aye, all right then.' Haig gave his slanted, ugly smile. 'English killing dragoons! That was clever.'

Helena pressed her advantage. 'You British also have fired on the white flag,' she cited instances that Selkirk knew nothing about, 'And how about Hendrina and Hansie? Are they so evil? Are they your enemies too?'

'You leave Hendrina out of this.' Haigie had developed a strong bond with Hendrina during his stay at her farm. The elderly Boer woman had been one of the few people in his life to show him affection. 'She's all right.'

'Indeed she is.' Reaching forward, Helena touched Haig's face with one gentle finger. 'Thanks to you. Thank you, David, for what you have done for her.'

For a second Haig stared, then he blushed. 'Och, loop woman, and dinnae be stupid.' He looked away. 'English killing dragoons. That was a good one.'

Selkirk nodded to Helena. 'You've won another admirer, Field Cornet Boadicea.'

'Another?' She sounded confused; 'who was the first?'

'I think the Captain is referring to himself,' Johannes said, but before Helena could reply the Aasvogels attacked.

They came in a mad rush, a press of mixed horse and foot crashing across the open space in front of the Reivers' position. 'Wait until they get close!' Selkirk shouted, 'then fire. Campbell, watch the left flank; Gray, you watch the right. Steady now!'

The Aasvogels yelled as they advanced, a mixture of English curses, Afrikaans invective and a melodious chant from the tribesmen. Used to the rapid charge of Boer horsemen, Selkirk had not experienced the sense of terror that these people created. He knew that, unlike the Boers, they would not care for the wounded, or treat the prisoners with respect. This fight was to the death, for surrender would bring worse torments than he could imagine.

'Steady. Mark your targets.' Selkirk spoke from habit; he knew the quality of his men. They knew exactly what they were doing. He saw the carbines level and was grateful that the Reivers were far better shots than the average British soldier. Helena was settled behind a fever tree, the green cockade in her hat giving a jaunty, feminine touch, but her rifle held steady in capable hands.

About eighty yards in front of the Reivers, a lone thorn tree squatted under the late afternoon sun. Lightning must have struck it some time in the past, for there was a curious split in the trunk, causing the branches to grow at each side, but leaving the top black and bare. A honey bird sat on one branch as if unconcerned about this war. Selkirk waited until the leading attackers were level with this lightning tree before giving the order.

'Now Reivers! Now's your time!'

The volley crashed out, followed by a more irregular crackling as each man fired into the mass. This was not the wild, undisciplined firing of recruits, but a controlled killing fire by experts who had learned their trade at Magersfontein and on a dozen skirmishes on the veldt. The leading attackers were swept away, horses and men falling in a tangled horror of mangled limbs and screaming bodies. As the Reivers fired, Selkirk became aware of another force on his left.

'Campbell! Watch your flank.'

'No! That's my boys!' Helena screamed the denial, 'let them be!' She twisted in her position, anxiety in her eyes.

'Do as she says!' Selkirk countermanded his order, 'fire to your front.' He gave Helena a wave, but she was already firing into the screaming mob that continued to charge on them.

The Boers came in at the gallop, shooting from the hip, then wheeling their horses, unsaddling and loosing two shots before up saddling again and galloping away. It was beautiful to watch, and devastating for the Aasvogels. Hit on two fronts, their attack faltered and they fled back, leaving half a dozen bodies writhing on the ground and three men dead. A horse screamed in agony, until Macpherson shot it.

Silence descended, and the bitter reek of cordite.

'They won't come again before nightfall,' Helena said. 'They like a massacre, not a fight and they did not expect my boys to come.' She smiled to Coenraad, who had popped his head up from the shelter of the riverbank. 'Hello Coenraad. You keep out of harm's way now.'

The boy looked around, until his mother snatched him back.

'Your rooinecks fought well, Captain Ogler. I was surprised. You must have learned from us.'

'Captain Ogler?' Johannes had spent the skirmish with the Fouries. 'I thought your name was Selkirk?'

Never one to withhold knowledge from the less privileged, Haig grinned. 'Aye, but Selks and Helena like to ogle each other. He did it to her first, then she stripped all of us and had a good decko.' He nudged Selkirk, 'isn't that so, Selks! Captain Ogler! That's another good one.'

Johannes, the stern minister, raised his eyebrows and looked away. 'I hadn't heard about that. Is that where the term vitschudden commando comes from?'

It was the first time that Selkirk had seen Helena looked embarrassed. He felt genuine pleasure at her discomfiture.

'If that's what you two do as enemies,' Johannes wondered, 'what would you do as friends?'

'We will never be friends,' Helena denied, 'he is a rooineck. This is a temporary alliance only.'

Selkirk avoided her eye. He looked up gratefully when Hendrina appeared, muddy, haggard but smiling. 'You have found more trouble I see, Andrew.' Shaking her head at the foolishness of youth, she distributed mugs of coffee. 'It is only lukewarm, but the best I could do.'

Selkirk sipped gratefully, then drank with sudden thirst. He had not realised how hungry and thirsty he was, and devoured the strip of biltong that Hendrina next produced.

'You are a strange man, Andrew, risking so much to save the enemy.' Hendrina had one arm around Helena as she watched him eat. Her eyes were old and wise, and very bright. 'And fighting alongside a woman who only makes temporary alliances.'

'You were never my enemy,' Selkirk told her. 'And I doubt that Sergeant Campbell would think that Hansie is his.'

'They are man and woman,' Hendrina said simply. 'They belong together. But you? Where do you belong?'

Selkirk looked up. He felt that Hendrina was testing him. 'I suppose that I belong in the Fethan. That's my home.'

There was something angry about the tilt of the green cockade when Helena turned away. 'So go to your Fethan home, rooineck, and leave us in peace.'

The muddy brown water of the spruit flowed sluggishly past their position, rippling around the hindquarters of the patient horses. Ben was closest to him, the bullet scar white on his shoulder as he nibbled at the sour grass that grew at the riverbank. Colourful birds flitted about the vegetation and the honey bird returned to the lightning tree, calling hopefully to these men who hunted and fought and slaughtered so close by. Up above, high in the already darkening sky, a kite circled slowly, watching for prey. The chatter of the birds stilled.

'This is a terrible country.' Selkirk said. 'A place of death and horror and disease.'

'Ja. A terrible place.' Hendrina agreed. 'With terrible people. That is why the British want to add it to their Empire. That is why Sergeant Campbell is making big eyes at my daughter-in-law. That is why you are here with my daughter, Captain Ogler.'

'I am not with your daughter,' Selkirk denied. He glowered at the woman who had fought him so often. 'We just have a temporary truce.'

'Of course. I forgot.' Hendrina nodded understandingly. 'So it is just by chance, then, that you are admiring her legs through these ripped trousers?'

Selkirk looked hurriedly away as Helena shifted her position. The tear was high on her thigh and her skin was startlingly white against the dull khaki. He heard Hendrina mutter, 'No wonder she calls him Ogler,' and wondered why she spoke in English.

Gray nudged Selkirk with a harsh elbow. 'Look, sir.'

A twelve foot long black mamba slithered through the Reivers' position, its triangular head alert, small eyes expressionless.

Selkirk felt the fear squeeze something inside him. He could cope with Boers and Aasvogels. Heat, thirst, privation, fatigue were all part of a soldier's life, but snakes terrified him. He watched the sliding death glide past his men, then slowly removed his revolver from its holster.

'No, Andrew.' Helena's hand was cool on his arm. 'It will do no harm if you leave it alone.' Despite the presence of the snake, he could not help his eyes drifting to the rent in her trousers.

The snake vanished into the long grass, sliding purposefully away from the Reivers. 'As I said,' Selkirk repeated, 'this is a terrible place.'

'You said that,' Hendrina agreed. 'And I said there were terrible people.' She smiled to Helena, who still held Selkirk's arm. 'It is up to the good people to come together and take control.'

'Sir! They're coming up the river.' Blackdown had been very quiet until now, but he aimed and fired two quick shots into the middle of the river. 'I saw a ripple.'

Naked save for loincloths and holding short stabbing spears, half a dozen men rose in the midst of the Reivers. Water glistened on their black skin as they threw themselves toward the defenders. There was an instant of fear, a glimpse of water dripping from sharp steel, then Selkirk jumped forward. Without time to draw his revolver, he shouted to Gray and Campbell to keep watch as he wrestled the first man into the water. He felt the man slither from his grasp, felt iron hands close round his neck and lashed out aimlessly with his boot. There was no shock of contact and the kick put him off balance so his protagonist gained an advantage, pushing him backward and downward.

The hands seemed to be immovable, constricting his throat, tearing the life from his lungs; Selkirk heard something roaring inside his head and knew that he was about to pass out. He tried to kick again, missed, and felt his feet slip on the bottom of the river. His head was below the surface of the river so water burned into his nostrils as he scrabbled to release the terrible pressure from his throat.

All his life had contracted to this one agony. Nothing else mattered as the black whirlpool opened beneath him. Death would be welcome, death in a skirmish in this nameless stream in some obscure part of Africa. The pressure increased and Selkirk felt himself relax. The faces of friends and family came to him; his sister Jenny, Tam, his childhood friend, the Nobleman who had guided him through the early months in the Royal Borderers, Donnelly with his ever calm Arizona drawl, even Helena, teasing, taunting, reading his mind.

Selkirk's hand trailed in the cool water, until his fingers brushed against cloth. The loincloth of his killer. As he died, Selkirk spread his fingers, grabbed on to his attacker's testicles and squeezed as hard as he could. He had to crush to live, so he exerted all his remaining strength, feeling something like rubber give beneath his fingers. The pressure on his throat relaxed a little, so he squeezed again, twisting away from that terrible grip, opening his mouth and drawing a deep breath of African water that choked and gagged in his lungs.

'Bastard!' Selkirk emerged from the river, spewing water and bile, but still keeping a hold of his attacker. The man was screaming frantically, writhing in his agony.

'Here! Selks.' Haig was smiling. He had been born for this type of vicious scrimmage. Joining the army had only made it legal. 'Leave him to me.'

Haig lifted his bayonet, stabbed once into the man's neck and pushed away the body. 'You can let go now Selks. Unless you're enjoying yourself too much.'

Gasping, with each breath a searing agony in his throat and lungs, Selkirk looked around. There were four dead black men floating on the blood-clouded water. Blackdown was lifting a fifth high in the air, bending him backward until his spine snapped. Then he tossed away the body. A sixth was splashing back downstream. Gray took careful aim and fired once. The man jerked and fell silently forward.

'Here did you see that? I killed two of them. Just like that, slitted them wide open while Captain Selks was playing in the water.' Haig was grinning as he recounted his part. Helena was staring at him, her eyes wide.

'I've never seen anyone fight like that before,' she muttered. 'He was so fast!'

'Aye, that's Haigie, the British army's secret weapon!' Selkirk tried to joke but it was painful to speak. Sitting down at the bank, he massaged his throat. 'Any more movement Sergeant?'

'No, sir. Dead quiet.' With Hansie secure at his side, Campbell was back to his laconic best.

'Thank God for that.' Selkirk nodded to Haig. 'You did well Haigie. So did the rest of you, but I don't intend to stay here and wait for them to attack. We're going to break out. Helena; do you want to come with us, or return to your commando?'

Helena looked to her mother. 'I will stay with you just now. But remember we have a truce. You must return as my prisoner.'

'And that'll be bloody right.' Haig spat into the river, and immediately glanced at Hendrina. 'Sorry missus.'

'We made a bargain Haig.' Selkirk felt the rasp of pain as he spoke. 'I gave my word.'

'Bugger your word, Selks. You can't just go in hands up to the boojers.'

'Keep a civil tongue in your head Haig.' Campbell's roar echoed around the river. 'And say sir when you speak to an officer.'

'We're moving up river tonight. One hour after dark.' Selkirk made his decision. 'I'll lead. Campbell, you're rear guard. Helena, if you and Haig could look after the Fouries, the rest of my Reivers would watch the banks.'

'They'll expect something of the sort,' Helena warned. 'Remember, there are British and Boer deserters as well as renegade tribesmen with the Aasvogels.'

'I know.' Selkirk rubbed his throat. 'So we will do our best to deceive them. I only wish we could alert your boys so they could arrange a diversion.'

'Denys is a good man. He will not sit all night and do nothing.' Helena slapped at one of the thousands of mosquitoes that came with the fading light. 'What a verdomte country! I wish I were back home.'

Selkirk moved slightly, breaking a branch underfoot. The broken piece swept downstream, turning slowly in the current. He watched it for a second, then smiled as the idea came into his mind. 'Maybe we don't need Denys.'

McGann had been cleaning his carbine. Now he looked up. 'Here we go boys. The Captain's planning something.' He grinned to Hendrina, 'every time you see that expression on his face, Hendrina, you know something's going to happen. We call it the Devil's look, because there's always the devil to pay afterward.' Immediately contrite, he held up a hand to Johannes, 'No offence, minister.'

'None taken, Mr McGann, I'm sure the Lord understands.'

'Right lads,' Selkirk spoke rapidly as the idea formed in his head, ' I want you to gather all the dry wood you can. Anything combustible, that means anything that can burn, Haig!'

'Dinnae get bloody clever, Selks, or I won't save your hide next time.'

161

Campbell looked at him, 'McGann was right, sir. What devilment are you planning now?'

'The Aasvogels will be expecting us to do something, Sergeant, so we'll oblige them. We're going to send a couple of blazing rafts downstream, something to draw their attention while we go upstream.'

Helena nodded. 'You're a slim devil, Captain, but so am I. Don't just have fire; they'll soon realise the truth. We could maybe add something else?'

'Remember the explosive cart sir?' Applewood reminded. 'Maybe we could do something similar?'

Selkirk thought for a moment, then nodded. 'Of course. Everybody count your cartridges. Tell me how many you have left.'

The Reivers always rode with at least two hundred rounds each. Between them they had over a thousand cartridges remaining.

'Enough to start a small war,' Selkirk said. 'I want everybody to keep a hundred and give me the rest. McGann, you're Irish so you'll know about bomb making. You help here.'

'I've never made a bomb in my life.' McGann protested, until he saw the humour in Selkirk's face. 'Right you are, sir.'

It was fully dark before they finished, and the night sounds of Africa echoed eerily through the trees as the Reivers worked with cordite, matches and anything that could burn. There was little dry wood in the humid forest belt by the river, so Selkirk compromised with a raft of green logs piled with whatever they could find. He wondered if anybody could feel his fear as he stumbled in the dark, thinking of that evil triangular head of the mamba. Even the thought of the snake caused cold sweat to soak through his shirt.

They constructed five rafts. Two were larger, with a six-foot square framework of boughs and a bed of woven branches on which the dry wood was stacked. These were the fire rafts. The other two were half the size, with a more solid base on which cordite was coiled, with piles of bullets placed a few inches apart.

'God bless our endeavours,' Johannes said softly, and gave a short sermon. The words were simple, reminding Selkirk very much of Sunday morning in the tiny whitewashed kirk in Fethanbridge, with the birds calling outside and Jenny nudging him to stop fidgeting.

After the sermon Johannes started a psalm, the words and tune both familiar. Most of the Reivers joined in. The women also sang, their tones lighter, higher than the men, so that the praise ascended with the depth and range of a choir to the soft blanket of the African sky. Selkirk looked up. A million stars peered heedlessly down on the dirty, frightened men.

'I wonder if God's watching us now.' Helena was surely wiping a piece of grit from her eye as she also looked skyward. There could be no other reason for the bead of moisture that rolled slowly down her cheek. 'Sitting up there on his celestial throne.'

'If he is,' Haig said, 'he'll he swearing at us for the mess we're making of all his work.' After a quick glance to Hendrina, who nodded her approval, he also began to sing. Selkirk was always amazed that so ugly a man could possess such a melodious voice. It was possibly his only saving virtue.

'Listen.' Helena lifted her hand and the singing stopped. Reivers and Boers alike strained their ears as the reciprocal sounds of singing drifted through the trees. 'That's my boys! That's my commando.' Selkirk recognised the pride in her voice. He felt the same about his Reivers. 'They've heard us. They're letting us know that we're not alone.'

'Keep singing boys. Sing your hearts out.' This time there was no disguising the tears in Helena's eyes, but still she gestured to Selkirk. 'Time we got started, I think.' Her voice was low, husky even.

Once Selkirk checked that the coiled fuse of cordite was safely concealed beneath a mound of leaves, Helena grabbed the first raft. The river had ruined all the matches, but Campbell, Clydeside engineer to the last, always carried a tinderbox, which Helena had appropriated. Now she waded out to midstream and wedged herself against the raft, holding it by the weight of her body until she was ready. There was a moment of hesitation as she fumbled with the tinderbox, then came the rasp of flint on metal.

'Verdomte!' Helena swore as the sparks refused to fly, then she sighed, blew softly on the edge of a homemade fuse. 'The river quickens further down, then broadens out,' she explained. 'If I've got the fuse right, the first explosion should be just where the broad stretch begins.'

'Let's hope you have it right then.' Selkirk manhandled the second, larger raft out. The singing continued, but now the Aasvogels were creating their own music, a discordant whistling and hooting, mingled with the deep, sinister beat of native drums. ' For God help us if that lot get hold of us.'

'Andrew,' Helena paused with her hands on the second explosive raft. 'If they do, if we lose, don't let us get captured alive. I mean us women, or Coenraad.'

For a second Selkirk saw the genuine fear in her face. 'I won't,' he promised. 'You have my word on it.'

'That means that you'd have to shoot us,' Helena warned. 'Could you do that?'

Selkirk pictured the scene as the hordes poured into the Reiver's camp. He imagined the black natives with their broad bladed assegais and the lust of blood in their eyes. He imagined Hendrina and Hansie and Helena in their grasp. Then he thought of the white renegades, offscourings of both armies. He knew from personal experience what some of the British soldiers were like; once released from the bonds of discipline, they would be worse than any African tribesman.

The Aasvogels would kill the Reivers first, but then the real horror would begin. Selkirk imagined the slaughter of Johannes and the worse aftermath of rape and slavery and vile, lingering torture. He imagined the sneering face of Nat Blunt looming over Helena, he imagined young Coenraad screaming as they swung him like a club and dashed his brains against a tree.

'Could I shoot you?' Selkirk blinked away the shocking images. 'I've been trying for years,' but the joke failed. Helena still looked at him, wondering if he were man enough.

'Yes,' Selkirk said. 'Yes. If need be.' He looked at her. 'It would be the last service of a friend.'

'Who is also an enemy.' Helena reminded, gently. She looked away at last.

Helena helped push the large raft into the stream and watched as Selkirk scraped at the tinderbox. She smiled as the flint refused to

164

spark, as it had failed for her just minutes before. Selkirk tried again, swearing, and the tiny sparks fizzed in the dark. A small flame appeared in the body of the raft.

'Push.' Helena urged, 'push it away!'

'Not yet, wait until it takes hold.' Selkirk delayed until the last possible second, then, with the flames scorching the coarse hairs on the back of his hands, he shoved with all his might. For a second he watched the flames coil toward the overhanging trees, with the red light reflected on water and sky, then he was heaving at the next raft, swearing as the Aasvogels began to fire. The shots echoed between the trees.

'Hurry now! Get the next one away.' Helena worked beside him as Campbell struggled with the largest of all the rafts. Selkirk saw Applewood lend his strength, the Englishman's muscles easily toying with the unwieldy construction. Firelight flickered downstream, showing red against the dark sky.

Helena launched the next explosive raft, with the cordite again hidden so the raft would be invisible on the dark river. Then the large fire raft followed, with Applewood grunting as he sent it spinning down the river.

'Just one more to go.' Selkirk ducked as a bullet whined past his head and smacked uglily into the water. There were other shots, but the Aasvogels seemed to be concentrating on the fire rafts.

'Everybody away, boys.' Selkirk had made a slight adjustment to his original plan. He ordered Campbell to lead the Reivers upstream, and kept the Boer civilians a compact group in the centre. They moved as quietly as they could, leading the horses and grumbling out of habit. Gray was the rearguard, for he would be least likely to shoot Selkirk by mistake.

As soon as Gray cleared the nearest bend, Selkirk positioned the last explosive raft in midstream, and again began to scratch at the tinderbox. Flint scraped on metal, but the sparks refused to come. Swearing, he bowed over the raft, and scraped desperately as the water surged around his legs, and bullets clipped and hissed among the branches overhead. A bullet smacked into the water in mid stream, then another, and a third thumped into the raft at Selkirk's side. He swore, a long, meaningless repetition of all the foulest oaths that he could devise as the resulting splashes showered him with water and rendered the tinderbox useless.

Selkirk glared at the raft that had been made with so much labour but which was now only a lump of floating timber. Lifting his carbine, he fired three shots toward the Aasvogels, working the bolt with such speed that the first of the ejected cartridge cases still gleamed brassily above the water even as the last left the carbine. As he fired he continued to swear, drawing on a vast repertoire of foulness learned in bothies and barracks from Berwickshire to Bloemfontein.

'What terrible language from such a well bred man.' The words were mocking as Helena slipped beside him. 'Hoe gaan dit Captain Rooineck?' 'How's it going, Captain?'

'The bloody tinder box is ruined.' Selkirk shouted.

Helena shook her head. 'Leave it then. Don't waste time here' Grabbing his shoulder, she unceremoniously shoved him upstream. 'Come on, we'll join the rest.'

The fire rafts were well downstream, their flickering light casting weird shadows on the sky, when the fuse touched the first cartridge. Selkirk heard a sharp crack, then another, followed by a whole succession, like a volley from British infantrymen. He did not know what happened next, perhaps a spark from the fire raft landed on the cordite, or the fuse was badly laid, but there was an explosion that tore the whole sky apart.

'Jesus.' Selkirk flinched as flames and sparks erupted in to the night, then descended in a brilliant display of pyrotechnics that showered the river and surrounding veldt with fire.

'Swearing's allowed,' Helena permitted graciously, 'but I won't stand for blasphemy. God, Andrew, run!' Her expression altered from mockery to panic. 'This verdomte raft's also alight.'

Chapter Thirteen :Northern Transvaal – June 1902

A blazing branch had landed on the explosive raft, catching the cordite fuse nearly two thirds of the way along its length. Helena stood with her hand on Selkirk's arm, both frozen as they watched the deadly flames hiss furiously toward the first cartridge. Rather than the three minutes that they had allowed themselves to escape, they had only sixty seconds before the collection exploded. It was Helena who moved first, shoving him brutally upstream. 'Andrew. Run!'

They ran together, heads down as they forced their way upstream, away from the sparking death that floated so innocently on the water. The river seemed to tug against them as if deliberately impeding their passage, while the occasional bullet hummed overhead.

The second and third raft exploded together, sending another volley of bullets in every direction and momentarily stilling the sounds of the night. There was a lifting chorus of shouts and screams from the rear, mingled with another sound that Selkirk knew he should have recognised. It was like the sough of wind through the Border hills, something familiar from the past that did not belong in this place of horror and fire.

'What's that?'

'I can't hear anything,' Helena pushed him in front. 'My ears are ringing. Keep moving, Captain Rooineck.'

They ran, stumbling over the uneven bed of the river, tripping over branches that snagged against their legs, cursing, shouting, feeling the cold sweat of fear drench their clothes. Three times Selkirk heard something heavy move on the riverbank and closed his eyes in fear. Worse than the terror of dynamite and Aasvogels were his childhood nightmares of snakes and lions and crocodiles.

There was more firing in front, a steady crackle that grew louder as they pressed forward. They moved quickly as worry overcame their fatigue. 'They've hit trouble!' Helena shouted above her own deafness.

'Campbell's a good man,' Selkirk said. 'He'll have everybody well in hand.'

'I hope so,' Helena tried to peer round a bend in the river to the darkness ahead, 'God, I hope so! I should never have left them.'

'Why did you?' Selkirk wanted to know.

'To help you, you ogling rooineck skelm.' Her reply was quick and cutting. 'I knew that you couldn't manage on your own.'

They negotiated a sudden sandbank, where the current rippled silver in the light of distant stars, then moved on, urgent, into the night.

'Look.' Selkirk pulled Helena to one side as the body of a horse surged past with the current. Blood smeared the surface of the water.

The river narrowed into a succession of curves, each one overhung by dense thickets of trees that nearly blocked out the stars. It was at the tightest of these curves, where a fallen tree protruded half way across the channel, that the Aasvogels had set their ambush. The Reivers had flattened themselves against the banks, but their enemy was positioned on either side, whooping and yelling as they fired. Bush-hatted men dodged and swore and shot at the invisible ambushers.

'Bad?' Selkirk sought out Campbell while Helena moved to comfort her family.

'They're in front and on both flanks sir.' Campbell had lost his hat and there was blood on his face. 'McGann's wounded; a round in the shoulder, and Pert's disappeared somewhere. Maybe he's hit but I can't see in the dark.'

'How many are there?'

'Dunno, sir. Plenty!' Campbell fired four quick rounds, grunting as return fire thumped into the bank at his side. One of the horses screamed and began to kick as a bullet smashed into its flank.

Selkirk ducked as a thrown spear sliced into the tree above him. 'Pull the men back, one at a time. We'll try and establish a barricade somewhere. Leave the horses; they'll have to take care of themselves.'

'Leave the horses?' Campbell stared at him, then nodded.

It was anathema for a cavalryman to abandon his horse, but Selkirk knew that they were only a burden in the river. Surviving the night was all that mattered now; escaping on the morrow was a whole world away.

Hansie held a crying Coenraad tight in her arms, while old Hendrina, scarcely built for river walking, struggled on. Haig was at her side, cursing fluently as he alternatively lent her a wiry arm and fired toward the enemy.

'Bastarding boojers! No offence missus. Come out, so I can bloody kill you, you cowardly buggers! Sorry about the language Hendrina, but these bastards annoy me.'

Gamely limping along the night-dark river, with her skirts hitched up to her thighs, Hendrina tutted, 'They annoy me too, David, but don't worry about the language. My Kaspar was a great man for the oaths. Especially when he thought I was not listening. But don't call these men Boers. They are Aasvogels.'

'They're arse somethings anyway.' Haig reloaded and fired again.

A bullet plucked at Selkirk's sleeve and he spun round, swearing.

'All right sir?' Campbell was at his side, teeth white in a dark face.

'Aye. Over there.' Selkirk gestured to a shelving beach. 'We can get ashore and settle down to defend ourselves.'

'Johannes! Has anybody seen the minister?' Hansie sounded close to panic, until Campbell splashed towards her, arms outstretched.

'Come here, Reivers. Come to us!' Selkirk loosed two quick shots into the bushes.

A mass of men appeared on the beach that Campbell had indicated. They aimed their rifles, jeering as they fired into the river. 'Come and die, but leave us the women!' Their laughter was crueller than the eyes of any black mamba that crawled.

'It's all right Hendrina, Selks will see us safe, he always does.' Haig reassured. 'He'll have something planned.'

'Not this time Haigie,' Selkirk said, so softly that only Helena could hear. Lifting his carbine, he fired, swore when he realised that it was empty, and fumbled for cartridges. He dropped two in his haste, hearing their dull plop with slight dismay. That was two more of the enemy that would live.

Mentally he traced their route, searching for a better defensive position. 'Helena. We'll make a stand at the sandbank that we passed. Try and hold out until morning.' McGann, struggling with his damaged shoulder, moaned softly in the dark

Helena nodded in the dark. She was supporting Hansie with her left hand, while trying to keep her rifle out of the water.

It was a relief, if only a momentary one, to leave the river for the slithering dry sand. Selkirk watched over his men as Helena helped Hansie up. Campbell carried Coenraad. Haig, struggling with the bulk of Hendrina, was last.

'Told you that Selks would think of something, didn't I? Here we are, a fine wee defensive position with its own moat and plenty fresh water. We can hold this for days, can we no', sir? Until Donnelly comes for us anyway.' Haig helped Hendrina to sit on the sand. 'You'll like Donnelly, miss, even if he is American.'

The bank was elongated, about thirty paces in length and about one third that in width. A dead horse was bumping gently against the uppermost point and a few more horses clambered up beside the Reivers. Selkirk was glad to note that Ben was among them.

'Roll call!' Selkirk shouted. He counted his men. Pert and Gray were missing, and Blackdown was trying to ignore the blood that poured down his leg. Johannes the minister was also missing, but the Fourie family was intact.

The firing died away, leaving a forbidding hush that the nocturnal animals seemed reluctant to fill. Far downstream, the last flames of the rafts flickered against the sky.

'Build a barricade, boys. Use anything that we can find. Rocks, branches, dead horses. We'll make our stand here until Helena's commando drives away the Aasvogels.' Selkirk tried to sound confident, but he knew that as soon as the light strengthened they would be little more than a target. He knew that the Reivers would fight, but already he sensed movement on the banks of the river. The enemy was gathering there, vultures waiting for the kill.

'Are we going to die?' Coenraad asked, and his mother soothed him.

'We are in God's hands.'

'Are we going to die?' Hendrina asked, but it was Haig who answered.

'With Selks here? Nae bloody chance!'

'Your men have faith in you Captain,' Helena said quietly, 'but I ask you to remember your promise.' She touched his arm, her lips close to his ear, 'don't let the Aasvogels get my family.'

'I won't forget.' Taking Campbell aside, Selkirk informed him of the situation. 'If I'm dead, Campbell, I rely on you to do it.'

'I was on the Frontier, sir. We didn't let the Paythans get our boys either.' He looked at Hansie, sitting on the sandbank with Coenraad held between her knees. 'War's hard on the women.'

Selkirk nodded. There was nothing he could say.

Dawn brought a silvery mist that shaded the trees, so they seemed to bow in veneration of the impending sacrifice. A discordant chorus of birds greeted the morning, their song ugly in comparison with the deep music of the blackbirds that regaled the Fethan. A single snake slithered across the sand, but strangely Selkirk watched it without fear. Unlike him, it belonged here.

'Not long now sir.' Campbell worked the bolt of his carbine. He checked the barricade that they had erected. Thigh high at best, it served only to mark the boundary that they held. The Fourie family sat together at the strongest point, their backs deliberately turned to the river so they could not see the vicious death all around.

'Another hymn might be helpful.' Campbell suggested. 'Kirky would know what to choose.'

'So he would,' Selkirk heard something move on the left bank of the river. He swivelled toward it, feeling a growing pain where the bullet had grazed his arm. McGann was lying still, holding the shoulder that Hendrina had bound during the night. Applewood lay at his side. His bleeding had stopped, but he favoured the injured leg.

'Shall I start sir?' Campbell had the hard voice of a sergeant, but the others soon joined his rendering of the 23rd Psalm. They sung softly, an invocation of faith more than a defiant chorus, but the words seemed to strengthen them as the mist thinned. There were voices on the riverbank and somewhere the deep thrumming of drums.

171

'I wonder what they're saying?' Using Applewood as a crutch, McGann pushed himself upright. He walked to the furthest point of the sandbank and raised his voice. 'What are you saying lads? Summoning help because you can't beat the Reivers alone?' With his left arm in a sling, he raised his right, fists clenched in defiance. 'Run away and play, you bastards! The Reivers are here!'

The drums continued, sinister in the mist. Selkirk could see movement on the riverbanks now, vague shapes that hardened into a long line of ragged men, black and white and khaki. One stepped forward.

'Shall I kill him, Selks?' Haig sighted along his carbine.

'Not yet.' Selkirk held up his hand. 'I think he wants to parley.'

'Tell them that we'll accept their unconditional surrender,' McGann said, his voice rough with pain.

As one of the Aasvogels stepped forward, Selkirk recognised Nat Blunt. 'What do you want, Blunt?'

'The women.' The man's Midlands accent was ugly. 'Give us the women and the rest of you can go safe.'

'Bugger off!' Haig's shout was emphatic.

Blunt sneered directly at Haig. 'We'll keep you too, Jockey boy. We could do with a pet monkey!' He stepped back and signalled with his hand. A knot of men came forward, bearing something white and wriggling.

'That's Johannes.' There was a sob in Helena's voice.

They had stripped the minister naked and tied him spreadeagled to a wooden framework that they now erected on the bank of the river. Johannes looked toward the sandbank, eyes unafraid. Two men held flaming torches at his side. Johannes began to pray.

Blunt stepped beside Johannes, placed a hand on his chest. 'If you surrender your women, you and this man can go free. If you hesitate, we shall castrate him, then crucify him to a tree.' His sneer was infinitely more evil than the black mamba had been. 'You will all die the same way.'

Hendrina began to pray in Afrikaans as Hansie pressed Coenraads's face close to her body. Selkirk could not read the expression on Campbell's face, but knew the Sergeant was suffering terrible torment.

'Sir?' Haig gestured to his carbine.

'Not yet.' Selkirk stepped forward, his heart pounding. 'If you let that man free, I will come in his place. I am a King's Officer, worth far more in ransom than any Boer civilian is. Let these people go and I swear that I will talk for you in court.'

Blunt shook his head, took one of the torches and slowly pressed it into Johannes' chest. The minister stiffened and began to intone the Lords Prayer. The acrid stink of burning hair reached the Reivers. Selkirk saw the first flames.

'Wait.' Selkirk held up his hand and the torch was removed. Johannes emitted a long gasp and sagged against the ropes that held him.

Haig began to sing, not the peaceful psalms of the Bible, but *Defence of Dunkeld*, the old Royal Borderers' fighting tune, that retold the day when the regiment had stood in their trenches amidst the burning town, as Cannon's screaming Highlanders had launched an attack on them. It had been a day of pike and bayonet against the silver claymore, and the song told of the blood and agony and glory. Haigie sang it well, standing his full five foot three as he fitted the wicked bayonet on to his carbine.

'You're deid, Blunt you bastard. That man never did anybody any harm.' The Edinburgh accent was more pronounced than normal as Haig reverted to the gang fighter of his youth. 'You're deid, man.'

Blunt's sneered as he blew on the torch and thrust it against Johannes stomach. 'Lower each time, eh Jocky? I'll do worse to you. I hate the Scotch.'

'You'll hate me worse before I've done with you!' Haig abruptly stopped shouting and cocked his head to one side. 'Hear that sir?' He was smiling, not his fighting smile of pure sadistic pleasure, but something else, something deeper. 'Can you bloody hear that? It's the boys! They've come back for us.'

'What?' Selkirk listened, but he could hear nothing but the sinister hiss of flames, the beat of drums and the stifled sobs of Hansie. Johannes tried to flinch away as Blunt dragged the torch lower down his body.

'Bloody listen, Selks, you Johnny Raw bastard!'

Then Selkirk heard it, faint at first but growing louder. 'That's the pipes! It's the pipes, by God.' He closed his eyes, remembering the sound that he had heard the previous night.

Haig was laughing, capering on the sandbank as the women stared at him, and Campbell hugged Hansie and shook hands with the Reivers.

'Andrew, what is it?'

'It's the pipes.' Selkirk explained, 'not the great Highland pipes, not the kilties, but our pipes, the pipes of the Border! The Royal Borderers are here!' He lifted Helena high into the air, held her close, kissed her once and then, realising what he was doing, replaced her carefully on the ground.

'Sorry. But it's the pipes.'

With their ears attuned to their own instrument, the Reivers had heard the Border pipes long before the Aasvogels could. Suddenly remembering the plight of the minister, Selkirk nodded to Haig.

'Shoot that bastard, Haigie, would you?'

Shrugging, Haig levelled his carbine and fired. The sneer ended as Blunt fell, clutching at his thigh, which was pumping blood. His long screaming sob raised the hair on Selkirk's neck.

'Bad shot Haigie, remind me to reprimand you for that later.'

'Bugger off Selks.' Haig lowered his carbine. 'I said that I would kill him, but I'll do it my way. I'm a bayonet man, myself.' His eyes were back to their customary poisonous glare.

'That's bugger off, sir! Campbell barked. 'I won't tell you again, Haig! Show some respect when you swear at an officer!'

The column came from both sides of the river, catching the Aasvogels in a neat pincer movement. While horsemen galloped along the far side of the river, the Royal Borderers combed the bush on the near side. The regiment had no pity, shooting or bayoneting any that refused to surrender. Selkirk watched as a small group of horsemen splashed across the river to the sandbank.

'Thought you would be here!' Cloete rode alongside Colonel Elliot of the Reivers. 'It was very good of you to lay on all the bright lights to guide us in though.' The third man grinned at Selkirk from beneath the rim of his bush hat.

'Typical bloody Pom officer, can't do anything right unless there's an Aussie to take control.'

'We thought we had lost you Gray.' Selkirk ignored the deep purple colour that Elliot was turning at this new example of Colonial insubordination.

'Naw, Perty and I got separated at the ambush, so we guided in these boys.' Gray dismounted with a typical flourish, 'I believe that you already know my good friend Denys?' He nudged the fourth member of the group, who glowered morosely at Selkirk

'Is he a prisoner?' Selkirk could not imagine Denys surrendering so tamely.

'The war's ended, sir. Both sides signed a treaty at Vereenging at the end of last month. The column was coming to let us know when it heard all the noise you were making.' Gray waved cheerfully to Coenraad, who was crying with a mixture of reaction and exhaustion.

'And you, Cloete?' Selkirk asked. 'Where do you fit into all this?'

The big Boer shook his head, 'I can't say, Captain, but Colonel Hume wishes you all the best.' He paused, significantly. 'So does General de la Rey. After all, you escorted me nearly to his camp.'

Selkirk stared at him blankly. 'Is that so?'

'Somebody had to contact all the scattered commando leaders to tell them of the peace talks. What better way would I pass through hostile territory than with a Reiver escort? That was your task, Captain.' Cloete smiled to him. His uniform bore the insignia of a full colonel.

'But Akersdorp and Helena Van Vuren? What about them? What about their threat to the Empire by holding British territory?' Selkirk could have continued. He could have asked about the blood and deaths, the suffering and torment, the worry and wounds suffered by his men and Helena's commando. He could have mentioned the horrors suffered by Johannes, who was even now being treated for burns by a concerned army medical orderly.

'Fleabites, Captain. Your real job was to take me north in safety. Akersdorp did not matter; it was just a dorp to place you, somewhere that you could be found again if you were needed.'

'I see.' Selkirk touched the bright ribbon of the DSO. Was that also insignificant? A bribe to ensure that he would risk his life again, and again, for the schemes of some politician?

But there was nothing deceptive about the man who waded the river and grabbed hold of his shoulders, grinning and talking and laughing.

'Selks! Hey Selks.' The Nobleman stepped back a pace, lifted the hunting horn that had travelled with him across half the world and blew a single derisory blast. 'Captain Selks now, eh? Man! They must be hard up for officers if they promote you.'

'Haigie's here too.' Selkirk said, 'and somebody else that you might recognise,' he glanced around the crowded sandbank, 'where's Helena?' The sudden panic was alien to him as he imagined Helena being hit by the last shot fired by the Aasvogels while he was dancing with the Nobleman. ' Hendrina, where's Helena?'

The old woman shook her head. 'She's gone, Andrew. Did you really think that she would surrender to the rooinecks?'

'She can't be gone!' Selkirk ran to the water's edge. There were hundreds of soldiers, Colonials with their Herculean bodies and cynical attitude, Borderers with their pith helmets and Lee-Enfields, horsemen with jaunty bush hats, watchful Boers in rags and stubborn pride, but no Helena, and no Ben.

'She asked me to give you this,' Hendrina passed across a ragged, damp square of folded paper.

Selkirk opened it. 'Remember meneer Ogler,' it read, 'I have your word of honour. You are my prisoner.'

Chapter Fourteen :Edinburgh - October 1903

From the ramparts of Edinburgh Castle, the South African War seemed long ago and so far away. Captain Selkirk DSO of the Royal Borderers gazed downward on Princes Street and the adjacent Gardens. From this height the busy trams looked like toys, while the strolling crowds, from the long-skirted ladies with their parasols who inspected the splendid shops to the crossing boys who swept clear the horse muck, looked insignificant. Yet these were the people of Empire. It was for their sake that the Royal Borderers, the Gordon Highlanders, the Imperial Yeomanry and all the rest had fought so hard, half a world away.

'Company ready for your inspection, sir!' Sergeant Hetherington saluted as ponderously as he did everything else, yet Selkirk would not have exchanged him for any soldier in the regiment.

There had been big changes since their return from South Africa during the summer. Many of the long service men had left, including Private Haig, much to Selkirk's surprise. Some of the others had been invalided out due to sickness or wounds. A new intake of Johnny Raws had taken their place, and Selkirk had spent much time and a great deal of unrefined language on licking the newcomers into shape.

'Ready for your inspection, sir!' Hetherington repeated. He stood so rigidly at attention that his limbs trembled.

Selkirk nodded. The Edinburgh damp had washed away much of Hetherington's tan, but the blunt, honest features were the same, although the scarlet full dress uniform fitted more closely than the field khaki of the veldt. 'Thank you sergeant.'

'It's not right sir, what they're doing.' Typically, Hetherington remained at attention when he made his protest.

'Thank you, Hetherington. I'll come and inspect the men now.' Selkirk put an edge to his voice.

'Yes sir, but it's not right.' Hetherington remained obstinately at attention.

Selkirk sighed. He was now paying the price for his relaxed attitude to discipline on the veldt. If he had kept a firmer grip of the men then, he would not have to endure this level of insubordination now. With the war ended, the British army had promptly forgotten most of the lessons that it had learned at Spion Kop, Colenso and Magersfontein. The old, rigid divides had returned, with firm class barriers and virtually no communication between officers and men. At the same time, this was Hetherington, who had stood side by side with him in half a dozen skirmishes. 'What's not right, Hetherington?'

'It's not right that he should get decorated, and not you. It was you that held Akersdorp, not him!' As he voiced his indignation, Hetherington's Northumbrian accent strengthened.

'I don't think that's entirely correct, Hetherington. We all held Akersdorp, you, me, the Reivers, the men of the garrison, and Colonel Drongan.' It had come as a bit of a shock to learn that Charles Drongan had recovered from his wound and survived the war. With the death of his brother in a hunting accident, Charles was now Lord Drongan, and as such had been awarded the Victoria Cross for his gallant action in repulsing a Boer attack on Akersdorp.

'Yes, sir, but it's not right, not after all that happened.'

'That's enough, Hetherington. Return to the men.' Selkirk acknowledged the now slightly sullen salute. 'And Hetherington,' Selkirk waited until the sergeant turned to face him. 'I appreciate your point. Thank you. If I had my way every member of the Reivers would be awarded the Victoria Cross, but that's not the way it works.'

'Maybe we should change the system sir.'

It was late October, with a chill North Sea haar creeping over the barren expanse of the Esplanade. The Royal Borderers were drawn up in their scarlet and gold, with the green sleeves that told of early service in India, and the colours that boasted of half a hundred battles in a score of campaigns across the world. The most recent battle honours, 'Modder River', 'Magersfontein' and 'South Africa, 1899 to 1902' glared out in defiance. The simple words meant little to the crowd that had gathered to watch the ceremony, but the old soldiers knew their significance, while Selkirk vowed that the young recruits would learn.

The band struck up the old songs, first the *Defence of Dunkeld* then the *Border Reivers* followed by a medley of rousing marches that lifted the chins of the military and set civilian toes a-tapping.

Selkirk marched out to the front of his men, inspecting their dress and bearing, adjusting a button here, commenting on a minor matter there. As always, the youthfulness of the recruits, and their lack of size struck him. Did we really go to Africa with an army of boys, he thought. Was I like that when I joined?

Salted among the thin, pale faces and stunted bodies of the Johnny Raws were the veterans. Here was Charlton, twice wounded and proud holder of the Queen's and King's South Africa Medal. Here was Lance corporal Bell, who held a drift against De Wet's commando, and Romanes, who got lost in the Transvaal and rescued a starving Boer family on his return, and Faa, who was first into the wagon laager at Paardeberg.

Selkirk stopped in front of Noble, as saturnine and cynical as ever, who stared intently at nothing. 'You're looking good, Nobleman.'

'Forty six, sir.'

'What?'

'Forty-six days and my twenty-two years are up. Then I retire with a pension. I've got a little put away Selks, and I'm going to buy a pub.' The Nobleman winked and relapsed into his expressionless stare.

Buy a pub. That must be the dream of half the infantry in the army. Survive their time and put away enough money to buy a public house. Only the most fortunate made their dream. Selkirk could see Noble's pub now, with the veterans gathering to swap lies and the battered bugle above the bar. 'Good for you Nobleman. I'll be your first customer.'

It was General Hector MacDonald who presented the medals, and when he appeared the attitude of the men altered immediately. Where they had been disciplined but bored, now they became attentive, for 'Fighting Mac' was one of their own. MacDonald had spent nine years in the ranks before being commissioned, and had since risen to the heights of command without losing his reputation among officers or rankers.

Erect in front of his men, Selkirk saw the famous general, handsome as any man in the British army, bedecked with honours and awards, standing in the middle of the hollow square of the Borderers. For a moment Fighting Mac's eyes were far away, as he surveyed the regiment and the grey stones of the castle, then he snapped back into reality.

'There are many brave men in the British army,' MacDonald began, his voice carrying to the silent soldiers and beyond, to the swelling crowd of spectators and upward to the grim stonework of the castle itself, 'but few to match Lieutenant Colonel Lord Charles Drongan. Left in command of Akersdorp, the most northerly village in the Transvaal, Lord Drongan gathered together a scratch force of British and colonial infantry, with a few irregular horse, and held out against all the armies that the Boers could muster.'

Selkirk studied Drongan as he stood to attention in front of the Borderers. He was just as tall, but had lost a little weight, while the face was as handsome and powerful as ever. His uniform was tailored to perfection, his boots gleamed, and the hilt of his sword shone gold even in the dullness of Edinburgh. He looked every girl's picture of the perfect officer.

General MacDonald brought his version of Drongan's virtues to a close with a ringing, 'and so I have the greatest pleasure in pinning the Victoria Cross to the breast of one of the bravest men in the British Empire! !'

The band struck up a fanfare, most of the crowd cheered, although Selkirk thought he heard a low hissing from some, and the General called for three cheers from the men.

There was a mixed response, with the recruits cheering this hero with great spirit while the veterans were more restrained. Selkirk remained at attention. He felt the thump of medals on his own chest and glanced down to admire his DSO, his Queen's Medal with clasps for the Modder and Magersfontein and the King's Medal. He knew that he had earned them, but still felt vaguely ashamed, perhaps because of the men that were left behind, or of the devastation caused throughout South Africa.

The ceremony was nearly complete. Lieutenant Colonel Lord Charles Drongan was saluting, turning smartly and marching toward his own regiment, the colourful Ettrick and Cheviot Militia, which had played such a magnificent part in the farm burning and general harassment of Boer civilians. To get to his position, Drongan had to march past the Borderers, coming within a few paces of Selkirk.

The band was playing *Soldier of the Queen* as Drongan approached. Selkirk pulled himself even further erect and tried to keep the loathing out of his face, but could not restrain his eyes from fixing on the Colonel. He saw the slight check in Drongan's step, the momentary hesitation before the man recollected that he was a Colonel and the holder of the Victoria Cross. Drongan marched past, his sword at his side and his right arm swinging, slightly stiffly due to the bullet that Helena had planted there, but still as straight as a sergeant major.

Then it was over, the men marched off parade, the crowds dissipated to their respective homes or chosen pubs and the officers could relax deep inside the cold stone walls.

The Royal Borderers carried their home with them, so their mess was redolent of regimental culture, from the pipes on the wall to the trophies of war that sat inside glass fronted cases. There were crossed Afghan jezzails and Indian tulwars, with a drum that was captured at Waterloo and a glove that Marlborough had lent a long dead colonel. The most recent exhibit was the Vierkleur, the flag of the Transvaal that had once flown from the square in Pretoria. Selkirk also allowed his eyes to rest on the battered Mauser that the Nobleman had rescued from the smoking carnage of Paardeberg. Past now, if not forgotten.

Memories of war brought back another worry. It was strange how he had received regular letters from Jenny while he was in Africa, but they had dried up once the war ended. She had not replied to any of the last four of his letters, although she must know the amount of labour he took with each carefully scribed note. As soon as he could arrange leave, he would take a trip to the Fethan.

The thought of seeing the old familiar place was very cheering, with the gentle green hills where he had played as a boy, and the soft rippling water, and his father and the girls. His mother had died of hard work and bad temper only a year ago. That was the last thing Jenny had written, and it had taken Selkirk weeks to recover from the shock. Although they had seldom been the best of friends he could not imagine the Fethan without her.

'Well, Selkirk.' Colonel Elliot's terrible eyes surveyed Selkirk. He had grown up in the Royal Borderers and remembered him as a raw recruit. 'Your men looked well enough.'

'Thank you, sir.' Selkirk fought the desire to stand to attention when Elliot spoke to him. Such behaviour was just not done in the officer's mess.

'Do you have a partner for the dance tonight?' With the close of the war, Selkirk's Reivers had been disbanded and the men returned to their parent regiments. Selkirk had retained his rank and rejoined the Royal Borderers, but as an ex-ranker he was not always accepted among the officers. By this public approach, the Colonel was obviously trying to sway the opinion of his officers.

'No, sir.' In the brilliant gaslight of the mess, Selkirk was extremely aware of the deficiencies of his borrowed dress uniform. The patches and darns were clearly visible. 'I had thought about volunteering for duty officer.'

'Again?' Elliot raised his eyebrows. 'I want you to attend the dance, partner or not. I know that there will be some friends of yours there.' The smile was genuine.

'Oh?' None of the Reivers would be invited, so Selkirk could only think of Colonel Hume or Major Scott. It would be good to see either of them again. 'Thank you, sir. I'll be there.'

'Glad to hear it.' Elliot half turned away, 'and Selkirk, stop calling me sir in the mess. It's bad form, don't you know?'

Only the Royal Borderers could stage such an event. They had commandeered the Great Hall of Edinburgh Castle, with its massive hammer beam ceiling and the fireplace that had seen the birth and intrigues of royalty. Now the entire solid building was thumping with the noise. Pipers lined one wall, blasting out the wild Border music on their Northumbrian pipes, while the floor swayed and thundered to the rhythmic pounding of hundreds of military feet and their daintier female companions. Soldier servants glided through the throng, balancing trays of whisky and claret, champagne and brandy as easily as they had once lugged Lee-Enfields across the veldt.

Peacetime soldiering had returned, bringing with it all the privileges of rank and class.

Standing against the wood-panelled wall, Selkirk sipped carefully at the Glenfiddich malt whisky and watched the dancers. This was his third dram, which was two more than he normally allowed himself, and already he could feel the effects. He heard the music change to Dashing White Sergeant and the dancing increased its tempo further. The room was filled with scarlet-faced men in scarlet uniforms panting in unison, while the long skirts of their women swirled in kaleidoscopic brilliance.

'Hoe ganan dit?' How goes it?

'Vrot, danke,' Rotten, thank you. Selkirk answered automatically, if truthfully, before he realised he was speaking in Afrikaans.

Major Scott nodded. 'I thought so. Who's the looker?' He nodded to the most central group of dancers.

Selkirk peered through the blue haze of tobacco smoke. Even among a room full of elegant women she was outstanding. The curve of hip and flank and breast could have belonged to a statue of Venus, while her face, now in profile, was classically perfect. Everything, from the royal blue dress that revealed just enough of her cleavage to tantalise, to the carefully coiled hair, spoke of breeding and wealth and sheer class.

'That?' He tried to sound nonchalant, although his heart was suddenly pounding. 'Oh that's Georgina Montgomery. Lord Drongan's sister.'

'Heard that you knew her.' Scott drained his glass, rescued another from a passing tray and half emptied it in a single swallow. 'Good looking woman, right enough. Wonder where her husband is?'

Selkirk quickly searched the bounding dancers. He saw Drongan, smiling charmingly into the eyes of a plump redhead, but could not see James Montgomery. 'No idea. Where is he?'

'Elsewhere.' Scott replaced his now empty glass with another. 'Topping champagne this Selkirk. Much better than the syrup that they served at the Mount Nelson.' He followed Georgina with his eyes. 'I was there for some time you know, watching over the Rand

Lords. Bumped into the gorgeous Georgina more than once. And Montgomery too, now and then. Foul fellow, handsome as be-dammed and always smoking a long cheroot.'

Selkirk knew that Scott was leading up to something. 'Carry on, Major.'

'Heard your name mentioned too, more than once. When they argued, mostly.' Scott tapped the medal ribbons that lined Selkirk's chest. 'My room just happened to be next to theirs. Seems that Captain Montgomery has an eye for the ladies. Strange, when he's married to something built like that. Georgina told him that you were twice the man he was, which did not please him much.'

Scott gestured to the nearest servant and helped himself to two glasses. 'Anyway, just thought I'd let you know. There's a waltz coming soon, by the way, and I added your name to Georgina's card.'

'What?' Selkirk felt sudden panic. His dancing experience amounted to the occasional gallop around the local hall while he had been a ploughboy. The prospect of dancing with the highly proficient Georgina, with his brother officers watching and criticising, appalled him.

Major Scott was obviously enjoying Selkirk's discomfiture. 'Here you are, Andrew Selkirk DSO, the man who saved the Empire, commander of the famous Reivers, and you're afraid to dance with a girl that you've known all your life?' His laugh was deep and loud and deliberately coarse.

It was then that Georgina turned round and saw Selkirk. Her cheekbones were still too tanned to be fashionable and her eyes still crinkled at the corners when she smiled, but marriage had matured her so she was more beautiful than ever. She paused for a second, resting her white-gloved hand on the arm of the stocky major with whom she had been dancing then glided across to him. Half the male heads in the room watched her pass.

'Andrew!' Her pleasure appeared unfeigned as she presented her hand, which Selkirk kissed as gallantly as he could.

'Georgina,' he said then added, foolishly, 'Mrs Montgomery.'

'Both are correct, Andrew,' Georgina was entirely unfazed, 'but with you I prefer the former. After all we have been more than friends for some time.' Retrieving her hand, she touched the badges of rank on Selkirk's shoulder. 'You've made quite a name for yourself, Captain Selkirk.' Perfume enclosed him as she fingered his medal ribbons, 'DSO, King's South African Medal, Queen's South African Medal with clasps.' Her fingers drifted across his chest. 'And all well earned, I hear.' There was laughter in her eyes as she took his arm and guided him to the centre of the floor. He had forgotten how tall she was, with the top of her hair rising higher than his cap.

Georgina seemed to expect officers and their ladies to step aside and let her pass, but it was a novel experience for Selkirk. They danced an eightsome reel first, with much changing of partners, and to Selkirk the dance was little more than a whirl of panting men and bouncing ladies, but then the music slowed and gentlemen were more selective with their choice of partners.

'Are you free, my dear?' the stocky major enquired of Georgina, who made a point of examining her card before shaking her head.

'I'm so sorry, John, I'm already booked with Captain Selkirk.' Georgina's smile was so obviously genuine that the major could only bow politely before searching for his next victim.

'He's such a tiresome little man,' Georgina said, 'but I'm sure he means well.' Her giggle was all the more appealing because it was childlike. 'Do you know he spent the entire last dance with his eyes fixed on my breasts. I would be quite flattered, only he did exactly the same thing with Mrs Captain Paxton, and she's nearly forty years old.'

Despite himself, Selkirk emulated the tiresome major, and blinked as Georgina arched her back to make his task easier. This time her laugh was deeper. 'Oh, I don't mind you looking, Andrew. There's nothing there that you haven't seen before.'

She was firm yet feminine in his arms as they waltzed through the swaying crowd. Twice Selkirk nearly trapped her foot, but she manoeuvred deftly away, giving gentle words of encouragement and advice as her right hand alternately pressed and relaxed on his back.

'That's the way Andrew, easy on the left foot, I'm your dance partner, not your horse, now turn, slowly, slowly, then right hand higher.' Her eyes seemed bottomless, her grace ethereal as Georgina whispered him back into her life.

'There now, you danced like a master.' She released him with seeming reluctance, only to slide her arm through his. 'Is it not hot in here?' Georgina did not appear warm, the glow from her body radiated control as she manipulated the situation effortlessly. 'Could you escort me outside for a moment, Andrew? I feel in great need for a breath of cooler air.'

Again the crowd parted in front of her and they walked across the greasy cobbles, arm in arm under the dark Scottish sky. There were sputtering torches for light, and khaki-clad soldiers who saluted them punctiliously as they passed.

Georgina halted them beside Mons Meg, the huge fifteenth century cannon that thrust its long iron snout toward the invisible Forth. Together they stared over the gaslit city. 'Isn't it beautiful, Andrew?' The lights seemed to flicker amidst the dark rectangles of the New Town, with the Walk descending into the black canyon of docks and warehouses that was Leith. This was the romantic capital of Scotland, the hometown of Walter Scott and Robert Louis Stevenson, the city where the castle separated the Jekyll of the Georgian New Town from the Hyde of the Auld.

She pressed closer to him, and he felt his body respond as the combination of malt whisky and warm Georgina eased away his unhappiness. 'I've missed you Andrew.' Her hand eased round his waist, then she suddenly shivered. 'Oh it's cold out here! Don't you think it's cold out here?'

Naturally Selkirk unbuttoned his jacket and slipped it over her shoulders before suggesting that they return indoors.

'Not yet Andrew,' Georgina snuggled closer, 'after all, I haven't seen you for so long. We've got so much to catch up on.'

Selkirk breathed deeply, inhaling the scent of perfume and vibrant woman. Out here on the castle battlements with the damp Edinburgh air around him and his medals and rank secure, Selkirk could nearly forget that Georgina was married to somebody else. He could imagine that she was his woman and that their future stretched before them. He closed his eyes, wondering what it would be like to return home as the gallant Captain with the princess of the Fethan on his arm.

The hands of the princess were busy, wriggling inside his shirt, caressing his stomach, stealthily moving downward.

'So how is married life, Georgina?' For a minute Selkirk had been tempted. Georgina remained the most beautiful woman that he had ever seen, and one of the most desirable, but she was not for him. Selkirk remembered the pain of their last meeting, when she had explained that there could never have a future.

'James Montgomery is the master of twenty thousand acres in Berwickshire. His family has known mine for decades. But you, you're nice, but, Andrew, you're only a ploughboy, a farm servant and the son of a farm servant!' The words were all the more cruel for being true and Andrew wished that he could just stand up and run from the house. None of the persecutions that Charles Drongan had inflicted upon him came close to his sister's no-doubt kindly meant words.

'I see.' Selkirk nodded. 'But I am also an officer in the army.'

'You are.' Georgina agreed. 'And a very handsome one too. But you see, Andrew, that does not matter either, not really, because you're not a real officer, not a gentleman.'

The memory was bitter.

Georgina's hand stilled. 'Oh Andrew, this is not the right time to ask that.' Her voice was as melodious as ever, but something had changed. 'That wasn't fair!'

'Perhaps we had better return to the dance,' Selkirk said, 'you are getting cold out here.'

She returned in silence, barely looking at him, and Selkirk sought solace in another whisky. The amber liquid exploded in his stomach, spreading its warm friendship through his veins. Selkirk had another and watched as Georgina allowed another man to sweep her on to the floor. Her laughter mocked him and all his life.

'Fine looking girl, your Georgina.' For all his rotundity, Major Scott had the ability of drifting through the crowd.

'She's not my Georgina,' Selkirk said.

'More yours than any other man's,' Scott smiled as a waltzing couple flicked past. The woman waved with the fingers of her right hand. 'That's my wife by the way.' He threw back his champagne. 'You could still have her. That's Georgina I'm talking about, not my wife. She's spoken for.'

'So is Georgina.' Selkirk's speech was slurred as the whisky bit. 'She belongs to somebody else.'

Scott put a hand to his ear. 'Hark! Did you hear that?' he looked at Selkirk and grinned. 'It was the sound of a cock, crowing! Wasn't it three times that Peter denied Christ before the cock crowed?' He pulled Selkirk into a corner. 'Listen, Selkirk, I've watched you. You did well in South Africa, but your personal life is a mess. You've no friends except rankers and no influence. If you found a woman with position and power, she would push you upward for her own sake.'

'Upward? Upward where?'

'Higher rank, you dimwit! You're young and you have a reputation. Not many people coming back from Africa can say that. If you pulled the right strings, smiled with the right people, you could rise all the way to General rank maybe. Another Hector MacDonald, another Bobs! And Selkirk,' Scott's smile was as sober as a Free Kirk Minister, 'Georgina Drongan does not belong to anybody. She is her own woman, not Montgomery's'

The music stopped then and a press of people pushed past, with Scott's wife taking hold of the major's arm. Tall and slender, she seemed genuinely fond of him, removing the glass from his hand to peck him on the cheek before disappearing again.

'Women.' Scott retrieved his glass. 'Always wanting to change you.' He smiled fondly after his wife. 'As I was saying, Selkirk, Georgina Drongan could help you rise high. We both know that she likes you.'

'She seems to like everybody,' Selkirk pointed out as Georgina walked past, deliberately emphasising the swing of her hips as a leering Lieutenant clung to her arm.

Scott sighed. 'God, man, you've a lot to learn about women. I was watching you out there. You rejected her, so now she's paying you back. She's trying to show you what you could have.'

'And her husband? The master of twenty thousand acres?' Selkirk did not disguise his bitterness.

'Twenty thousand acres? Didn't you hear?' Scott shook his head. 'No you wouldn't. You were far too busy talking to the rankers and fighting the Boer. Montgomery's a gambler. That was the reason for the sudden interest in Georgina. He wanted the Drongan money to pay back his debts. He's not interested in her; or rather, no more interested in her than he is in any of the other women in his life.'

Selkirk sampled another whisky. The sudden surge of sympathy was genuine. 'God. Poor Georgina, does she know?'

'She does now. She's grown up a lot in the last year, has your Georgina.' Scott tapped the glass that Selkirk was holding. Gaslight sparked from the intricate cut of the crystal. 'I'd go easy on that if I were you old boy, she's already got one drunkard in the family, she would not care for another.'

Suddenly there was something pathetic about the tall, beautiful woman who danced with such grace. She looked suddenly vulnerable as she pirouetted among her peers. Selkirk moved toward her, just as Charles Drongan stepped forward.

Chapter Fifteen : Edinburgh - October 1903

'You're not sniffing after my sister again, Selkirk.' Drongan kept his voice low.

Selkirk held out his hand, 'Congratulations on your Victoria Cross, Colonel.' He forced a smile, 'I don't think I ever witnessed a braver act than your attack in Akersdorp.' He heard the murmur of approval from those officers nearby. Some guessed at the animosity between Selkirk and Drongan, although nobody knew the full story. Now here was one of the adversaries offering friendship and forgiveness in the good old British manner.

In such a public place, Drongan could only take Selkirk's hand. 'Thank you, Selkirk,' his grip tightened with every word and once again Selkirk was shocked at the sheer strength of the man. His wounds did not seem to have weakened him at all, although Selkirk had detected a hint of a limp, and he carried his left shoulder slightly higher than his right.

'I was honoured to serve with you sir,' Selkirk saw Georgina watching, hiding her surprise behind a well bred smile, 'and I hope I may do so again sometime.'

'Oh, I hope so too, Selkirk, I hope so too.' Drongan pushed his face closer. 'Perhaps next time my subordinates will not leave all the fighting to me.'

While the officers looked puzzled, for although they did not accept Selkirk as an equal, none doubted his courage, some of the women turned away at this implication of cowardice. Selkirk felt the colour rise in his face as Drongan abruptly dropped his hand and ushered Georgina away.

It was a few minutes before Selkirk could return to his position at the whisky tray, and he added a few more Glenfiddichs to his total as he watched the dancing. They never seemed to tire, these madly energetic officers and their normally languid ladies, but when the faces and dresses began to blur Selkirk decided that he had seen enough of the Regimental Dance and retired outside.

The sentries saluted as he passed, their young faces unfamiliar in the gloom. He thought of all the generations of soldiers that had guarded this castle, from the armoured knights who had fought for Bruce to the long siege under Kirkcaldy of Grange and the redcoats who listened as Bonnie Charlie's pipers screamed defiance along the Royal Mile. No doubt they also worried about women and reputation and the future, although history only recorded their deeds, not their thoughts.

Other dancers also seemed to be leaving, for there were smart uniforms and shimmering silk dresses drifting among the gaunt stone buildings. Selkirk turned aside as one couple engaged in a passionate embrace. The woman was giggling high pitched as they broke the clinch, and glancing over her shoulder to ensure that she was followed, she skipped down the Lang Stairs. The man, tall and powerfully broad in the dim light, reached for her, laughing.

'No, Charlie. Not here!' The woman spoke with the educated tones of breeding, but added some words that would not have been out of place in the barrack room. Charlie replied in a sonorous growl, grappled with her more meaningfully and stopped her squeals with his mouth.

Selkirk turned away. The shenanigans of other people did not interest him.

'Charlie, down there, in that room.' The woman was breathless as she led the way, passing within a yard of Selkirk. The tall man was Charles Drongan, running with his shirt untucked and half the buttons of his trousers unfastened.

So intent on each other that they did not see Selkirk, they stopped to wrestle amorously in the angle between an eighteenth century cannon and the castle wall. The woman was giggling; trying to struggle free of her dress as Charles slid his hands around her hips. There was a slight scrape from the ramparts above, and Selkirk stared drunkenly at the man who crouched there. Ragged and seemingly misshapen, he poised on the sullen stone, sillhouetted against the northern sky like a twentieth century gargoyle.

There was sudden movement as the man jumped, one hand on the broad cloth cap that covered his head. He landed on Drongan's shoulders, knocking him to the ground. The woman screamed, both hands to her mouth. Selkirk started forward. There was a blur of steel, rising and falling, twice, three, four times. He heard the sickening thud of a knife driving into flesh, heard Drongan cry out and saw the spreading stain on the cobbles at his feet. The woman screamed again, high-pitched, and backed against the cold stone wall.

The assailant was muttering as he drove home his knife, grunting with the force of each blow.

'Jesus!' His reaction slowed by alcohol, Selkirk could only stare while the man stabbed Lord Drongan. He saw the knife drawn back for another blow, saw drops of blood flicker on to the woman's dress, then the fumes cleared and he ran forward, his dress boots slithering on the greasy cobbles.

Only when Selkirk was within reach did the man stop. He looked up, face shaded by the cap but predatory eyes gleaming, and spat on his victim. As Selkirk staggered forward the man jumped on to the iron barrel of the cannon, poised for a second and leaped again, to land on the ramparts. Without pausing, he slipped over the wall.

'Charlie! He's killed Charlie!' The woman was hysterical, clutching hold of Selkirk as she added, illogically, 'can you save him?'

Lord Charles Drongan lay face up on the cobbles with the blood pumping from half a dozen wounds in his body. Three years of ugly experience told Selkirk that Drongan was dying, but for the woman's sake he wasted seconds examining him before chasing after the attacker. Hoisting himself up the wall, he looked over the side. The dressed stone dropped away to merge with the basaltic rock on which the castle was built, sheer and black and cold. Selkirk scrambled over, panicked for a second as he thought of the sheer drop beneath him, then his searching feet found a ledge. He stopped to listen.

There were faint scratching sounds to his left, as if somebody was inching down the face of the cliff, so Selkirk headed in that direction. The thought of that terrible drop sucking at his legs unmanned him, so he gagged, with fear rising in his throat. Suddenly Selkirk regretted the whisky and the soft living of the officer's mess.

His foot caught a pebble. It clattered downward, bouncing from ledge to ledge in a seemingly endless descent.

'Jesus.'

Voices from above sounded, echoing hollowly in the night. 'Who's there?' He recognised the voice.

'Selkirk! Somebody's murdered Lord Drongan!'

'I know that, dammit! What are you doing down there?' That was Colonel Elliot's voice.

'The murderer escaped this way, sir. I'm trying to catch him!' Selkirk thought that should be obvious, but thought it best to be diplomatic.

'Can you see him?'

'Can't see a thing, sir.' The clamour had killed Selkirk's concentration. He peered into the dark.

'I'll have a lantern hung down! Wait there!' There was a pause, during which Selkirk moved slowly in the direction from where he had heard the sounds. His boots slipped on the greasy rock and he shuddered as the wind whipped around him. The noises from the castle seemed muffled, while Edinburgh was grumbling beneath. The horrendous drop seemed to suck at his legs, willing him to fall.

There was a sudden scraping, a gasp and yellow light as somebody suspended a hurricane lamp on the end of a rope. The lamp swung, dangerously close to Selkirk's head. 'Can you see anyone yet?'

The light cast shadows that shifted shapes from a man to a tuft of grass and back to a man. There was another ledge a few feet lower down and Selkirk eased on to it, swaying as the wind caught him. He moved slowly forward, shouting directions to whoever held the lantern.

A soft Edinburgh rain pattered down, making the rock even greasier, more dangerous, as Selkirk probed further from the security of the castle wall. The cries of encouragement faded away, then Selkirk flinched as his foot slipped. For a second he balanced, one legged, with both hands gripping a small tree that gripped miraculously to the rock, then he found a foothold and slammed against the rock, shaking.

'Dammit!' Somebody swore loudly and dropped the lantern. It bounced down the hill, casting alternate light and shadow. Selkirk had a single glimpse of a man's face, uglily scarred, with vicious eyes under a flat cap, then the lantern was gone and he was gripping to a shelf on the castle rock, alone with a murderer.

'Captain Selkirk, sir!' Only a sergeant major could create that volume of sound, 'you've to come up now! The Colonel's despatched men all around the rock. The murderer can't get away.'

Thankfully, Selkirk grabbed hold of the rope that uncoiled at his side. He was shivering with cold and reaction when he clambered over the battlements into the waiting crowd of men.

'Did you see him?'

Selkirk nodded. His legs felt suddenly weak so he slid down beside one of the ancient cannons. 'Briefly.' He described the man. 'Small, ugly, with staring eyes.'

'Not much to go by, but he won't get off the rock.' Colonel Elliot shook his head. 'It's a bad business, Selkirk.'

'How's Georgina? Lord Drongan's sister? She'll be badly cut up about it.'

'She is.' Elliot agreed. 'We sent for her husband, and in the meantime Mrs Elliot is caring for her.' He touched Selkirk's shoulder, 'Good of you to think of her Selkirk, for I know that you were not good friends with the family.'

Standing at his back, Major Scott nodded. 'Selkirk knew them both in Africa sir. He cares for his own.'

Chapter Sixteen :Fethan Valley, October 1903

It was not the homecoming that he had expected. The beech tree of his childhood looked stark against the dull autumn sky, while the Fethan Water had shrunk somehow, although the sound was the same. Even the hills were different, bleaker, lacking the urgency and colour that he had grown accustomed to during his years in South Africa. . Selkirk remembered the last time he had been here, when he had left to become a man and only Jenny had remained to wave goodbye. He strode along the once familiar, rutted track and halted nervously outside the door of the cottage where he had been born.

He rapped once, noticing the peeling paintwork on the door and the grass that pushed stubbornly through the cracked paving of the garden path. There was nervous sweat dampening his palms and he looked eastward, to that gap in the hills that Tam and he always promised to explore. He had travelled much further now, half way around the world and back, yet he felt that he was returning with nothing resolved. In a second he would see the familiar face of his father, hear the welcome from Jenny's lips. Footsteps sounded inside and he took a deep breath to still his suddenly racing heart.

The door opened and a stranger stared at him, wordless.

For a second Selkirk did not know what to say. There had never been strangers in the Fethan. 'I'm looking for the Selkirks? Andrew Selkirk?'

The man's expression did not shift. 'Gone. Evicted.' He was unshaven, with small, bright eyes. 'Lord Drongan didnae like them.'

'Lord Drongan?' Selkirk thought of the tall, slender Lord of his youth, but of course Charles had been the last Lord Drongan. 'Lord Charles Drongan?'

'Aye. We go through a lot of lords here. The Fethan's gey hard on gentry, and suchlike.' The eyes moved slowly over the officer's uniform that Selkirk wore. Selkirk had not hoped to impress anybody with his success, for the Fethan folk were not an impressionable lot, but he had hoped to be accepted back into the family.

'Do you know where they are now?'

'Gone. Out of the Fethan. Good riddance. They were a bad lot, by all accounts. The son ran off for a soldier.' The man closed his door firmly.

Selkirk closed his eyes. Even in death, it seemed, Charles Drongan had the power to hurt. He must have hurried back to the Fethan as soon as he had become Lord and taken out his spite on Selkirk's family. But where would they go? His father had been a Fethan man all his life while his mother would refuse to live anywhere else. Tam might know; if Tam remained in the neighbourhood.

Tam Wilson had been Selkirk's boyhood friend, and was now the third horseman in Ettrick Mains Farm, some ten miles outside the Fethan. He greeted Selkirk with vague suspicion at first, then relaxed as he realised that some of the old Drew Selkirk still lurked behind the ribbons and uniform.

'I never expected to see you again, Drew,' he said, once the initial hand shaking and 'how have you beens' were out of the way. 'I heard that you were killed in Africa.' He shook his head. 'Then there was that terrible business with Lord Drongan. Bad that, he was a good landlord to us.'

Selkirk hid his frown. 'Charles Drongan? You hated him as much as I did.'

'No, not me.' Tam had grown up lean and straight, with hands the size and colour of spades and a wispy-haired wife who stared at this officer who had come to see her husband. Selkirk could hear a baby crying inside their cottage. 'Once you left, things quietened down round here.' His smile was slow, 'man we were the wild ones, were we not? Remember when we poached that deer and sold it to old Rutherford? I'm ashamed of the things we did then, Drew, really ashamed.'

Selkirk felt some of his reason for existing slide away. Through all the campaigns and carnage of the South African War, he had drawn his strength from the Fethan. Memories of the hills and the river, the moist air and the freedom, the scents and the people had kept him sane. It was for this that he had fought, and now even Tam had changed.

196

'Maybe you're right, Tam, but do you know where my family have gone? They were evicted.' He felt, rather than saw, the shock on the face of Tam's wife.

Tam looked away. 'I heard and I'm sorry for it, Drew, but Lord Drongan was within his rights. He said that they were a bad influence in the area, what with you running away to join the army and then Jenny getting herself with child.'

So that was why Jenny had not written! She was ashamed! 'With child? Well good for her. She'll make a marvellous mother.' Selkirk felt a glow of genuine pleasure as he thought of Jenny. Although she was the youngest, she had always looked after Selkirk, often deflecting the wrath of his mother from his person and concealing his many transgressions.

'She's not married to the father. It's a sin.' That was the first time that Tam's wife had spoken.

'A sin?' Selkirk thought of the concentration camps on the veldt, and the drifting smoke from burning farms. He remembered Rab Mackie with his arm blown off, and that legless trunk in the Modder Drift. 'A sin to create life?' Suddenly he had to be out of this place with its stunted parochialism. He controlled his anger. 'Well, we'll have to disagree there.'

'Lord Drongan did not permit any of his farms to employ that family. I heard that they were in Ettrick.' Tam's expression suddenly changed, as if something from the past had landed, fleetingly, on his shoulder. 'I liked Jenny too, Drew, but she did bring it on herself.'

'Ettrick eh?' Selkirk held out his hand. 'Thanks Tam.' He shook hands firmly, knowing that they had drifted too far apart ever to be friends again. Africa and the Fethan had moulded different men.

The first time Selkirk had visited Ettrick he had been awed by the size of the place. Now he realised that it was only a small Scottish town, with ponderous stone buildings, half a dozen tall-chimneyed mills and as many churches. The people, close faced and suspicious, carried their business close to their chests while talking about rugby and the textile trade. If anything, they were even less tolerant of strangers than the inhabitants of the Fethan had been, but they fawned to this decorated officer from the African war. One even offered to point the direction to the tenement in which the Selkirk family lived, but lost his enthusiasm when no tip was proffered.

'Jenny!' ' Selkirk stood in the stair well and bellowed at the top of his voice. He listened to the echoes, screwed up his face at the stench of damp and human urine and carefully mounted the stairs.

There were three doors on each landing, most complete with names. The very last door of the third floor was open, and a thin, worried looking woman peered out. 'Was that you shouting? You might have wakened young Andy here.' If nothing else, Jenny had retained her spirit. It showed in the fine light of her eyes, and in the teeth that were still white and even. 'What do you want?'

'Is that any way to talk to your brother, home from the wars?' Selkirk grinned as Jenny stepped back, automatically tidying her hair.

'Drew?' her voice was uncertain, 'Oh, please Drew, go away. You can't see me now. Not like this.'

'Not like what?' Selkirk held her, feeling the lack of flesh on her bones. 'Man, Jenny, there's nothing of you. We'll have to feed you up.'

Shaking her head, Jenny looked down as Selkirk eased into the flat. A scattering of newspapers covered the floorboards, and the single table was bare of a cloth. There was a box bed in one corner of the room, where a baby threshed amidst a tangle of ragged covers.

'Where's the others? Where's father and the girls?' Selkirk tried to speak quietly as he moved toward the baby. 'This is Andy, is it? Named after me, I hope?'

'Don't touch him. He's sick.' Jenny's eyes were heavy, red-rimmed with exhaustion or tears, but her breath was sweet and she kept her back straight as she walked.

'Oh? What did the doctor say?' Not having known the baby, Selkirk was more concerned with Jenny. In his limited experience, babies were nearly always sick, or being sick, or about to be sick.

Jenny shook her head. She sat on the only chair. 'Oh Drew, why did you come here? You shouldn't see us like this.'

'Is that right?' Selkirk glanced around the room. He saw no food and precious little else. What light there was filtered through a tiny window that looked on to the grimy stone wall of a textile mill. 'Where are the others, then? Father? Agatha and Margaret?'

There was a silence, broken only by the restless stirring of young Andy and the harsh clatter of machinery from the mill. At length Jenny looked up. 'Father's dead, Drew. He died the same day that Andy was born. Agatha and Margaret are both married now. They don't speak to me any more. Not since Andy.' Although Jenny tried to sound brave, her voice faltered at the end.

Selkirk closed his eyes. His father was dead. The quiet, kindly man who had always been dominated by the relentless will of his wife, yet who had lived a decent, honest life, had died. He must have been a deeply disappointed man, with his only son lost to the army and his favourite daughter giving birth to an illegitimate child.

'Well, we make a nice pair, don't we? I'm sorry about father, but he would have hated to live in the town anyway.' Selkirk had seen too much death and suffering to allow his emotions to show, while his relationship with his other sisters had never been deep. He remembered them carrying tales about him to their mother purely to get him in trouble. Maybe that had all been a very long time ago, but childhood memories hurt.

'All right, let's get this mess sorted out.' Selkirk glanced around the room. He could smell the rat droppings, while dry rot spread its fungus through the bare plaster of the walls. 'You still didn't tell me what the doctor said about Andy.'

Jenny no longer disguised her tears. She looked at this tall officer, stripping away the uniform to find the brother that she had known so well. 'He wouldn't see me,' she whispered.

'Oh?' Selkirk felt a sudden surge of anger. Was this the Scotland for which he had fought? 'Why not?'

'Because I've no money. And because Andy was born out of wedlock.' Great tears rolled down Jenny's face.

'Is that so?' Selkirk stood up. 'Well, if he won't see you, he'll bloody well see me! Take me to him.'

'When?' Jenny dashed an arm across her face. She had been alone for so long now, trying to be brave, that it was good to allow somebody else to take over.

'Now.'

Jenny remembered her brother as a brash youth always getting into trouble. Now Captain Selkirk took command. He waited until Jenny fed and cleaned Andy, then escorted her to the other side of town, where fine villas with neat gardens proclaimed the respectability of their owner. The doctor's house was two storied, with dormer windows and an impressive entrance. It stood at the intersection of two streets, with stained glass on the windows and blue slates on the roof. The maid opened the door to Selkirk's repeated knockings. Jenny remained at the gate, hidden by a neatly trimmed privet hedge.

'The surgery's shut,' the maid started, then noticed the officer's uniform and array of medal ribbons, and curtseyed deeply. 'Oh I'm sorry, sir, I thought you might just be a mill worker. They often come here, bothering the doctor with their complaints.' She was a youngish woman with large brown eyes that she used on Selkirk.

'Terrible.' Selkirk sympathised, 'they shouldn't let people like that into decent homes.' He allowed the maid to survey his height, tan and rank. 'Could you tell the doctor that Captain Andrew Selkirk, DSO, of Selkirk's Reivers and the Royal Borderers, is here to see him?' He gave his broadest smile. 'There's a good girl now.'

The maid ushered Selkirk into a large, comfortably furnished waiting room. After she lit the hissing gas light and bustled away to fetch the doctor, Selkirk brought Jenny inside. She perched uncomfortably on the edge of one of the chairs and wiped her tears away with a shaking hand. All the time, she was juggling her baby, muttering soft words and throwing Selkirk an occasional wondering glance.

They heard the heavy footsteps of the doctor before he arrived. He opened the door, still fastening a necktie over his stiff white collar and with his suit incorrectly buttoned. Ignoring Jenny, he smiled to Selkirk. 'Captain Andrew Selkirk? And may I congratulate you on your DSO, sir, richly deserved, I'm sure.'

Selkirk grasped the damp hand that was extended to him. 'I am Andrew Selkirk, doctor, but it's a different Andrew Selkirk that I want you to see.' Without releasing the doctor's hand, Selkirk indicated Jenny. 'This lady is holding your patient. He is also named Andrew.'

For a moment it seemed as if the doctor would refuse, but with Captain Andrew Selkirk, DSO, grasping his hand, he decided to co-operate. Selkirk stood over him while he examined the baby, while Jenny hovered anxiously at his back.

'There's nothing wrong with this baby that good nourishment would not cure,' the doctor announced. He glanced at Jenny, 'Are you the mother?'

Jenny admitted the fact with a guilty nod.

'Then you should be ashamed of yourself. Letting your son get to this condition.' The doctor seemed genuinely angry as he faced Selkirk, 'and you should be even more ashamed sir, treating your wife like this. You're a fine husky man, and she's nothing but skin and bone.'

'She's not my wife,' Selkirk found himself liking the doctor a little more, 'she's my sister.'

'I see. And her husband?'

Selkirk glanced at Jenny, who shook her head very quickly. 'Dead,' he said quietly. 'He died while I was in South Africa, leaving my sister with child.'

'Oh.' The doctor was a stout, fussy looking man who had spent the best part of his working life worrying about the immorality of mill girls. Faced with the unfortunate, but obviously respectable, sister of an army officer, the dedicated caring that had originally drawn him to the profession emerged. 'I will have to examine your sister, Captain Selkirk. She is very underweight.'

Jenny glanced desperately at her brother, obviously about to refuse, but gathered her courage together and followed the doctor into his private preserve. While they were gone, Selkirk reminded them of his presence by whistling loudly. Although he had no desire to embarrass Jenny, he was quite prepared to burst in on the surgery if he felt she was not being treated properly.

After Selkirk paid the bill, they left with a prescription for beef tea and other nourishing food, which Selkirk purchased from the Borders Co-operative store. He dumped the collection of paper bags and cardboard boxes on the table and helped Jenny cook. Amazed at the condescension of her now awesome brother, Jenny ate all she was given, still keeping her eyes averted.

Few British officers managed to exist on their pay alone, but by shunning most social activities and living as frugally as possible, Selkirk had amassed some savings. He could think of no better way of spending them than on Jenny.

'You'll not be living here then.' Once he had started, Selkirk decided to make a whole new existence for Jenny. He glanced around the room, dark with the late afternoon gloom. 'I'll wash up and you'll pack up. We're off to a hotel for the night until we find somewhere better.'

'A hotel?' Now she had eaten her most substantial meal in over a year, Jenny already looked better, but a hotel was far above her expectations. 'We can't do that.' She gestured to her clothes. 'I've nothing to wear, Drew. Lord Drongan said we had to leave right away, before we even had time to get our things.'

'Aye? Well Charles Drongan won't be bothering you again.' Selkirk decided that it was not the best time to go into details. 'Are there any clothes shops in Ettrick?'

'Of course there are.' Jenny looked amazed at his ignorance. 'There's Graham's in the High Street. Why do you ask?'

Selkirk grinned to her. 'You'll see.'

The assistant in charge of ladyswear was delighted to attend to the sister of an army officer. 'There was a house fire, you see,' Selkirk lied easily, 'so we need a complete wardrobe. Two of everything,' he smiled at the awed expression on Jenny's face, and repeated, 'absolutely everything. Including underwear.' Remembering the pleasure of sliding Georgina's most intimate articles of clothing down her thighs, he broadened his smile. 'And none of your second rate rubbish. Silk, if you stock it, or only the finest linen if not!' This time Jenny looked scandalised, so he hugged her close.

'No, you can't,' Jenny whispered.

'Yes, we can.' Selkirk waved to the assistant. He felt the old urge to be mischievous for its own sake. 'I've many years of neglect to make up for. And clothes for the baby too.'

'What a lovely little boy.' Forty years old and comfortably plump, the assistant smiled with genuine pleasure at young Andy. 'You must be very proud of your son.'

'My nephew,' Selkirk corrected. 'And my Godson. Or he will be soon.' He felt Jenny's eyes on him and grinned. For the first time since he returned to Scotland he was enjoying himself.

Leaving Jenny to preen herself in front of the mirror, Selkirk sauntered along to the Cross Keys Hotel and booked them into two adjacent rooms. The hotel was surprisingly full, 'some special party, sir,' said the booking clerk, 'but we can always find room for such a distinguished officer as yourself, sir.' By the time Selkirk returned to the shop, Jenny was admiring Andy's new appearance, 'Drew, I don't know how we can thank you.'

'Don't be silly.' Feeling for his wallet, Selkirk peeled off the top note. He did not allow Jenny see how little remained. 'Is that enough? If it's not, just send me the bill. And could you have the rest delivered please. We're at the Cross Keys Hotel.' He squeezed Jenny's arm under his. 'The name is Selkirk. Captain Andrew Selkirk.' He hustled Jenny out before she could protest.

'Drew. We can't stay there. It's too expensive!' Jenny's shock lasted only until Selkirk steered her into the foyer of the Cross Keys Hotel, reputedly the finest hotel in the Central Borders. Familiar with the extravagances of Cape Town and Pretoria, Selkirk was less impressed than Jenny, accepting as his due the attentions of uniformed staff and dark-suited manager.

Their rooms were side by side, lit by soft gaslight and furnished in the most modern taste. Knowing that his funds would not last for long, Selkirk was determined to make the most of them. Smiling, he carried a now laughing Jenny over the threshold like a bride and deposited her on a bed so soft that she sunk almost without trace.

'Bathroom through there,' he told her, 'and I'm next door. We dine at eight and I want you bright, shiny and as pretty as a picture.' His pleasure was genuine when he looked down on his sister lying in disarray on the bed. 'And don't worry about young Andy. The hotel has its own nanny to look after children. There will just be the two of us tonight.'

Selkirk was still smiling when he entered his own room and walked straight into the tall man who stood there, smoking a long cheroot.

Chapter Seventeen : Ettrick – November 1903

Blue smoke hazed his head as the man gazed down on Selkirk, his slow smile amused. 'You're living high for a ploughboy, aren't you? And separate bedrooms? That's not the same Corporal Selkirk that tumbled Marie in Kimberley!' The Arizona drawl was as slow and relaxed as ever, but Donnelly looked more prosperous.

'Have you forgotten how to salute a superior officer?' Selkirk was laughing as he shook Donnelly's hand, 'but it's good to see you again. I thought you would be poking cattle in America, or digging for gold in some other unknown place, miles from the back of nowhere.' He stepped back, 'Man, you're looking fine though, all fancy suit and expensive cigar. And is that a diamond tie pin?'

'Diamond it is, and the suit's the best that dollars can buy.' Donnelly looked a little puzzled as he surveyed Selkirk. 'How about you, Selks? You seem to be living the high life yourself.'

It was easy to talk to Donnelly, but while Selkirk explained his situation, some of his good mood evaporated. He had been so busy making Jenny feel better that he had nearly forgotten the death of his father, but now the grief came mingled with the guilt and sorrow.

Donnelly listened, nodding his head when required. 'Bad business, Selks. I'm sorry for your loss. And for your sister; you always spoke highly of her.' He pulled hard on his cheroot and exhaled scented smoke into the room. 'Fact is, though, we've all done it Selks. We've both loved them and left them and thought nothing more about it. Maybe we've caused a few tragedies in our own lives.'

Selkirk narrowed his eyes at this new viewpoint. 'They were easy ladies though,' he protested.

'And we were easy men. I doubt there's a whisker's worth of difference between the two.' Donnelly shrugged and slumped into one of the two vast armchairs that graced the room. 'We're all human, but it seems to be mostly the women that pay the price.'

Selkirk was silent. He had accepted Jenny's mistake as a weakness of character and forgiven her at once, but Donnelly's words made him realise the hypocrisy. There was nothing to forgive, and no weakness except that of being a human. 'You're right of course,' he conceded, then grinned, suddenly feeling guilty himself and even closer to Jenny than he had ever been before. 'Thank you.' Donnelly made a mock bow from his seat. 'And now, Captain Selks, you can tell me why you invited me here?'

'What?' Selkirk sat in the other armchair. 'I didn't invite you. I didn't even know that I was coming here until an hour ago.'

Donnelly shook his head. Reaching inside his jacket, he produced a square envelope and unfolded a letter. 'Dear Donnelly,' he read slowly, 'it is my pleasure to invite you over to Scotland. Please arrive for the first week of November. You will find that a room has been reserved for you at the Cross Keys Hotel, Ettrick.' Donnelly looked over to Selkirk, 'there's no signature, but I naturally imagined that it was from you.'

'Donnelly,' Selkirk leaned closer, 'I might manage to pay my bill, and Jenny's for a couple of nights, but after that I'm flat, stony broke. I have no idea who sent that letter, but it certainly was not me.'

'How about the others then?' Donnelly looked more amused than confused. 'You don't know what I'm talking about, do you?' Abruptly rising, he pointed his cheroot at Selkirk. 'You're slipping my boy. There was a time when you would have scouted this hotel and marked every entrance and exit, and every guest. Now you just walk in, and with that beautiful sister of yours too, without checking anything.'

Jenny stood in the doorway, slightly awkward in her grand surroundings. Bathed and with her hair washed and brushed, she looked respectable, but her new cream dress was too large for her, and she still looked desperately tired. 'I heard voices,' she said, 'but I didn't think you would mind. Should I have knocked?'

Selkirk felt as if his heart was breaking. This was his favourite sister, and she was confused and hurt and lost. 'No.' He stood up. 'This is Donnelly, my old friend from Kimberley and the Reivers.'

'Mr Donnelly,' Jenny held out her hand.

'Walter.' Donnelly glanced at Selkirk. 'Or Walt if you prefer.'

'Walter? I didn't know you were called Walter.' Selkirk grinned at this new revelation.

'Don't be impolite Drew.' It was the old Jenny that put him in his place, 'I must apologise for my brother, Walt,' she used the name with deliberate emphasis. 'He can be very childlike sometimes.' When she gave Selkirk a glare that could have curdled milk, he wondered if she was quite so lost as he had believed. 'However, he has told me all about you, in the few letters he bothered to write.'

'Not all about me, I hope,' Donnelly's smile hid mischief that Selkirk had not noticed before, 'for then you would certainly not wish to meet me.'

Jenny's laugh was so spontaneous that Selkirk grinned. He saw her toss her newly washed hair and glance over Donnelly appraisingly. 'Don't worry, Walter. My brother would leave out the bits he did not want me to know. But I can guess what sort of thing you two have been up to.'

Selkirk felt his mouth open. Was this his Jenny? The little minx had only just met Donnelly and already she was flirting with him. Suddenly he realised, belatedly, that she had also grown up during his absence. She was a mother and a woman. As she laughed at a sally of Donnelly's, and touched his arm, he realised exactly how much of a woman she had become. For a moment he was shocked at the thought of his sister acting in such a manner, then he remembered young Andy sleeping in the adjoining room and examined Jenny with new attention.

How could he have missed it before? She was thin, certainly, but well shaped, with the wide hips of a woman and nicely proportioned breasts. She was attractive too; no, he corrected himself, she was very attractive, with her high cheekbones and straight nose. When she smiled like that, with the tip of her tongue protruding through her slightly parted teeth, he was not surprised that Donnelly should respond.

He watched as his sister and his friend talked, ignoring him completely. Twice he tried to interrupt, but both times they brushed him aside, and when Andy began to cry, he left the room. He knew little about babies, but if he could organise the Reivers, he could surely change and wash a child.

Jenny rescued the screaming Andy five minutes later, laughingly rebuked Selkirk for his lack of skill and quite calmly introduced Donnelly to her son.

'This is Andy,' she said, 'I was never married to the father and I will never see him again.' She faced Donnelly with her stubborn chin protruding in a manner Selkirk found profoundly familiar.

Donnelly picked up Andy with a skill that told of past practice. 'He's beautiful,' he said, choosing exactly the right thing to say to any new mother, 'and as you've no interference, you can mould him properly.' He nodded toward Selkirk. 'Just make sure he doesn't turn out like your brother.'

'My terrible brother that you've travelled thousands of miles to see.' Jenny's smile encompassed them both, and she listened while Donnelly explained his presence. 'So if Drew didn't send that note, then who did?'

'The same person that sent the others,' Donnelly said. 'You'll see what I mean in the dining room.' He leaned back in Jenny's seat and lit another cheroot, looking very pleased with himself. His eyes followed her as she bent to wash Andy.

The Cross Keys had been built nearly a century before as a staging hotel, and had expanded when Walter Scott's novels had generated interest in the Borders. Donnelly led the way to the dining room, as he had so often guided them across the veldt, and Selkirk walked arm in arm with Jenny. Deep pile carpets muffled their footsteps in the long corridors, on whose walls hung frowning portraits of characters from Scott's books. There was a creaking staircase that led to the ground floor, and glazed doors opening into a splendid room with two chandeliers and tall french windows. There were some thirty tables set for dinner, and a hubbub of noise and conversation.

The nearest man grinned mightily when Selkirk entered the room. 'There's the Captain! Stand to attention boys.' Applewood appeared quite at home in the black dinner jacket and it seemed that the Reivers had taken over Ettrick.

Many of them were there, smiling in genuine pleasure or standing with habitual wooden faces. There was red haired Mackie, with one sleeve empty but a welcome on his face, Burke the witty Connaught man, Thomson the Welshman and John Blackdown the massive saddler from Somerset. There were Fairweather, Pert and Ogilvie, looking uneasy in their formal suits and as brown faced and lean as ever. There was Kirky Macpherson, supple as a sprig of his own Badenoch heather, with his perennial sunburn at last cleared. He looked small beside McGann the Ulsterman, who seemed to have completely recovered from his shoulder wound.

Selkirk looked at them all with a mixture of pride and affection. They had been his men, his Reivers. However he noted the gaps in the ranks. None of the Australians were present, not Grey or Cobb or the lanky Smith. Nor were any of the serving Royal Borderers there; Hetherington or Charlton, utterly reliable Northumbrians. There was no Haig, which might be a blessing, or Campbell, or Newman, or any of the men who remained behind in Africa, by choice or fortune of war, buried on the veldt or the scorching Kalahari or the dark forests of the north.

'Stand easy, men.' They broke ranks to talk to him, and to lift Jenny's baby and pass him from hand to calloused hand. They mocked Selkirk's uniform and teased the waitresses who attempted to restore order, and only when Selkirk took control did the noise subside. They returned to their seats, leaving Jenny laughing and breathless and Andy in Blackdown's arms.

As relieved waitresses scurried to serve them, Selkirk asked if anybody knew why they were there. There were blank looks, a ribald remark from Mackie that was followed by an immediate apology to Jenny from Macpherson and the shaking of many heads.

'We thought you invited us sir,' Pert explained. Young Andy had been passed to him, and he balanced the baby with as much aplomb as he handled a horse or rifle. 'We all thought the same.'

Only when everybody was adequately fed and watered did the maitre-domo approach Selkirk, 'I understand that you are all here for the Installation sir?'

'The Installation?' Selkirk repeated, but Jenny kicked him under the table.

'Who told you that?' All of Jenny's uncertainty had vanished with the attention of Donnelly and the Reivers. She now looked very much at home in the hotel.

'The gentleman who made the reservations, madam.' The maitre-domo remained unruffled. 'He said you would all be remaining for two nights. Except yourself, Captain Selkirk. It seems that you were booked in twice, once by the gentleman, and once by yourself. ' He glanced at Jenny, 'there was however, no mention of a lady, or a child. I presume that they should be billed separately?'

'Of course.' Selkirk said. If somebody else was paying his bill, he could afford to pay for Jenny.

'Are neither of you going to ask then?' Jenny shook her head, 'I don't know. You men and your ridiculous pride.' Leaning forward, she put a small hand on the maitre-domo's sleeve. 'This invitation was a surprise. Could you tell us who is paying for everything?'

'Of course, madam. It was Captain James Montgomery. He is being installed as the new Lord Drongan tomorrow.'

Chapter Eighteen :Ettrick – November 1903

The Scottish Borders is an area rich in tradition. Every town and most villages possess a proud heritage of bloodshed, battle and butchery that they have distilled into a week-long pageant of entertainment. Peebles has its Beltane, Selkirk its Common Riding and Ettrick its Ettrick Fair and Rantin' Maggie Nicht. The story behind each is long and complicated, with as many twists and turns as a Border burn, but the locals, be they Gutter Bluids of Peebles or Trickians of Ettrick, remained immensely possessive of their own town. Every Trickian knew the story of Rantin Maggie, a local woman who had helped rally the townsfolk to repel an English assault during the Rough Wooing, and who had fought at the battle of Hadden Rigg.

> *'Maggie ranted a' the lads to fight the foe sae sair*
> *And when her arms were cutted off she ranted a' the mair!'*

Ettrick, however, possessed a second ceremony that created nearly as much pride. As the largest town within the ancient Lordship of Drongan, Ettrick was the natural focal spot for the Installation of the Lord. The ceremony followed a pattern that had remained unchanged for at least four hundred years, with certain aspects stretching back far longer, so that some Kirk ministers had refused to participate in events that they thought so pagan that they were positively lewd.

Naturally these ancient practices were the most popular among the Trickians, who hid a native bawdiness behind the dour conservatism that they presented to strangers. For sheer bacchanal roistering, the evening of any Border festival is hard to equal, but even the most toughened veteran of the common ridings reeled before the prospect of a Drongan Installation. It was said that more illegitimate babies were created that night than in any month of the year, while alcoholic drink was consumed in vast quantities.

Naturally the Reivers looked forward delightedly to playing a full part in the Installation of Lord Drongan, particularly as they were not paying a penny for the privilege.

The morning traditionally began with a procession to the High Kirk of Ettrick, which stood on an ancient pagan site high above the rugby pitch. Selkirk remembered his mother's fury when he climbed up the surrounding rowan trees as a youngster, and still flushed at the memory of the public retribution that had followed. The trees remained huge and gnarled with age and the sin that they had witnessed, but he no longer had the desire to clamber up the branches.

'See these trees?' Jenny told Andy, pointing to the branches that dripped moisture from the morning mist. 'Your uncle used to climb to the very top! Wasn't that naughty of him? You won't do that though, will you?'

'Of course he will, given the chance.' Donnelly had fought off a queue of hard-bitten Reivers for the privilege of carrying the baby. 'Getting into trouble seems to be what young Selkirks do best.'

Spread out among the crowd, the Reivers waited for the procession to pass. The good and the great and the invited gentry of half the Borders had gathered in the grounds of the ruined Abbey before walking in solemn dignity along the High Street of Ettrick. Led by the minister and under the shadow of the same huge Celtic cross, under which Rantin Maggie had rallied the men of the Lordship at Hadden Rigg, they ignored the stares of the curious peasantry.

Immediately behind the minister marched the Lord Provost of Ettrick and the Lord Lieutenant of the County, closely followed by half a dozen riders of the Ettrick and Cheviot Militia, before the body of gentry appeared. Many were red faced and panting, for on their shoulders they bore a wooden platform, on which sat the soon-to-be installed Lord and his Lady.

Selkirk spent a few minutes studying the faces of the militia riders, before deciding that none were familiar. They all seemed to be young and fresh faced, the Callants of the town rather than men who had ridden across the African veldt.

Sitting on the elaborately carved Lord's Chair, James Montgomery appeared to be in his element. Heir to the Lordship of Drongan by right of marriage to Georgina, he was tall and handsome and debonair, with his carefully clipped moustache and the uniform of a militia Captain. So why had he not only invited, but also paid for so many of the Reivers to be present? Had he wanted them to see his ultimate triumph? Looking at him, Selkirk remembered Montgomery's fist smashing into his face. There was no future for Selkirk on the Fethan once Montgomery became Lord Drongan.

Nonetheless, Selkirk did not spend much time concentrating on Montgomery, for at his side Georgina looked as composed as any queen. A Drongan by blood and looks, she was the true heir to the Lordship and the crowd knew it. As she passed they howled their appreciation with that two-syllabled cheer that was unique to Ettrick and always raised the hairs on the back of Selkirk's neck. Their devotion was genuine, for many had known Georgina as a girl, and most appreciated that she had led a team of nurses to treat the wounded in Africa.

Georgina responded regally to their loyalty, lifting her hand to the baying proletariat. Her dress of pure white silk trimmed with gold shimmered every time she moved, so she appeared more like an angel than a woman of flesh, bone and desire. Twice she touched the Drongan Cross that hung in splendour around her neck. This cross was so old that even antiquarians hesitated to date it, but some said that St Cuthbert himself had first worn it. Local folklore claimed that only the Lady of Drongan could hold it, so there were one or two among the crowd who mumbled about bad fortune, as the Installation had not yet taken place.

'Doesn't she look well?' Jenny lifted Andy high above her head. 'Take a long look Andy, for you won't see many Installations.'

Georgina must have caught the movement. She deliberately turned in her seat to wave to the baby, a gesture that pleased the crowd, who roared again, 'Hoo-rah! Hoo-rah! Hoo-rah!' the double bark of the Ettrick hound that had sounded from Carham Field to Philliphaugh and had echoed in diminishing volume around the butchered king at Flodden. Georgina's eyes met Selkirk's, opened slightly wider, and then she turned away. She touched the arm of her husband, whispered something and they both laughed. Montgomery kissed her soundly and the crowd cheered once more. 'Hoo-rah! Hoo-rah! Hoo-rah!'

'They seem happy together.' Jenny eased Andy down. 'You must be pleased to see her again, Drew, after you meeting her in Africa.'

Selkirk exchanged glances with Donnelly, who shook his head, once. 'Yes, we spoke once or twice.'

'I know. She told me all about it.' There were still tired lines around Jenny's eyes, and strain showed in her mouth, but she had brightened up considerably over the last day. 'It was Georgina, or should I say, Lady Drongan, who told me where you were. She wrote to say that you were in hospital but would recover.'

Selkirk relived the memory of Georgina walking into a ward of sick, naked men during the terrible enteric outbreak of early 1900. 'She did her bit,' he said.

'She didn't actually nurse you, did she?' Jenny looked shocked at the thought. 'I mean, she wouldn't do any of the, the necessary bits, did she?' She searched for words that would convey her meaning without upsetting the delicacy of Georgina's gentle breeding.

Selkirk helped her out. 'Yes, she washed naked men and emptied stinking bedpans,' he told her brutally. Donnelly's angry glare carried its own intriguing message.

There was some difficulty when the procession mounted the steps of the church, but they managed eventually, and the chosen few filed inside. A tolerant man, the minister allowed the great, iron studded doors to be thrown back so that the masses could have an insight into the lives of their betters. The ceremony was brief, with a prayer of benediction for the Lordship, five hymns and a splashing of Holy Water on the heads of the soon-to-be-installed couple. Once they emerged, arm in arm at the top of the stairs, the crowd cheered again.

'Is that it then? Can we get drunk now?' Applewood voiced the question that was uppermost in the mind of most of the Reivers.

Selkirk shook his head. 'It's hardly started. There is a procession, then the Installation ceremony on the Green, then the fancy dress competition, games and frolics and drunken debauchery.'

'Which you won't be taking part in, Andrew Selkirk,' Jenny said severely, and laughed. 'Much!' Yet it was Donnelly to whom she smiled.

Having been blessed by the Kirk, Montgomery and Georgina now mounted horses and led a great cavalcade around the bounds of the town. Following an ancient route, they traditionally stopped at certain spots to shout the Ettrick Slogan, which was once a warning to scare off any neighbour who might dare to trespass on Ettrick soil. Some places had to be ridden at the gallop, the Tweed was forded in a curtain of spray, and then they touched on various landmarks with long wands of peeled ash.

'What's the purpose of that?' Donnelly wondered. Being an American, he was both fascinated and amused by the centuries-old tradition.

'They are maintaining the lands of Ettrick,' Jenny explained. 'You see, at one time all the men had to know the boundaries of the town, including the common grazing land. That way outsiders, or stoorifeet as the Trickians call them, could not encroach. In the olden days the men used to beat the boys at these places.'

'That would help them remember,' Donnelly agreed. 'Nice traditions you have here.'

'The last Lord, Charles Drongan, wanted to revive that idea. I don't know what James Montgomery thinks.' Jenny pulled Andy closer to her breast. 'He's getting hungry, so if you gentlemen would excuse me, I'll have to return to the hotel room for a while.'

The city fathers had allowed a certain relaxation of the drinking laws during the Installation Ceremony, so that those licensed establishments that native Trickians owned were permitted to open all day. The Reivers were not alone in making full use of this freedom.

'Things are becoming lively,' Donnelly observed as a group of singing Trickians surged out of a doorway, men and women together.

'They'll get livelier still,' Selkirk promised.

There were games on the rugby pitch, tug of war, foot races, horse races and other sports that were less salubrious. There was always a maiden versus wives rugby game, where old scores were paid off as wives met suspected mistresses in face-scratching and hair-tugging conflict. There was also a boxing booth, where Selkirk watched local Callants being beaten to bloodied disaster by a granite eyed professional from Dublin. Tempted to enter the competition himself, he was upstaged by Blackdown, who accepted all that the Dubliner had to offer, then felled him with a single punch. The crowd cheered the muscular man from Somerset, and more than one Ettrick girl slipped towards him to offer more meaningful congratulations.

All these festivities were interesting, but did not divert Selkirk from the true reason for the gathering. By the end of the day his enemy, James Montgomery, would be Lord Drongan, married to Georgina and he would be exiled for life.

The prospect of returning to the Fethan had kept Selkirk sane through two and a half years of war. Although he was now aware of the faults of the Borders, he could not think of a future anywhere else. He was Drew Selkirk of the Fethan; without the Fethan, who would he be?

'The crowd is restless Selks.' Donnelly pointed to the park gates, from where there was a general drift of people.

'They're going to see the main event.' Suddenly Selkirk felt sick. What had been the point of all his strivings? He was a man out of place, for if he no longer belonged in the Fethan, he had never been comfortable in the officer's mess of the Royal Borderers. His rank was a sham, the product of a unique war that was now finished. Was he destined to moulder in a captain's rank, shunned by his peers, sneered at by the troops, unwanted, underemployed, despised, until he retired? He was no career soldier, but he had no other trade, for no self-respecting farmer would employ a ploughman who had once been in the ranks.

'The Installation?' Donnelly touched his shoulder. 'Come on then Selks. After all, the man himself invited us.'

'Round the boys up, will you?' Selkirk felt very old and immensely weary, 'and we'll see this thing through.'

From time immemorial until the early eighteenth century, the Lords of Drongan had lived hard by Ettrick. Their original dun had been on the largest island in the River Tweed, which ran so close to the town that its autumnal floods habitually immersed the High

Street. Through time, the dun had been enlarged and improved, burned and destroyed, built and altered, until the 15th Lord had built himself a much grander edifice on newly enclosed land. Never a family to give anything away, the Drongans had held on to the original island, but allowed the castle to crumble into ruin. The 22nd Lord, Georgina's grandfather, had sold the remaining stones to the town for building material, so now the island was bare save for unkempt grass and the remains of that summer's weeds.

Drongan tradition declared that every new lord should be installed on this island, with his naked feet placed firmly in a natural depression in the rock and the Cross of St Cuthbert held over his head. It was a ceremony of great power, after which the new Lord travelled in state to Drongan House while all laws were relaxed in Ettrick for a full twelve hours. It was that last part that the town looked forward to most.

The crowds had gathered early, some singing the traditional Ettrick songs, others giving a bawdier version, while those most drunk simply lay on the grass muttering incoherently. Some wore fancy dress, ready for the later festivities, with one nearly naked Maid Marion becoming very friendly with her Robin Hood while a pair of hooded Friar Tucks seemed content on silent meditation. The Reivers arrived in a more or less disciplined body, although Mackie was a little under the weather while the girls who hung on to each of his arms encumbered Blackdown. They moved to the front of the crowd, where Jenny was already waiting with a fed, cleaned and sleeping Andy held securely in her arms.

The main players rode slowly through the crowd, acknowledging the well-deserved cheers of their tenants. The Callants had erected a wooden bridge between the river bank and the island, which the ministers and civic dignitaries crossed, but Montgomery and Georgina trotted through the Tweed, splashing the crowd, who cheered all the louder at this display of daring.

'Bloody show offs.' Pert gave his opinion.

Georgina had never looked more beautiful as Montgomery handed her from her horse. Somewhere along the route she had changed her white silk for a more practical riding dress of navy blue and gold, the colours of Ettrick, and her hair was tied back in a long pony tail that tapped enticingly against the smooth swell of her buttocks. Patting her horse in reassurance, she transferred her riding crop to her left hand, lifted her right hand for Montgomery to hold and stepped firmly to the centre of the island. As if in homage, a single shaft of sunlight slipped through the November clouds to drape her in warmth.

'She's some girl, your Georgina, sir.' As a Welshman, Thomson was less inclined to accept the local forelock-tugging tradition. He grinned over his shoulder to Selkirk. 'It's a pity you let that bastard pinch her from you.' His face altered as he saw Jenny at Selkirk's side, 'beg pardon about the language miss, I didn't know you were there.'

Jenny was more concerned about the implications of Thomson's words than the content. 'He said your Georgina, Drew. What did he mean by that?'

'Georgina Drongan helped us, out on the veldt,' Donnelly soothed her, 'she helped find horses for the Reivers, so the Captain sort of adopted her as a mascot.'

'That was not very respectful,' Jenny said.

Selkirk had a flickering vision of Georgina lying naked on a Pretoria bed, her arms draped across the pillow and her hair spread enticingly across her breasts. Perhaps he should have been more respectful then, too. 'Don't forget that it was her brother that evicted you,' he reminded. He was beginning to feel the strain of the day and wished that it were all over. When Jenny coloured and dropped her eyes Selkirk wished that he had kept his mouth shut. He put his arm around her but she shrugged free and edged closer to Donnelly.

The crowd fell silent as Montgomery and Georgina knelt on the smooth stone in the centre of the island. The caring husband, Montgomery, signalled to a man in the crowd, who passed over a square silk cushion to protect Georgina's knees. In front of them, partially filled with rainwater, was the natural depression that an unknown mediaeval craftsman had enhanced as he carved it into the shape of the footstep that signified ownership of the Lordship.

As tradition demanded, the parish minister, who represented the Almighty, and the Lord Lieutenant of the County, to represent the Crown, mounted the four steps to the small wooden platform that had been placed there. The two men seemed to loom over the assembled congregation.

The minister raised his voice. He was a large man with a massive bushy beard and he was renowned for the power of his lungs. For the second time that day he blessed the couple, then demanded that the Lord bring them into His Grace and shower their Lordship with bounty and prosperity. The crowd listened, some hoping to share in the last part, others hoping that the ceremony was not too protracted. The two Friars Tuck seemed intent on the ducks that paddled in the dull water, while most of the Reivers were more interested in the antics of Maid Marion, who seemed intent on losing the prefix to her name and her reputation to an obliging Robin Hood.

'She must be bloody freezing,' Pert said, eying her entirely without shame.

'Aye, they breed them hardy in the Borders,' Mackie replied.

At length the minister halted and the crowd shifted restlessly until the Lord Lieutenant stepped forward. He was a tiny man, resplendent in the scarlet uniform that he had worn when he marched through Afghanistan in the army of Bobs two decades previously, but he dominated the island by sheer personality.

The crowd stilled as the Lord Lieutenant held up his right hand. He smiled as a gust of wind lifted his cocked hat, introduced himself and started with a paean of praise for the late Lord Charles Drongan that ran easily into the reason for his presence.

'We are all here for the installation of the next Lord of Drongan, Captain James Montgomery, who has lately returned from sterling work in the South African War.'

The crowd watched, silent save for an occasional cough. Nobody knew James Montgomery; a landowner from Berwickshire was as much a stranger in Ettrick as a Zulu or a South Sea Islander. The sound of the Tweed was very loud as it lapped on the grass fringes of the island.

'We are also here for the installation of Georgina Montgomery as Lady Drongan.' This time the crowd cheered, for Georgina had always been the most popular of all the Drongans. Montgomery smiled thinly as the Lord Lieutenant waited for the hubbub to subside.

'So without further delay, I will ask once, twice and three times if there is any in the crowd who knows of reason for James Montgomery not to undertake the privileges and responsibility of Lord of Drongan!'

The crowd waited. Twice in the last three years, a new Lord Drongan had been installed, and on each occasion the ceremony had been performed without a hitch. Some of them knew that this part of the ceremony stretched back to the old Celtic laws, when a chief could be challenged by any of his tribe who could claim a better right to the position. Most did not care, wishing only for the ceremony to end so they could begin the real celebrations. More people joined the watchers, including a troupe of fanciful Highlanders, a Turk with a tilted fez and a third Friar Tuck in a costume far too large for him.

'I ask the first time,' the Lord Lieutenant raised his voice 'is there anyone present who knows of reason for James Montgomery not to undertake the privileges and responsibilities of Lord of Drongan?'

There was no response, save a muttered, 'Get on with it man' from Thomson. Selkirk looked at Georgina as she stood tall and proud, a single footstep away from becoming Lady Drongan. He caught her eye and smiled encouragement, but she did not respond.

'I ask the second time,' the Lord Lieutenant repeated, allowing his voice to echo across the rippling Tweed, 'is there anyone present who knows of reason for James Montgomery not to undertake the privileges and responsibilities of Lord of Drongan?'

Georgina straightened her back, reached for Montgomery's hand and prepared for the Installation. Above them, framed by the long Border hills, the clouds parted fully. Sunshine eased over the Tweed, bringing a blessing to the ceremony. Even the ducks seemed to be silent as the Lord Lieutenant raised his hand expectantly.

'I ask for the third and final time!' His voice thundered over Ettrick, 'is there anyone present who knows of reason for James Montgomery not to undertake the privileges and responsibilities of Lord of Drongan?'

Georgina looked away as Selkirk tried to nod approval to her. Montgomery lifted his foot, preparatory to placing it in the ancient carved footstep in the rock.

'I do!' One of the Friars Tuck claimed.

Some of the crowd laughed others tutted at this crude attempt at humour, but the Friar stepped boldly on to the bridge, his footsteps echoing on the untrimmed wood.

'What the devil do you mean?' Montgomery took a half step forward. Georgina clutched his arm, her face suddenly pale.

Momentarily nonplussed, the Lord Lieutenant peered at the hooded man. He seemed to swallow hard, then, glancing apologetically at Montgomery, continued. 'It is anybody's right to so challenge,' he said, but his voice had lost much of its timbre. 'Step on to the island and state your reason.'

The Friar strode forward, halting a few paces from Montgomery. His mediaeval costume looked fitting in such a setting. 'I state that James Montgomery cannot claim the Lordship of Drongan, for I have a more direct claim to the title.'

Georgina looked ready to faint. She was holding tight to Montgomery's arm, staring at this hooded apparition in front of her.

'Don't talk nonsense man! If this is some hoax I'll have you locked up.' The Lord Lieutenant abandoned all attempts at formulaic speech as he dismissed the friar's claim. 'James Montgomery's claim is through his wife, the sister of the last two lords. Nobody else has a better claim!'

'I have.' The friar shrugged back his hood and stood bareheaded. Georgina gave a little gasp and put a hand to her mouth, while Montgomery stared in incomprehension. 'And I claim the Lordship of Drongan.'

'You can't do that,' obviously confused, the Lord Lieutenant held to the legal procedures that he knew so well, 'you need a gentleman backer, and proof of your claim.'

'I have proof.' Still with his back to the crowd, the friar produced a thin sheaf of paper from a pocket of his robes, and as backer, I call upon Captain Andrew Selkirk, DSO.'

'Sweet Jesus,' Selkirk closed his eyes as Albert Newman, now publicly revealed as James Drongan, beckoned him on to the island.

Chapter Nineteen :Ettrick – November 1903

It was Georgina who spoke first, gesticulating wildly toward Selkirk. 'He can't be a backer! He's only a ploughboy, one of my tenants!'

'Damned right!' Montgomery's face had diffused with blood; 'he's no gentleman!'

The Lord Lieutenant raised a suddenly chilled eyebrow. 'An officer who holds the King's Commission and medals that show he had faced the King's enemies is always a gentleman, Captain Montgomery. Whatever his antecedents. I had the honour of serving with General Hector MacDonald before he gained his commission. I would ask you to remember that.' He pointed toward Selkirk. 'Pray step this way, Captain.'

Selkirk felt the weakness in his legs as he stepped on to the bridge. Newman, now James Drongan, was smiling to him, extending a hand in friendship. 'Sorry to put you on the spot sir, but I'm afraid there's nobody else that I trust, much.'

'God, Newy. You're dead! Haigie saw you killed.'

'Sorry about that too, sir, but Charles was very suspicious of me. He knew my face, you see, but wasn't quite sure who I was. If he had worked it out, I would really have been dead, and probably you too.' James Drongan grinned, 'So Haigie and I devised a plan to make things easier.' His grin widened, 'There was another factor too, but we'll come to that later.'

'Andrew.' Georgina had released Montgomery to place a hand on Selkirk's arm. 'You won't let this happen, will you? We're more than friends, you and I.' There was desperation in her eyes, 'Please Andrew? For me?'

'Nothing he can do about it sis,' James Drongan told her. 'I am the correct heir, and rules is rules. Anyway,' he jerked a scornful thumb at Montgomery, 'he's not fit to own Drongan. A drunken, womanising gambler! He'll have you ruined within five years.'

'James.' Georgina transferred her attention to her brother, 'please! We need the money. We do!'

'No doubt.' James Drongan patted her hand, 'but so do I. Don't fret, Georgie, I'll see you right.'

The Lord Lieutenant had been examining the papers that James Drongan had produced. 'These seem in order,' he said. 'I'm sorry Montgomery, but this is the heir.'

'The man's a cad, sir!' Montgomery looked ready to commit assault; he stepped forward, fists clenched and mouth working furiously.

'I wouldn't advise that, Montgomery,' James Drongan shook his head. 'I have a dozen picked men in the crowd, you don't have your bully-boys with you and there are hundreds of witnesses.'

'Picked men?' Selkirk asked.

'The Reivers of course.' James Drongan's grin widened even further. 'You didn't really believe that Montgomery invited you all, did you? I learned a lot from you, sir.'

Once again the Lord Lieutenant mounted his platform. He held out both hands to still the crowd.

'We have an alteration to the programme,' he said. 'James Drongan, who we believed lost for good, has come back to claim his position as Lord of Drongan. As the nearest male heir, he has precedence over the claim of Georgina, and so I ask, for the first time, is there anyone present who knows of reason for James Drongan not to undertake the privileges and responsibilities of Lord of Drongan?'

Ignoring the incoherent protests of Montgomery, the Lord Lieutenant rattled through the procedures, hardly giving time for any protest to be registered before inviting James Drongan to divest himself of his footwear and step into the carved footstep.

With Selkirk at his side, James Drongan did so. 'I never thought that I'd do this,' he said, then winced. 'That water's damned cold.'

'Oh Jamie. How could you?' Releasing Montgomery's arm, Georgina ran from the island, her footsteps hollow on the wooden bridge. Some of the crowd parted in front of her, but others simply stared, enjoying her distress. After a moment's delay, Montgomery followed, shoving through the now hostile crowd.

'And now, would you take the oath, my Lord?' the Lord Lieutenant held up a card for James Drongan to read, which he did.

222

'I James, Lord of Drongan and the Fethan, swear to uphold the rights of my rightful sovereign and protect the people of my Lordship. So help me God!' He grinned to Selkirk. 'It's very mediaeval, isn't it?'

'Indeed.' The Lord Lieutenant answered for him. 'And will your supporter also swear?'

As if in a dream, Selkirk held the printed card, filling in the gaps where appropriate and hardly stumbling over the sonorous sentences. 'I, Andrew Selkirk, Captain in His Majesty's Royal Borderers Regiment, swear that to the best of my knowledge, James Drongan is the true Lord. He will act for the people of the Lordship to the best of his ability.'

The Lord Lieutenant claimed back the card. 'Congratulations, my Lord Drongan.'

James Drongan nodded. 'Thank you Peter. I will expect that you'll call round in a day or so?'

'Of course, James. We can shoot some of your birds.'

'Good for you, Newie!' The voice from the crowd was familiar and Selkirk saw the third Friar Tuck flick back his hood. Haig grinned uglily to him. 'Morning Selks!'

Shrugging off his Friar Tuck costume, the new Lord Drongan used the long robes to dry his feet. Wearing Norfolk jacket and tweed trousers, he looked every inch the Lord of Drongan. 'You haven't met my wife yet Peter, so I'll take this opportunity to introduce her to my people.' He nodded to Selkirk. 'Captain Selkirk knows her well.' Donning his boots, Charles Drongan mounted the platform and pointed to the second Friar Tuck, 'come on over, my dear.'

Lady Drongan walked elegantly across the bridge and, retaining her hood stood beside her husband. Enjoying this free entertainment, the crowd cheered as she waved to them.

'Good morning everybody.' Lord James Drongan spoke to the crowd. 'Most of you have heard of me. Some of you even knew me as a child. You are aware of my reputation as the black sheep of the Drongans, the man who was expelled from Eton, the man who wasted his youth on drink and dissipation and loose women.'

They were silent now, watching him, wondering what he was going to say. Even the Reivers stared at this man who had once been their colleague and who had returned from the dead. Selkirk sought out Jenny, who smiled to him. She was standing arm in arm with Donnelly.

'Well, that reputation was well earned, I'm afraid.' Lord Drongan waited until the buzz of surprise dissipated before he continued. 'However, three people dragged me from the mire. The first was Captain Andrew Selkirk here, a native of the Fethan.' He indicated Selkirk, while the crowd cheered and Jenny wiped a sudden tear from her eye.

'The second was Private David Haig, who taught me the meaning of loyalty.' Lord Drongan indicated the diminutive Haig, who swore audibly and threatened violence on the men who tried to pat him on the back.

'The third was this lady, who is undoubtedly the most gentle and loving person I have ever met and one who I married before she found somebody else.' Very gently, Charles, Lord Drongan, folded back the hood of the second Friar Tuck.

Looking more beautiful than ever, Marie, Lady Drongan, smiled at her tenants. The crowd stared, for most had never seen a black woman before, but one or two began the double Ettrick cheer that echoed from the hills. Marie lifted her hands in acknowledgement then, still smiling, kissed her husband.

'Now we can get drunk!' Mackie said, and the crowd cheered again.

'Of course, some people won't accept Marie as Lady Drongan.' They sat in the dining room of Drongan House with a large fire in the marble fireplace and scented smoke spiralling from the cigars. Lord Drongan looked as if he had never been a trooper of the Queen, with one elegant leg crossed lazily over the other and his bow tie immaculately tied above the crisp white shirt.

'I'm sure Marie will win them over.' Even when surrounded by his friends, Selkirk felt slightly ill at ease inside Drongan House. 'She'll make you a good wife, Newie, My Lord.'

'I will, Selkirk.' Marie sat calmly beside her husband. She had refused to bow to convention and head an exodus of ladies to the withdrawing room. 'I have known many British soldiers, including you, but only Newman Drongan has never let me down.'

Selkirk felt Jenny's eyes flicker from him to Marie and knew that she would be asking many questions later. 'I had not realised that you two had become so close.'

Charles Drongan leaned back and smiled. 'God, but it's good to be home!' Reaching out, he patted his wife's leg. 'Remember when we rode back from Bechuanaland and I was wounded? You left me at Hendrinafontein?'

'I remember.' Selkirk would never forget that wild time, from the ambush in the Kalahari Desert to the attack at the waterhole and the scramble across the veldt.

'That's when I began to like Marie. But she left for the North with Thomas Duff the hunter.'

'He was a bad man.' Marie shook her head. 'He didn't just want me. He wanted every black woman.'

'But you're not black, Lady Drongan?' Jenny sounded puzzled. All her education had informed her that black women lived in grass huts, worshipped the sun or pagan gods and wore very little clothing. Now here was Marie, no more dark skinned than many a Scot, as beautiful and graceful as Georgina, so educated that she could speak three languages, a devout Christian and totally at ease as Lady Drongan.

'I am Griqua, a half cast.' Marie spoke simply, but it was obvious that the term hurt her deeply.

'You're bloody Scottish now!' Haig lifted his head from the drinks cabinet, where he had been sampling something from every bottle. 'And I'll slit the first bastard that says otherwise.'

'Thank you David.' Marie awarded him one of her most charming smiles. 'With you as my champion, I know I will always be safe. But please don't swear in front of Selkirk's sister. I don't think she likes it.'

'Sorry Miss Selkirk. Nae offence.' Haig slumped into his seat with a bottle of brandy that must have cost fifty guineas.

'So where did you meet Marie again?' Selkirk continued his questioning.

'At Akersdorp.' Lord Drongan smiled as Marie signalled to one of the servants, who quietly closed and locked the drinks cabinet. 'When Haigie and I were escorting Lieutenant Cloete to the Boers,

225

we came across Duff. He was with a bunch of wild men, Aasvogels they called themselves.'

'We met,' Selkirk said.

'Well, they had Marie with them, and some other women.' Lord Drongan glanced toward Marie. 'We cut some free and took Marie with us. Then you organised an ambush and we rode into it.'

Selkirk remembered Marie's companion that day. He decided that it was easier to let that incident pass. 'You did well, Newie, My Lord. What happened to Duff.'

'I happened to Duff.' When Haig looked up his eyes were primeval.

'Duff was going to sell me to the Aasvogels and Haigie saved my life,' Marie said simply. 'But Newie saved my soul.'

'As you know, Haigie returned to the unit. He was too good a soldier not to, but I couldn't. The Boers had a pastor with them, a wee man named Johannes. He married us there and then, and we made our way to Scotland.'

'You're still officially dead, or a deserter,' Selkirk pointed out, but Lord Drongan shook his head.

'No. Albert Newman is officially dead. For all the world knows, James Drongan has been living a life of dissipation in London until he returned here.'

'Best leave it like that, sir.' Donnelly leaned across the table. 'Leave sleeping dogs to lie, eh Selks?'

For a second there was tension in the room. A log slipped in the fireplace, sending a shower of hissing sparks on to the tiled surround. Selkirk looked from Lord James Drongan to Marie. Both returned his gaze, one with a mixture of defiance and apprehension, the other with complete faith.

'All the same,' Selkirk said softly, 'it was lucky for you that somebody murdered Charles Drongan.'

'Indeed.' Lord Drongan said softly. 'Some passing thug, perhaps, or an ex-soldier with a grudge. He was always hard on his men.'

'That must have been it.' Selkirk felt the atmosphere change. He heard Haig's chair scrape softly and knew that the small man had been poised for one of his lethal assaults. 'I chased the murderer you know,' he said. 'I saw him quite clearly on a ledge of the Castle Rock.'

'So you said, sir.' Donnelly had placed himself between Haig and Selkirk, his Arizona drawl relaxed and friendly. 'You said that you did not recognise him, didn't you sir?' There could not have been a more direct hint.

Selkirk remembered the small stature and the predatory eyes of the killer. There had been thousands of men like that in the British army, and more were to be found in every industrial slum in Britain. 'No, I didn't. I've no idea who he was.'

Haig grinned to him, scarred face wary. 'Probably just as well, Selks. You dinnae want to get caught up in stuff like that. Anything could happen.' He tasted the brandy. 'Anyway, Charles Drongan was a bastard. Look what he did to Hendrina's farm. He deserved to die, that one.'

'Now that that's out of the way, I have a small proposition for you sir,' Lord Drongan poured a generous amount of whisky into Selkirk's glass. 'Just listen before you decide.'

***

Selkirk was only half-asleep when the door opened. He started up, reaching for the carbine that should have been beside his bed, swore softly when he realised that it was missing, and rolled quickly out of bed.

'It's all right Andrew, it's only me.' Georgina Montgomery lurched into Selkirk's room and closed the door with a deft flick of her heel. It was obvious that she had been drinking, and when Selkirk applied a match to the candle that stood in its brass holder on his bedside table, he saw that she had also been crying. Her eyes were puffy and red, and tears had carried great black streaks of mascara down her perfect cheeks.

'Georgina.' Selkirk helped her on to the only chair, where she slumped, with the black silk nightgown flowing around her. 'Are you all right?'

'All right?' She looked up at him through liquid eyes. 'Of course I'm all right. I'm Georgina Montgomery, nearly Lady Drongan, nearly rich, nearly well liked, nearly important, always bloody nearly.' She looked away again, taking a deep sigh to compose herself. 'No Andrew, I am not all right. I am anything but all right. Indeed, I am all wrong.' Her face twisted into a parody of the beautiful Georgina smile.

'I'll fetch you a cup of tea,' Selkirk decided. He wondered if he should call Jenny.

'No.' Georgina placed her hand on his arm. 'No, thank you Andrew.' Her hair, normally so immaculate, hung loose and tangled, but still shone in the candlelight. 'Do you know something Andrew? I admire you. You are always so, so capable, whatever happens. You never protested, even as a child when Charles beat you in the horse racing. That was fixed you know, so he had the fastest horse. It would never do for Charles Drongan to come second to the son of a ploughman.'

'Aye? Well he never did, did he?' Selkirk forced away the bitterness that had burned within him for the best part of his life. 'He died a hero, Lord Charles Drongan, VC. And do you know something, Georgina? He won that medal well. It was one of the bravest acts I've ever seen in my life.'

'God! There you go again, Andrew! Always capable, capable of praising a man that hated you, capable of winning a ploughing match or a war, capable of being a private or an officer, capable of making me love you, despite your position.'

'You love me?' Selkirk stared at her. This was Georgina, the beautiful daughter of Lord Drongan, the girl he had admired from afar, and the woman who had rejected him because he was only a ploughboy.

Georgina pushed herself to her feet and stood, swaying, in the centre of the room. 'We made love didn't we? Yes? Well then.'

'So why choose James Montgomery? I would have done anything for you.' Selkirk tried to clear the confusion from his head. He knew that he was speaking the truth, even though he had to tear it from the bottom of his soul.

'I told you why. He had lands, power, influence. You had nothing. But now the situation has changed, hasn't it?' Georgina laughed. 'He's gambled away his inheritance and failed to take mine. So what am I now? A petitioner for favours at the court of Lord James? And with a husband that's no use to anyone.'

Selkirk wished that Jenny would walk into the room, or Marie. Anybody to save him from this torture. 'He's still your husband; the man you chose, for better or worse, remember.'

'I remember,' Georgina said, 'God, I remember! But nobody told me that it would be worse. Look!' Shifting her shoulders, she unfastened her gown and let it slide silkily to the ground so she stood naked in front of him. 'Do you like that?'

'Of course.' Despite himself, Selkirk admired her smooth curves. He remembered the softness of flank and breast, the suppleness of legs and buttocks strengthened by a lifetime of riding, the manner in which her nipples had hardened under his fingers. 'You must be the most beautiful woman that I have ever met, Georgina. No man could fail to like that.'

'No man? James doesn't! My husband doesn't like that!' The obscenity of her next gesture shocked Selkirk. This was not the behaviour he expected from Georgina. 'Oh no, not him. Do you know what he likes?'

'No.' Lifting her robe from the ground, Selkirk draped it over her shoulders. 'I don't know Georgina, and I don't want to know. You're drunk and you're not thinking straight.' He stopped her next sentence with his fingers. 'Go back to bed, Georgina, and we'll both forget everything that happened tonight. Goodnight now.'

Hoping that nobody would see them together, Selkirk escorted her to the corridor where her bedroom was located. Despite the affair of the Installation, the new Lord Drongan had insisted that his sister remain as long as she liked. 'Off you go now Georgina. Back to your husband. Back to where you belong.'

Georgina took three steps and when she turned round her eyes were clear and her speech sober. 'I think I belong with you, Andrew. I do love you, you know. If only things had been different.'

He nodded. 'We would have been good together, Georgina, but things are not different. Things are just what they are.' He paused for a second, allowing his eyes to drift over this woman who had meant so much to him. 'Goodnight, Georgina.'

Selkirk returned to his room and quickly dressed before lifting the sealed agreement that he and Lord Drongan had both signed. Walking through the cool corridors of this house that he had often dreamed of visiting, he opened the door to Jenny's bedroom and quietly entered. She was lying face down in the bed, with one arm curled around Donnelly. Both were naked, and young Andy snored purposefully between them. Selkirk smiled. They made a good couple, for both would look after the other. Neither stirred when he pulled up the sheet to cover them before crossing to the desk that stood in a corner of the room.

He and Lord James Drongan had spent over two hours working on an agreement. Now Selkirk placed the carefully worded document on the polished surface of the desk and lifted a pen. Carefully inspecting the nib, he dipped it into the ink-well and worked furiously for a few minutes. Using the faint light that filtered in from the corridor, he inspected his handiwork. He had scored dramatically through his own name and added two others. The remainder of the document was untouched.

'Agreement between James, Lord Drongan, Jennifer Selkirk, and Walter Donnelly' it now read. 'To lease the farms and lands of the Fethan in perpetuity, or until such time as both parties wish to end the agreement. Rent to be agreed by mutual consent.'

For a second Selkirk hesitated, then he scribbled his name across the bottom of the page. Once he would have asked for nothing better than to farm the valley in which he had spent his childhood but not now. He no longer belonged. He was no longer Andrew Selkirk of the Fethan.

Chapter Twenty : At Sea – January 1904

Last time he had travelled in this direction he had been crammed below decks along with hundreds of other soldiers of the Queen. Then, he had been young and inexperienced, with no power to control his life. Now he was a few years older, a retired and distinguished captain in His Majesty's army and vastly more knowledgeable in the ways of the world.

Selkirk glanced down as the screws of the lavender hulled steamer turned the sea into creamy froth. He had stared into that same sea for days now as the ship churned southward, leaving the damp coolness of Scotland far behind. Not long now, and the massive table would begin to unfold from the bottom of Africa. Not long now and he could disembark, with only a few pounds in his pocket and the rest of his life before him.

Selkirk wandered forward, nodding to the excited passengers who had never before been this far from home. He stopped on the promenade deck; reached in his pocket and, for the hundredth time that voyage, brought out the folded square of paper.

'*Remember meneer Ogler,*' it read, '*I have your word of honour. You are my prisoner.*'

Selkirk smiled and stared toward his horizon.

Malcolm Archibald
March 2005

Glossary

Aasvogel – vulture
Bergschotten – Scottish highlanders
Commando – mounted unit of Boers
Khaki – Boer word for British soldier
Kliphok- ruins of African stone huts
Mooi - beautiful
Pom pom – type of fast firing light artillery
Rooineck – redneck – British soldier
Spantau – riem, used to tie a cow's legs while milking
Trek jou – move quickly
Verneuk - cheat
Veldcornet – field cornet – commander of small commando
Vitschudden - stripping
Vrot – rotten

Historical Note

Concentration camps were one of the most controversial innovations of the Boer War. The British interned up to 100,000 people, both black and white, but mainly women and children. These camps may have been intended to remove the women from the farms so that they could not supply the Boer commandos. They may also have been intended to keep the civilians safe and fed. However, the Boers were not used to camp life and the loss of life was appalling.

Toward the end of the war there were many small groups of extremely unpleasant people roving on the veldt. The memoirs of Deneys Reitz mention his encounters with some. Doyle's Australian Scouts were among the British units used to help defend isolated Boer farms from these people.